VISIBLE SPIRITS

VISIBLE SPIRITS

STEVE YARBROUGH

PICADOR

2002

First published 2001 as a Borzoi Book
by Alfred A. Knopf, New York

This edition published 2001 by Picador
an imprint of Pan Macmillan Ltd
Pan Macmillan, 20 New Wharf Road, London N1 9RR
Basingstoke and Oxford
Associated companies throughout the world
www.panmacmillan.com

ISBN 0 330 48637 3

1 3 5 7 9 8 6 4 2

A CIP catalogue record for this book is available from
the British Library.

Printed and bound in Great Britain by
Mackays of Chatham plc, Chatham, Kent

For Lillian Faderman

TOOLS OF ADVANTAGE

THE MUD on Main Street was half a foot deep and mixed with enough horse shit to make him wish he had something to clamp over his nose. But he'd lost his handkerchief on the train coming up, and anyway, it was stained with blood: in New Orleans a fellow had punched him in the mouth. He couldn't remember who it was, though he did recall how much it hurt.

A supply wagon loaded with hundred-pound sacks of feed grain and hog shorts waited in front of Rosenthal's General Merchandise, and a couple horses were tied up in front of the hardware. But he knew, because he knew his brother, that Leighton would already be in—he'd probably been at the office since five or five-thirty. He went to bed every night at nine o'clock and rose at four so he could get an hour's worth of reading done before setting to work. He'd always done that and always would, especially now that he had two jobs instead of one.

THE LEGEND on the window said *LORING WEEKLY TIMES*. The building had once been a saloon, but that closed down back in '96 when the drys won the local option election. Leighton had played a role in their favor, editorializing at length, arguing that the whole community should be outraged at the sight of drunks staggering along the sidewalk, bumping into women.

Through the window this morning, Tandy could see him sitting at his rolltop desk, back where the poker tables used to be, reading a big leather-bound volume. He wore a gray suit, and Tandy knew the suit was clean and fresh-smelling, that the collar of his white shirt had been pressed this very morning. He knew who had pressed it, too.

The door was unlocked; he opened it and stepped inside. Blank sheets of newspaper were stacked on the floor near an old copper-plated handpress, and on the counter were metal baskets with copy in them. A Western Newspaper Union calendar hung on one wall. Instead of smelling like cigarettes and whiskey, as it used to, the place stank now of ink and dust.

Leighton didn't even look up. "I was wondering when I'd hear from you," he said.

Tandy stomped each boot on the floor, and clots of mud flew off.

Leighton laid the book down. He stared at Tandy's boots. "Most folks would've stomped the mud off outside."

"Course, I'm not most folks. I'm family."

Leighton stood. As always, when Tandy had been away for a while, the size of his brother took him by surprise. Tandy was not a small man himself, but Leighton stood six foot five, an inch taller than their father, and even though he lacked their father's weight, he could still fill a room by himself. When Leighton was present, Tandy felt he had less of everything—less space to move around in, less air to breathe.

A big lightbulb hung from the ceiling. Pointing, Tandy said, "I heard y'all had got electric power."

The civic booster in his brother asserted itself: you could almost see his chest swell. "Got it last fall. Right now, it's only on from six till midnight, but that's a big help to us on Wednesday evening, when we're actually printing the paper."

He smiled and crossed his arms. "You hear what happened over at the livery stables?"

"No."

"Uncle Billy Heath decided he needed him some electric power. Said he wanted to be able to check on his horses without worrying about toting a coal-oil lamp in there and having one of 'em kick it over and set the whole place afire. So he had Loring Light, Ice and Coal string a cable in and suspend a big old bulb from the rafters. When they turned on the power, all the horses went crazy. They kicked open the stall doors and took off down Main Street. One of 'em ran right over Uncle Billy. Broke his arm in two places."

Tandy laughed. Eight or ten years ago, in a poker game in this very building, Uncle Billy Heath had beaten him out of a good-looking saddlebred mare. Tandy had owned the mare for only three or four hours before losing her, and it pleased him now to think maybe she was the one who'd broken Uncle Billy's arm.

"When a person leaves town," he said, "all sorts of things start happening. You don't hardly know the place when you get back."

"Yeah, there's a few things that have changed, I guess." Leighton stuck his hands in his pockets. "I imagine you know A. L. Gunnels passed on."

"No, I hadn't heard that. Who's the new mayor?"

"The truth is, you're looking at him."

This was the moment Tandy had dreaded, the worst thing about coming back. At two o'clock this morning, as he sat on a hard bench at the depot, batting away mosquitoes and doing his best to stay awake, he had imagined what it was going to feel like when he stood face-to-face with his brother and acknowledged another of Leighton's successes, and it had almost been enough to make him jump on the next train leaving town. The problem was, he didn't have the money to buy a ticket on the next train. He'd traveled just as far as he could.

"Well now, damn if we don't have a politician in the family," he said. "Congratulations."

He offered Leighton his hand. When his brother took it, Tandy felt how puny his own fingers were. The handshake almost crushed them.

"All I plan to do's serve out the rest of A.L.'s term. Some folks got together and asked me to do it, and I felt like I couldn't say no. I don't know if congratulations are in order, though. Maybe condolences would be more appropriate."

"How come?"

"We've got some troublesome issues to confront. For instance, there's a group of folks who want to pass an ordinance making it illegal to construct any more frame buildings, because they're scared a fire'll sweep through and burn the whole town down. But brick's expensive, so some folks are claiming this ordinance'll discourage new businesses and retard progress—*retard progress* is a phrase you hear in the board meetings every two or three minutes. People get all heated up over stuff like that, and by virtue of being both mayor and editor of the local paper, I'm smack-dab in the middle."

If being smack-dab in the middle displeased him, Tandy couldn't tell it. Leighton seemed, as always, quite happy with himself.

He did not, however, look particularly happy with Tandy. He let his eyes travel down his brother's torso to his pants, which a year ago had been white but were now a dingy cream color, with spots of mud and dried blood on the knees. The boots had last been shined five or six months back and were in need of repair.

"What happened?" he said. "Somebody catch you dealing from the bottom of the deck?"

"Nobody does that anymore."

"Well, it looks like somebody caught you doing something."

Nobody had caught him doing anything. A little more than a week ago, he'd been in a game where the pot had reached six thousand dollars, and a fellow he'd never seen before, a wiry little man with a funny accent and a gold watch chain that had a miniature jockey's cap and a saddle hanging from it, had convinced him and the other three players to follow him over to the bank, where he'd request a loan based on his hand. Tandy had bought the key to the deck, he held a strong hand, and it never crossed his mind, not for one minute, that one of the other players might have bought the key, too. He believed he'd found the perfect sucker. He believed it right up until the man with the watch chain— having received his loan from a banker who Tandy figured must not know the first thing about poker—played a king and four aces.

The money hadn't been Tandy's to lose. People wanted that money, believing it was theirs, and if you looked at things in a certain way, they were right. He'd heard that if he didn't leave town, somebody might kill him.

"You're broke, aren't you?" Leighton said.

"Temporarily insolvent's how I'd put it."

"Temporary's got its limits. After a while, temporary becomes permanent."

"There was a three-day period six months ago when I could have bought you and everything you call yours."

"No," Leighton said, "you couldn't have."

For a moment, while Leighton stood there facing him, letting his words sink in, Tandy hated his brother. It wasn't the first time, nor would it be the last. But he knew that if he could just keep a grip on himself for a few more seconds, the moment of hating would pass and he'd be left with the same old bunch of feelings, which were far too complicated to bear a single name.

Leighton turned, walked back over to his desk. He flipped open a ledger that lay near his typewriter. He made a show of staring at it, running his finger down the page as if he were checking figures. "Where are you staying?"

"Thought I'd take a room at Miss Rosa's."

"Room and board at Miss Rosa's is about four dollars a week. I imagine you're a few dollars short?"

Tandy was tired: he hadn't slept for two days or had a drink for three, and all he really wanted was to get into a nice soft bed with a bottle of whiskey and drink till he passed out cold. But one thing you could always do when you couldn't do anything better was bluff. If nothing else, it kept you in the game. So he did his best to sound rakish, untroubled. "Briefly."

Leighton opened a desk drawer and took out a metal box. He raised the lid, pulled a few bills out, counted and laid them on the desk, then put the box back in the drawer. The entire operation probably took only a minute or so, but to Tandy it felt like ten years.

Leighton picked up the stack of bills and walked over and handed them to him.

"Thanks," Tandy said.

"Sarah and Will'll want to see you. Why don't you come over tonight and eat supper?"

"All right." He crammed the bills into his pocket. "Leighton . . . that board you mentioned? Has it got the power to give out jobs?"

"Jobs?" Leighton said, sounding as if he couldn't believe he'd heard right.

"You know. City jobs."

"Yeah," Leighton said. "It's got the power to hire folks to sweep up the marshal's office and cart garbage over to the town dump. You want to cart garbage, Tandy? Is that what you're saying?"

Beneath Tandy's feet, the floorboards creaked. He was sweating now. He smelled his own odor.

THROUGH the inverted letters on the front window, Leighton watched his brother shamble across the intersection at Main and First, his head down, his eyes on the ground. He looked whipped, the very picture of failure and dejection, until he heard the sound of a horse's hooves and looked up. Sally Stark, the wife of a local planter, was driving along in a carriage. Instantly, Tandy's bearing changed. Straightening himself up to his full height, he doffed his fedora and swept it through the air, then executed a graceful bow.

Sally Stark pulled back on the reins, and the horse slowed down. Leighton watched while her face broke into a smile. Her lips formed a single word.

Tandy!

THE HOUSE stood on the banks of Loring Bayou. A big white house surrounded by a white picket fence, it had a broad veranda overhung by cedars, pecan trees and locusts. Leighton had designed it himself, in concert with his father-in-law, and it had cost him $2,500. Tonight, it was brightly lit.

Walking up from the street, he heard music: Sarah playing the piano, Tandy singing "Danny Boy." For a moment, he stopped and listened. He'd always loved hearing Tandy sing, but if he was in the room while the singing was going on, Leighton had to shut his eyes to enjoy it. Seeing the man behind the voice ruined the effect.

They had just finished the final chorus when he opened the door. Tandy was clean now, his pants and jacket sparkling white, his boots shining in the lamplight, though they still looked a little worn around the toes. He'd shaved and waxed his mustache and combed his hair.

He stood beside the piano. Sarah's cheeks were rosy, and she was smiling up at him. Upstairs, in a walnut cabinet near the bed, there was a photograph of her sitting beside Tandy in a buggy. In the picture, she wore a lace dress and a tall hat with taffeta trim, and she was looking at him with that same bright smile on display.

Tandy was at home among women, always able to make them smile, whereas Leighton never quite felt comfortable in their presence. He liked them and wanted to be around them, but whenever they were near, he became aware of his size. He tended to bend toward them, ducking his head in compensation. More often than not, they instinctively pulled away.

"That sounded pretty darn good," he said. He removed his hat, hung it on the rack and walked over and laid his hand on Sarah's shoulder. "Maybe y'all could go on the road and make some money."

"Tandy can't make money. It's beneath him."

"Well, I wouldn't say it's beneath me. I'd say it's somewhere off to the side."

"It seems there are some people in New Orleans to whom Tandy owes more than six thousand dollars."

"Give or take a dollar or two."

"And they've suggested he might come to harm."

"They're not bad folks. They're just a little too quick to rile."

"So Tandy is here, as it were, in hiding."

She hadn't looked at Leighton since he'd walked in. He willed himself now to lift his hand from her shoulder, but he couldn't. She was wearing a voile frock so sheer his fingertips could feel her pulse through the fabric. He felt the heat of her body as well, and something else—moisture, the sheen of perspiration on her skin. His free hand rose as if of its own volition; he almost laid it on her other shoulder and caressed her. What stopped him was the sight of a blackish smear on his palm. His hands had always looked rough, and now they frequently bore ink stains. He could never quite get them all off.

"Tandy can't hide," he said. "Tandy draws crowds like a dog draws fleas."

THEY SAT at the supper table, lingering over the remains of an apple pie Sarah had baked that afternoon. Tandy was telling a story about his adventures in New Orleans.

"So the driver, he looks over his shoulder at me and says, 'The one on the left, sir, he rough-gaited, and the one on the right, well, she a shirker. This crushed gravel on the street, it get up in the frog on the horse's foot, and it can make 'em go lame. Well, the one on the right there, she know I know that, so she start acting like that what's done happened. But there's one other thing she know I know. She know I know her just as well as she know me.' And you know what the driver did then?"

"No," Will said. "What'd he do, Uncle Tandy?"

"Well, he pulled the whip out of the socket and whacked the mare on her tail. But instead of picking up her pace, she got her tail up over the dashboard and cut loose with about five or six pounds of the stinky stuff."

Will burst out laughing.

"Tandy!" Sarah said.

"The old nigger was naturally the color of blackstrap molasses, but when the horse did that, he gagged and turned green. He had to pull his hat off and hold it over his face all the way back to Jackson Square. Tell you the truth, it like to killed me, too."

"Yeah," Leighton said. "It just about killed me now to listen to it."

He glanced at Will. He was nine, a tall skinny boy who sometimes got so excited he forgot to eat. He also forgot to sleep. "It's about time for you to go to bed, son."

"Daddy!" Will balled his hands up into fists.

"William Lee Payne," Sarah said. "Can you imagine your father or your uncle behaving like that if their father had told them to go to bed?"

Face sullen, Will kissed Sarah good night, then walked over and leaned against Leighton.

"Good night, son."

"Night."

On his way out, he paused long enough to shake hands with Tandy. "You'll still be here tomorrow?"

"For tomorrow and for many days to come."

"And you'll tell me some more stories?"

Tandy leaned back in his chair. Light glinted off the buttons on his jacket. "I'll tell you stories," he said, "that'll make hair spring up in your armpits." He grabbed Will and tickled him under the arms, and Will shrieked and ran for the stairs.

Tandy watched him race up them two at a time. "He's going to be a big one."

"Well, there aren't any small ones in our family."

"I'm the runt of the litter."

"It wasn't a very big litter to be the runt of," Sarah said.

"It was litter enough. Sometimes, when I was sitting at the table like this, across from Leighton and Daddy, I felt like I lived among giants."

"Oh, come on. Till I was fourteen or fifteen, you were just as tall as I was."

"I felt like I lived among giants. A war hero for a father and a brother who was clearly destined for the greater walks of life. And now, in addition to being a man of letters, he's the mayor."

"Yeah, and these civic posts are highly distinguished. That's why last year we reduced the membership on the Board of Aldermen from five to four. Couldn't convince a fifth man to run."

"Speaking of civics," Tandy said, "what else is new around town? Old Percy Stancill still buying up every piece of land he can?"

"Owns upwards of ten thousand acres."

"Didn't his wife pass on?"

"Two wives passed on. He's on the third one now."

"Good for him."

"You probably noticed the hitching posts along Main,"

Sarah said. "Now it's illegal to tether the beasts to porch columns. And Rosenthal's sells ice. They bring it up the river on a boat, and he stores it in sawdust. Oh, and we have a Negro serving as postmistress."

You could tell, knowing Tandy, when something aroused his interest. If he was sitting at a table, he would place both hands palm-down before him, as if he meant to push himself up. The hands were out there now. "A colored postmistress?" he said. "How and when did that come about?"

Leighton picked up his coffee cup and glanced at Sarah. She said, "I'll get some more."

He waited until she'd left the dining room. "The postmistress got the appointment during McKinley's first term," he said. "I think Jim Hill recommended her."

"One of 'em scratching another one's back."

"Well, somebody's always scratching somebody's back, Tandy. I reckon colored folks itch from time to time, same as we do."

"Yeah," Tandy said, "I guess so. So who is she—this postmistress?"

Leighton lifted his fork and picked at the remains of his pie. "Actually, you know her."

He looked up just as the light went on in his brother's eyes.

WEARING her carpenter's apron, she moved down the row, pulling those speckled butter beans off the vines and dropping them into her pockets. She'd planted late this year, toward the end of April. Now the garden was full of beans and squash, cucumbers and tomatoes. The cantaloupes weren't looking too good, but you couldn't have everything. She had plenty.

The garden was hers: she'd laid the rows out, erected oak posts at the ends of her bean patch, strung wire between them and tied saplings to the wire with rag string; she'd sown in springtime and hoed on June days so hot she almost swooned. Seaborn P. Jackson was nothing if not industrious, but he would not lift a finger to plant or tend a garden. Dirt, as far as he was concerned, was a substance to stand on. He derived no pleasure from its presence on his hands.

First thing each morning, he heated water for washing. In the back room, behind a gray curtain, he stood in the washtub and bathed himself meticulously, his bald head visible above the curtain rod. Then he shaved and brushed his teeth with baking soda, and once he was finished, he donned his suit and tie. He would not appear at the breakfast table until fully dressed for business.

He sold insurance—health, life and burial, mostly burial—for the Independent Life Insurance Company. For no more than twenty cents a week, you could assure yourself a hundred-dollar funeral. Seaborn himself oversaw the proceedings and was fond of stating he'd never let a dead person down. People called him "the policy man." Behind his back they called him "a biggity nigger," or just "Biggity."

She walked over to the back porch and emptied the beans into a pan, then carried it inside. She was sweating now, her legs and back and armpits wet. She went out back and, after scanning the shrubs lining the rear of the yard, she pulled her blouse off. She primed the pitcher pump, then began sloshing cool water on her arms and her belly, her shoulders and breasts. Seaborn had warned her never to do this. A white man had stopped him on the street one day right in front of Rosenthal's and told him that his son and one other boy had been walking by one day and noticed his wife out back with her shirt off.

"It's fine for y'all to live where you live," the man had said, "but there's a certain amount of responsibility that goes with the ground."

The only way the man's son and the other boy could have noticed her with her top off would have been to squat and peer in through the bushes, and while Seaborn surely knew that, he just as surely never said it.

"Don't *sir* 'em," she'd once heard him advise a young man of their acquaintance. "*Suh* 'em. There are sounds we can make which cause them discomfort, and an *r* on the end of the word *sir* is one of them. Say *uhh* after *sss*. Lay down hard on that last syllable, draw it out, make that good lasting impression, and they won't notice you again for three or four months."

So Seaborn would have rolled his eyes, nodding his head at this word to the wise, then come down hard on that last syllable. "Yes, *suh*." The man would quit noticing him, though he and his son and his son's friend would keep right on noticing her.

THE POST OFFICE stood directly across the street from Rosenthal's, in between the Bank of Loring and Farmer's Drugstore. This morning, when she got there, a mail sack was propped against the door. Sometimes the train came a few minutes early, and even though she'd asked the man who drove the wagon for the C & G not to leave the mail standing out front, where just anybody could take it, he was white and did as he pleased.

She unlocked the door, then grabbed the sack by its drawstring. She spent the next half hour distributing the mail, popping envelopes into boxes, bending over and glancing through the little windows from time to time to make sure nobody had entered the lobby without her hearing them. To keep customers waiting was not her policy. She'd even installed a telephone at her own expense so people could call and find out if they had any mail.

She'd just finished putting the mail out when the front door creaked open. She grabbed a rag and wiped the ink off her hands, then straightened her hair and walked out to the counter.

It was Blueford. He had his hands in his pockets and was wearing the funny-looking little tricornered white hat Rosenthal insisted on during business hours. The hat would've looked ridiculous on most men—she could scarcely imagine it atop Seaborn's bald pate—but somehow Blueford always bore it with dignity, even when he had a fifty-pound sack of cornmeal balanced on his shoulder.

"What you doin' this morning, Loda?"

"Same as every morning."

"Mail done come yet?"

"Sure has."

"I don't reckon I got nothing from my auntie, did I?"

She kept the mail for general delivery stacked on a shelf behind the counter. There was only a handful of items today. She went through them quickly, finding nothing for Blueford. "Sorry. I hope it wasn't money you were expecting."

"Not hardly. She done supposed to had a picture made of my cousin's little baby. I ain't never yet seen him."

"Is this the aunt that lives in Vicksburg?"

"Aunt Florice. Only one I got. Only natural aunt, anyway. Least as far as I know."

He must have noticed that her gaze had shifted, that she was looking beyond him, at the street. A couple wagons passed by, though no one was walking toward the post office. Nonetheless, he did what he knew she needed him to do: he began to take his leave.

"Well," he said, "old Rosenthal got twenty thousand things he expect me to do in the next twenty minutes."

He smiled at her and walked over to the door. He watched the street for a moment. Then, as if it were an afterthought—which it was not, because Blueford never entertained afterthoughts—he said, "By the way. Guess who I just saw this morning?"

"Who?"

"That younger one."

"Oh," she said. "So he's back."

"Yeah." He opened the door. "Reckon wherever he was at, they must of done run out of trouble."

TROUBLE.

She worried about it—you always had to—though she hadn't seen much of it in a pretty good while. She was not the only Negro in Mississippi with a government appointment, but she was the only one in Loring. Add to that the fact she and

Seaborn lived a few yards north of the railroad tracks and owned a twenty percent interest in Rosenthal's, and you became somebody folks couldn't help but pay attention to.

At dusk she closed the office, stepped around the corner at Main and First on her way home, and ran right into a white man, her head actually striking his chest. She bounced back and was about to apologize when she saw who it was.

"Oh, Loda," he said. "I'm sorry. I should've been watching where I was going."

"No," she said. "It's my fault."

"I didn't hurt you, did I?"

The truth was, her nose stung pretty good. "No," she said. Then: "Excuse me. No *sir*."

"Don't do that. Please."

She was looking up into his face. She could see his features distinctly: the square chin, the perfectly shaped nose, the powder blue eyes. He'd recently cut himself shaving; there was a nick near one corner of his mouth.

"It looks to me," she said, "like your daddy could've done a better job teaching you to use a razor." She stood back to observe her last word's effect: averted eyes, a faint bobbing of his Adam's apple, nothing more.

"I hear your brother's back in town," she said, then walked on.

SOME things had to be taken care of, and Tandy had taken care of the two most pressing issues right away. That was how he found himself in bed beside Miss Rosa Bates.

Miss Rosa was a widow, maybe forty-five or -six, a tall, solidly built woman with auburn-colored hair. Her husband had been a frail little man; Tandy used to see him emptying the slop jars behind the boardinghouse, but he'd passed away about fifteen years ago, during the yellow fever epidemic. Miss Rosa catered to the needs of drummers and other itinerants, and she had an agreement with Uncle Billy Heath: she sent folks his way, he sent them hers.

You could tell she had it in her to momma a man, and you could tell, too, that she was lonesome and hungry. He'd gotten her in bed the second night he stayed at her place. It hadn't taken much doing, just a couple shots of whiskey out of a bottle she herself had produced from a cupboard in her upstairs sitting room, and a perfectly honest admission from Tandy: that ever since he was fourteen or fifteen years old, he'd imagined himself alone with her at night. Maybe she hadn't ever set foot in places like Denver or St. Louis, he said, but she'd been to those places with *him*, whether she knew it or not. He carried her there in his imagination. He remembered one night in particular, when he was lying in bed in a hotel all the way out in San Francisco. The window was open, and it was raining, and you could hear carriages rolling down Geary. And he'd closed his eyes and thought of her, how she belonged in a big city, because big cities were exciting and she was, too. Her eyes got misty when he said that, and she laid her hand on his thigh, and the next thing he knew, her tongue was in his ear.

He wouldn't have been caught dead walking the street with Miss Rosa on his arm, but he'd walk the dog in bed with her any night of the week. Her private quarters had that well-stocked cupboard, her bed was big and soft, and her appetite for frolic matched his own. Best of all, she hadn't said a word about wanting a second week's rent.

She lay naked beside him now, her arms locked behind her head, big pink-nippled breasts lolling off either side of her chest. "Tell the truth, Tandy," she said. "You're a foot man."

"A foot man?"

"Some folks are titty men, some rump men. You, you're a foot man. You can't let 'em alone."

He did like her feet; they were big, but nicely shaped. Last night, when he had her on her back with both her legs over his shoulders, in a moment of real abandonment he'd pulled her left heel around in front of his mouth and licked it. He'd also sucked her toes. He'd had his drawers on when he did that, but he felt naked, and he liked the kind of naked it was. He'd been on the verge of telling her he wished she could see inside him, look right through the skin that covered his chest and tell him what was missing. He'd actually said as much once to a Negro woman he'd picked up in a policy shop in Memphis, and she'd looked at him with undisguised sympathy. "Honey," she'd said, "ain't nothing missing in you that ain't missing in everybody else—there may be just a little more of it gone."

What he told Miss Rosa now was, "I like everything about you."

She rolled onto her side. "You're lying."

"Lying how?"

"You don't like my age—and I ain't gone tell you what it is, by the way—and I daresay you don't like all these wrinkles on my neck. And you probably wish I wasn't quite so heavy." He started to protest, but she clamped her hand over his mouth. "And you know what?" she said. Her eyes were close to his, big and blue and a lot smarter-looking than he'd ever noticed. "There's a few things I ain't crazy about concerning you."

She removed her hand, so he could speak if he wanted to. But he didn't. His interest lay in what she might say, how she'd sized him up, whether or not she'd come close to his rotten core.

"You got a mean streak in you—don't forget, boy, I knew your daddy. But unlike old Sam, you're not always mean enough, and that makes you a little harder to predict. The lie you wouldn't tell if it suited you ain't been thought of yet, and if I had five hundred dollars—and I do have five hundred dollars, and a good bit more—I wouldn't no more leave it laying around for you to find than I'd go over to Uncle Billy's and lick a mule's butt. You're here at my place and in my bed because you need to be, and when you don't need to be no more, then you won't be. Question is, Which'll happen first? Will you find whatever it is you're looking for and move on, or will I get sick of your sorriness and pitch you out?"

She'd said all of that with a pleasant-enough look on her face, and the whole time she was saying it, she gently stroked his chest. But when she finished, she reached down between his legs and squeezed his balls. It didn't exactly hurt, but it didn't feel good, either.

"You tell me what it is you want from me," she said, "besides free room and board and a hole to poke your pole in, then I'll tell you what *I* want. And don't bullshit me, Tandy, or I'm liable to run you off right this minute."

Tandy licked his lips and said, "I need to rent a horse."

She stared at him for a second or two before she burst out laughing. "My God, Tandy," she said, "so do I. So do I."

UNCLE Billy Heath gave Tandy a long-winded seven- or eight-year-old bay that he claimed never stumbled and wasn't even scared of rattlesnakes. "Ever drummer that comes through here goes out to the Deadening sooner or later," he said. "More often than not, this is the horse they want. I expect he knows the way better than you do."

Tandy knew the way just fine, though he hadn't been out there since the day his brother signed the papers, selling the house and the land to a man from North Carolina named Ephraim Barnes. His brother had made out fine on that sale; he'd taken his portion of the money and founded the paper, then bought the old saloon and eventually built a big house of his own. Tandy had taken his share—which Leighton didn't even have to offer—and outfitted himself with a pair of new boots, a white suit, a nice trunk with bronze buckles on it, a case of bonded whiskey and a box of Cuban cigars, then boarded a big paddle-wheel steamer. When he got off the boat in St. Louis, he spent three straight days gambling, and at their conclusion, only a dollar and twenty-three cents remained to him. Later on, once he'd learned about the tools of advantage—the microscopic spectacles, the vest and sleeve holdouts all the professionals used so well—he understood that something besides bad luck had been involved.

What he'd done in St. Louis apparently wasn't that much different from what Ephraim Barnes managed to do with his new plantation. Tandy had already learned that Barnes had suffered through several poor crops in a row, and the talk was that he'd compounded his problems with ineptitude and neglect. Two years ago, he'd sold a large parcel of land, and then another last year, plus about half his livestock. Folks said he'd brought a woman down from Louisville, but she was incapable of withstanding the harsh summers; she'd left last year, supposedly to visit relatives, and hadn't yet returned. Folks said it didn't look like Barnes was going to make it.

Tandy rode southwest out of town along a narrow dirt road bordered on both sides by canebrakes that, in places, were twelve to fifteen feet tall. His daddy had cleared a couple thousand acres of cane. He and his men had cut it down, stacked it in huge piles and set them on fire. The joints in the cane were airtight. Burning, they popped like firecrackers.

There had been a great many fires back then: that was the only efficient way to clear large tracts. But trees, unlike cane, wouldn't burn while they were green. So his daddy ordered the men to ringbark them; then he filled an old vinegar bottle with poison and poured it into the rings through a cane spigot. The next year, once the trees were good and dead, the men piled up branches and set fires, which sometimes burned all night.

So much smoke was drifting in the air that Tandy's momma would soak handkerchiefs and bring them into the bedroom and lay them over his and Leighton's faces. Leighton could sleep like that, but he never could. He'd get out of bed and sit by the window until dawn, the damp handkerchief clamped to his nose, his eyes stinging while he gazed out on a landscape resembling the pictures of Hell in his momma's illustrated Bible.

THE OLD grinnell hole across from the front gate had just about dried up. He sat his horse and looked at it, recalling how when he was ten or twelve years old, sitting there with his feet in the water and a cane pole in his hand, he'd imagined that one day he'd be master of this place or one just like it. He'd holler an order and ten folks would jump. Trees would fall, woods would flame, a great mansion would rise from the ashes.

His father's structure, he saw when he turned his head, had begun to decay. One of the fluted columns along the front was sagging, the trim on the window casings was chipped and peeling, the roof missing shingles.

The house had seventeen rooms, an interior staircase eight feet wide and a ballroom big enough to hold half of Loring. His daddy once gave a lay-by party that lasted three days and included more than five hundred guests; for this event, he'd bought a thousand loaves of bread and eighteen hundred pounds of beef and had them shipped up the river from Vicksburg.

Building a house like this one and maintaining a six-thousand-acre plantation was chancy business, but his daddy had been a good gambler. He'd won his first thousand acres in a poker game, and he'd kept right on gaining, one way or another, until the day he went in the ground.

What it took to lose a place like this, or at least your share of it, was a question Tandy had often pondered, never arriving at a firm answer. So in the week that he'd been back, he'd decided the question itself didn't matter. What mattered, as his daddy and Leighton had both understood, was what you wanted. Tandy himself had never been sure, but now, for the first time, he thought he did know. And having figured that out, he meant to get it. All he needed was what his daddy used to win that first thousand acres.

A large vision. A small stake.

A DOG CAME around the corner of the house, studied him for a minute, then started barking. He was followed, a few seconds later, by an old Negro in a pair of blue overalls. Walking over to the gate, the man dragged the blade of a hoe along the ground. "Yes sir?"

"Mr. Barnes around?"

"No sir. Mr. Barnes ain't been here for nearabouts to two weeks."

"Where's he at?"

"Mr. Barnes done gone up to Louisville, Kentucky."

"What's he doing in Louisville?"

The old man leaned on his hoe. "I think maybe he might of gone up there to see somebody."

The cotton in the field south of the house was five or six feet tall, with blooms on top and the bottom bolls starting to open. It wasn't a bad-looking stand. In fact, it was pretty damn good-looking. "He's mighty stupid," Tandy said, "if he's gone chasing after some woman this close to picking time."

"Well," the man said, as if he hated to hear the reputation of his employer impugned, "he got somebody what handle things for him."

"Yeah, and I guess that's who's responsible for the house itself starting to look like a nigger shack."

The old man did not drop his head, as Tandy had expected, and instead looked him right in the eye. Tandy felt his blood rise. *Say just a word,* he thought, *and I'll slash you with the crop.* He could do that, or something worse if he wanted to, because he was Tandy Payne, and the old man was not himself but a colored extension of Ephraim Barnes, who did not belong here now and never would.

This was the realization Tandy had come to in the last few days: he'd spent most of his adult life in places where he didn't belong. He'd been played for a sucker by every sharper from New Orleans to Cincinnati, from there to Denver and back. They weren't better men than he was, they weren't luckier, they weren't even smarter. When you got right down to it, they were just men who felt at home with stamped cards in their hands and glass reflectors in the bowls of their pipes. Whereas he felt at home right here. Right now.

"You tell Mr. Barnes I came asking for him."

"And what'd be the gentleman's name?"

Tandy slacked the left-hand rein and pulled the other against the horse's neck, turning him back toward town.

"Mr. Terrell Andrew Payne."

"THE HOME Comfort Range got white porcelain doors on the warmer," Jakub Rosenthal said, swinging open a door above the cooktop. "Got two eyes above the firebox, two more over here on the right, less exposed to heat. Baking oven down here next to the firebox. And then, the best treasure of all, is this." He lifted a heavy metal plate off the range to reveal a medium-sized copper tank nestled in a compartment next to the oven. "You want a warm bath, you heat water down here, and you got a warm bath—just like that." To punctuate his last statement, Rosenthal snapped his fingers.

They always went through this routine, and Seaborn always enjoyed it. Without question, he would buy the range, since he had come here for that purpose; practically speaking, he already owned twenty percent of it. But it mattered that Rosenthal should go through the motions of selling him on it. And so, as with any large purchase Seaborn was about to make, Rosenthal complied. The one ground rule, unspoken by either party, was that these transactions must occur when no other customers were present. Nobody else was present right now, unless you counted Blueford, who was over in the corner among the cans of neat's-foot and mink oil, sweeping up, with that ridiculous hat on his head. Seaborn did not count Blueford. No amount of noise or motion could have made him look Blueford's way, just as Blueford would never turn in his direction.

"What woods would you recommend burning in there, Mr. Rosenthal?"

"Burn any wood. Best to burn oak and locust."

"What about pine?"

"Pine gonna be fine. Gonna burn fast, though."

"Now, about the price of this range—"

"A good price. Very good. Eighty dollars. You go over to Greenville, this stove got to cost you ninety-five."

"However," said Seaborn, arms crossed over his prominent stomach, "there's the question of the discount."

"Ah, the discount." Jakub Rosenthal—clad as always in his dark worsteds, with matching vest, tie and armbands—jammed his hands into his pockets. "Well now, *Mr.* Jackson, this eighty dollars, that already includes the twenty percent discount."

"I believe you just remarked that if I were to venture over to Greenville, this same stove would cost me ninety-five?"

"Ninety-five, that's right. That's what it's gonna cost you over in Greenville."

"Well now, Mr. Rosenthal, if I were to subtract twenty percent of ninety-five from ninety-five, I believe the figure I would arrive at would be somewhere in the vicinity of ... let's see ... I believe it would be seventy-six dollars."

"Yes indeed, Mr. Jackson. Your math is good. But that stove you not gonna buy over there in Greenville because you gonna buy this one here, that Greenville stove come right off the riverboat and onto the shop floor. This stove here, it come off the riverboat and they put it on a flatbed wagon and carry it over to the depot and then they put it on the C & G, and the C & G brings it over here and Blueford over there, he loads it onto the wagon and drives the wagon up here and then he takes it off the wagon with three other persons, and all these movements and all these persons cost Rosenthal's General Merchandise five dollars. Bringing the cost of this stove—this Loring stove—to one hundred dollars. Now, you take twenty percent from one hundred, and with your good math, you tell me what you got."

Seaborn had already reached into his pocket.

"What you gonna tell me you got, Mr. Jackson, because you're an honest man, is eighty American dollars."

Seaborn opened his billfold and began extracting fives and tens. Then he pulled out four ones. "I'll arrange my own delivery," he said. "Somebody will come for it tomorrow." He placed the bills in order, largest to smallest, and handed the entire stack to Rosenthal.

When Rosenthal was a young man, he had worked as an actor: if there was one thing he could do, it was follow a script. He counted the bills. Not once but twice. "Seventy-nine dollars," he said, ashen-faced with dismay.

"Twenty percent of that five-dollar movement-and-person cost is one dollar. And that one dollar belongs to me."

He tipped his hat to Jakub Rosenthal and bade him a very good day.

LEAVING, he glanced across the street at the post office. She was in there, standing behind the counter, waiting on a white woman, her mouth in the act of forming the words *Yes ma'am*. He watched as the woman laid some change on the counter. Loda waited a few seconds, lessening the chance of palm-to-palm contact, then reached out and picked up the money. No subservience marred her manner; she did what had to be done with style and grace and a perfectly straight face.

He had attended college, was conversant with physiology, knew a swollen heart was cause for worry rather than pride. But his heart was swollen now, and not from illness. Despite his determination never to grin in public, he made an exception, just this once, and allowed himself to do so.

THE GRIN, when she saw it, almost made her weep. On the far side of yet a second pane of glass, beyond spooled hemp and bolts of gingham, Blueford stood watching Seaborn walk away as if he owned the world. When finally he disappeared from view, Blueford raised his gaze. For a moment, his eyes met hers, and they locked gazes like that day she'd chased him through June cotton, laughing, right down to the banks of the river. Once she had him cornered, he'd grabbed the branch of a cottonwood and swung his legs into the air. Rather than wrap her arms around his knees and try to pull him down, she let him hang there, the muscles in his wiry arms rippling, until the effort began to show in the skin stretched taut across his cheeks. Finally, he let go, and as soon as his feet hit the ground, she lunged and shouldered him over.

Together, they'd lain there, heedless of the moccasins that surely were crawling nearby, her face a few inches from his.

"What you want?" he'd said.

"Not a thing in this world."

"Don't want nothing, how come you run me like I got some kind of scent on me?"

"I didn't say I didn't want anything. I said not a thing in this world."

"You a funny girl." Still he didn't touch her. "How come your skin so yellow?"

3 1

"Maybe I've got the yellow fever."

Then he did touch her, tracing his index finger along the bridge of her nose. She swore to herself that she wouldn't shiver. And didn't.

"Fever you got ain't none of no yellow."

So far back: it was the same year a Negro who called himself Dr. Sellers rode a sorrel gelding from plantation to plantation, exhorting all the freedmen to lay down their tools, to stop being hewers of wood and drawers of water and follow him to the land of Liberia, where he claimed they would have their own country.

He always wore a yellow saddle coat and black kip boots and a broad-brimmed hat with a black band around the crown. People said he was always armed, though nobody had ever actually seen a gun. Nobody had ever seen him eat or sleep, either, and nobody knew where he stayed. Some said that when night fell, he simply disappeared. Others claimed he lay down in the canebrakes.

One day in early autumn, when the pickers had taken to the fields, he rode onto Payne's Deadening. He rode slowly, tall and erect in the saddle. As many as fifty people walked along behind him, grown men and women, the elderly with their stooped shoulders and gray faces, some of the children so small they could hardly walk at all. One woman carried two babies, each in the crook of an arm. Old Miss Bessie got behind him, and her youngest son, Markham, fell in behind him, too.

All this was in the glance that passed now between her and Blueford: the sound of cotton leaves rustling as two pairs of young legs tore through a field, that stillness on the riverbank, the proud man on his gelding and those straggling along behind.

All of that, and more.

.   .   .

AFTERWARDS, whenever she tried to remember exactly what she'd been doing when he walked in, she couldn't. She knew her back had been turned to the door, so maybe she was post-marking mail. Or she could have been examining the figures in her ledger. But it always seemed to her that she knew it was Blueford who'd walked through the door. She reached up—this much she recalled with complete clarity—and scratched an irksome spot on her neck. Then she turned around.

"Morning," he said.

"Hi, Blueford."

"Seaborn been in."

"I noticed."

"Done come in and bought a Home Comfort Range. Said he'd arrange his own delivery."

"Well . . . you know he prides himself on taking charge of the situation."

"He didn't say it was no present or nothing. Hope I'm not saying too much."

For the first time in a long while, she detected a touch of bitterness. He was better than most people at concealing what he felt—usually, even from one who already knew. "You never say too much," she said.

The comment seemed to please him. He smiled and cocked his head slightly, and for a moment he looked like the boy he'd once been, back before all that time spent chopping and picking cotton in hundred-degree heat took its toll. Even though he'd worked in town the last few years, he still did his share of heavy labor, pulling those big sacks off the delivery wagon.

He lived in a shack with an old man named Scheider, a former slave who worked as a servant and driver for a white woman. Loda had ridden past the place one day in the hackney with Seaborn. Scheider sat barefooted on the front steps, drinking from a jug, swallowing hard, his Adam's apple bobbing. He spotted them, lowered the jug and hollered, "Yonder go the policy man!" Suddenly, Blueford stepped through the door. Gently, he reached down and pulled the jug from Scheider's hands, then placed his own hands under the old man's armpits and lifted him up. He led him back inside, without ever once glancing at the road. She could scarcely imagine what the moment must have cost him. She knew perfectly well what it had cost her.

"I ain't got no mail today, have I?" he said.

"Let me look."

She turned and made a pretense of riffling through the general delivery. "No," she finally said. "Sorry, not this morning."

"Well, reckon I best to be—"

He never got to finish, because the door opened and Tandy Payne stepped into the post office.

It had been a long time since she'd seen him—but not nearly long enough. He'd aged, the first traces of speckling in his mustache.

She remembered asking her mother why it was she didn't believe in the devil, as she often announced, and her answer was, "The Lord would never've needed to make Sam Payne if He'd already created Satan. Sam Payne's here among us, him and that younger son of his, and I'll tell you something. You ever see that white boy coming up behind you, you take off as fast as you can. You get to me and I'll do what needs doing. Because that boy may seem like a little worm now, but he's not a thing in the world but a big snake in the making."

He was not behind her, but in front of her, standing there holding an envelope in his hand and smiling at her as if he was glad to see her.

It took some doing for Blueford to attract his attention. He must have known the right thing for him to do was drop his head and shuffle out the door, yet he stood right there. She would never know whether it was his recent encounter with

Seaborn that made him stay, nor would she ever stop wondering.

"Believe I need me a few stamps, Mrs. Jackson." He reached into his pocket for change.

"Hey, there," Tandy said.

"Being as I got me—let's see, I got me two letters at home I need to mail—naw, now, excuse me, I got me *three*."

"Hey, there. Ain't you the one used to stuff rocks in the bottom of the sack coming weighing time?"

Nobody would have had the guts to weight a sack on Sam Payne. Not even Blueford. But Tandy Payne wasn't Sam Payne, and while Blueford should have seen the crucial similarities, for some reason they seemed to escape him.

He turned around and looked at Tandy. "I never stuffed no rocks in no sack. But I got docked a little too much from time to time."

"You saying my daddy cheated you?"

"His overseer was bad to melt lead and put it in the pea on them scales. Your daddy knew it, too. Miss Bessie was on him about it, but he never paid her no mind."

Tandy gnawed his lower lip. "You better tell him to straighten up, Loda."

She heard that whine in his voice, the same one she used to hear when he had trouble mounting his colt. His daddy had made him ride that colt because he knew it would buck him off and he wanted to toughen his son up. But the minute Tandy started whining like that, his momma would come running. She'd call one of the Negroes, and all he'd have to do was be lifted into the saddle.

"Tell him, Loda."

She wasn't his mother: there was no word for what she was to him, or he to her. She did his bidding nonetheless. "Go on across the street now," she said. "Go on now, Blueford. I mean it. I'll get you those stamps later."

Blueford dropped his hands and walked toward the door.

Payne stood directly before it, so she closed her eyes and prayed that he would step aside, but when she opened them again, he hadn't moved. He and Blueford were just inches apart.

This can't be happening, she thought. Seaborn had said it wouldn't, that it couldn't so long as they comported themselves in the proper manner. But Seaborn tended to forget they lived among others.

"What you aim to say?"

"Ain't gone say nothing. Ain't gone can leave, neither, lessen I can get through that door."

"Liable to get old standing there, then."

Blueford shrugged. "Somebody else gone get old with me."

Tandy stood there a moment longer, then finally said, "I aim to live in this town now, and stuff like this is fixing to quit going on. Why, it beats anything I've ever seen. And I've seen a few things. I sure have." He eyed Blueford's funny hat. "You ought to tell old Rosenthal you don't want to wear that thing. It's way too easy to draw a bead on."

He stuffed the envelope back in his pocket, opened the door and walked out.

IT WAS several seconds before Blueford faced her. When he did, he grinned at her and stuck his hands in his pockets. "Now don't act like it's Christmas," he said. "It ain't no Christmas. Nor New Year's, neither."

"No," she said. "It's not."

"Ain't nothing but a ordinary day."

"No," she said again, "it's hardly that. Not now."

"Well, it sure enough was. Except for I come in here and seen you. And that's what made it different from most days."

He left her standing in the hot, silent air, filled with his and Tandy Payne's absence.

WHEN Leighton rode into the livery stable, Uncle Billy Heath was coming out of the stall where a walleyed chestnut mare stood snorting. A halter strap dangled from the old man's hand.

Uncle Billy spat a stream of tobacco juice into the dirt. "Been out gathering the news?"

Leighton dismounted and handed him the reins. "Yeah. Traveled out to Brent's Landing. You remember when Devere Logan died?"

"Two, maybe three years ago?"

"Four years last month. They buried him under a big old oak in the backyard and left him there till sometime last fall, when they moved the remains over to the town cemetery. His wife claimed that as soon as they buried him, that tree lost all its leaves. Then this past spring, after they relocated him, the tree budded out again."

Uncle Billy led Leighton's mare into her stall, where he pulled her bridle off, slipped on the halter and tied her to the snubbing ring. "You believe she's telling the truth?"

"Well, I believe Devere had a fair amount of poison in him."

"Speaking of them that's poisonous, I hear your brother's keen on the old home place."

"Where'd you hear that?"

Uncle Billy pulled the saddle off and lugged it over to the tack room. Leighton followed.

"He come in here the other day to get him a horse. You can probably guess who paid for the horse, and you can probably guess what Tandy's done to deserve that person's patronage, and all I can say about that is, I guarantee you he'll earn every cent she gives him and then some. He didn't make no secret of the fact that he aimed to go out to the Deadening."

"I imagine he just wanted to go have a look around."

"Then yesterday I was in the barbershop," Uncle Billy continued, as if Leighton hadn't spoken. "Ben Huffnagle told me Tandy'd come in for a haircut. Said Tandy told him he was in the act of raising money to buy the place back from Barnes."

The sweat on Leighton's back and shoulders felt cold. "He told him *what*?"

Uncle Billy sat down on a bench and pulled out a plug of chewing tobacco, broke a hunk off and stuffed it in his mouth. For a minute or two, his jaws worked furiously. He closed his eyes, savoring the bitter sweetness.

"Now, old Ben Huffnagle, he can cut hair real good. But let's face it. Every horse in here, not to mention the mules, has got Ben bested when it comes to figuring out a problem. Ben thinks Tandy aims to raise his money by stirring Miss Rosa's coals, but as for me—well, I got my doubts. I believe Tandy's sharp enough to know Rosa don't have that much and wouldn't give it to him if she did." He spat. "What do you think?"

Leighton's mouth was so dry that he suddenly craved a drink of water, or maybe something stronger; but as he was not a drinking man, water would have to do. "I reckon I don't have an opinion."

Uncle Billy eyed him. "You the newsman. How come *I'm* the one telling *you* this?"

"Sometimes, I guess, the chicken loses an egg or two."

"That's as may well be." Uncle Billy chuckled and fired

another stream of spit into the dirt. "But between you and me, boy, you better quit worrying over who killed Mrs. Logan's damn oak tree."

HE SAT alone in his office, knowing he ought to get to writing and stop thinking about his brother. Tandy was an alchemist, always looking for a way to turn metal into gold, and almost none of his schemes ever worked out. "That boy's as worthless as a post-oak ridge," their father had said more than once. Yet Tandy had looked up to Sam Payne in a way that Leighton never had, though both boys had feared him alike.

Leighton pulled a sheet of paper from the stack on his desk and inserted it in the Underwood. Today was Friday, the day when he wrote "terry says" for the following week's paper. Allegedly a cockroach, "terry" did his work at night and wrote everything in lowercase letters because his method of composition involved leaping from one typewriter key to another, and for him to hold down the shift key was impossible. The column had become wildly popular, even though terry tended toward Republicanism in national politics and Loring County's mascot was still the yellow dog.

People forgave terry his leanings, just as they forgave Leighton his. The previous fall, when Booker T. Washington dined at the White House and papers all over the state reacted with outrage, calling for President Roosevelt's ouster, Leighton alone had counseled forbearance. *The president,* he wrote, *is not a Southerner, though he is certainly friendly to the South; he does not always think as we do, nor should he have to. As for B. T. Washington, we must ask ourselves whether or not one single ill-advised action should negate an entire lifetime of circumspect behavior. The answer, I suggest, is no. B. T. Washington is like the rest of us. He is not perfect. From time to time, he may make mis-*

takes. But on the whole, he has done a lot more good—for his own people as well as for us—than he has done harm.

Nobody held that editorial against him. People just smiled and shook their heads and said, "Aw, you know Leighton." Three months later, after A. L. Gunnels died, they asked him to be mayor.

Tentatively, he hit a key. As always, the words began to pour forth, the one thing he never had trouble with. Words had never let him down—though in his heart he feared he'd sometimes let them down.

everybody's worried about the pennsylvania miners' strike. when winter gets here, folks are saying, people are gonna freeze. folks are saying the president needs to get tough with those miners, tell them to get off their duffs and go back to work.

well, now, i'm a cockroach, and i know a thing or two about making do. and i'll tell you something. those miners had been working 12 hours a day, 6 days a week, for the princely sum of 50 dollars a month. out of that they paid their rent, paid for their food and fuel and had a charge deducted every month for the company doctor, though the company doctor rarely did anything for them except pronounce them dead.

here's what the miners are asking for now—a 10 or 15 percent raise, an 8-hour workday, and recognition of their union.

union, you say. why, unions are downright european.

but listen to what i heard the other day.

somebody came across a 12-year-old boy that was working down there in one of them dark holes for 30 cents a day and having every single penny going to pay off a debt left by his daddy, who'd lost his life in that selfsame mine 3 years earlier.

now like i said, folks, terry's a plain old cockroach, and a cockroach is supposed to live like a cockroach. but folks are folks, and they deserve to be treated like folks. so terry says let's go along with t.r. let's welcome him with open arms when he comes down here this fall to shoot bear, and let's let this strike work itself out. and in the end, we'll all be a lot better off.

and maybe that little boy can hang on to at least a few of them 30 pennies.

He read over the column, laid it aside, then looked at his watch: half past five. If he got home soon enough, he might grab the cane poles and take Will down to the bayou and see if they couldn't catch a fish or two before supper. They were biting. He'd walked over the bridge just this morning and seen three Negro men sitting there with their legs dangling over the water, poles resting on their knees, a couple frantic white perch splashing in a nearby bucket. The men all tipped their hats when he passed.

"Good mornin', Captain," one said. "How you, sir?"

"Just fine, Shine," he'd said, intending that the nickname apply to all three. He didn't know any of their names, nor whether any of them had ever shined shoes for a living. He just knew they were friendly and polite, as he meant to be.

He opened the door and stepped onto the sidewalk, the streets abustle with activity. Percy Stancill had sent several hundred bales of cotton to town, all of it loaded onto mule-drawn wagons that were creaking down Main Street in a caravan, bound for the compress. The Negroes driving the wagons were followed by an array of brightly dressed women from down in the Quarters, who called out to them, urging them to come over this evening.

His father, he suspected, had been to those places, and certainly his brother had. Sometimes, though it shamed him, he found himself wishing for it, too. He guessed if you could find it in yourself to go down there, you could quit worrying about your size or how rough your hands were; you could go on and grunt and slobber and moan, do all those things you'd always wanted to, and nobody would know but you and God and the woman you'd done them with, and she'd never tell anybody who mattered. But sooner or later, you'd have to walk past her on the sidewalk, and even though all those things you'd done with her had meant the world to you right when you were doing them, you wouldn't be able to tip your hat and say hello or wish her good day. And that just was not any way to behave.

He locked the door, pocketed the key and started across the street.

"Leighton! Ho—*Leigh*ton!"

It was the last voice he wanted to hear right now, the last he ever wanted to hear, and for an instant he contemplated darting across the street to disappear in the crowd surging along beside the wagons. He could slip away, go on home, and maybe Tandy would take a fancy to one of the women and forget what was on his mind.

But Leighton stopped and waited while his brother hurried toward him waving a sheet of paper. A cigar was clamped between Tandy's teeth, but it didn't stop him from grinning in a worrisome way.

"Looks like a little bit of the literary impulse has rubbed off on me," Tandy said, handing Leighton the sheet. "I'd like you to put this in next week's paper."

Dear Mister Editor

"Figured I'd start off formal," Tandy said. "Just so folks wouldn't think anything untoward was involved, what with us being kin."

"The word *editor* is misspelled."

"Well, I ain't had the benefit of all the reading you've done." With his forefinger, Tandy thumped the page. "Go on, now—read it."

It has come to my atention in recent day that a unhappy situation exists here in Loring. There is to put it planley a colored woman running one of the most important institutions in our town which is the United States Post Office. The other day yours truly happened to venture into said institution only to discover that there was in adition to this woman another member of her race hanging around there and in this case it was a male.

Well you may say it was most likely her husband a respected enough member of that race and a bisiness man in his own right and there is nothing wrong with him droping sometimes by there to see his wife and it could be that he needed to send something. Well I happen to know that it was not her husband nor a member of the colored bisiness comunity of Loring Miss. but a laborer who used to work on a local plantation and is now employed as a porter at a bisiness on Main Street.

I will leave aside for now the mater of what he was doing there at all clearly to me engaged in low voiced conversation with this woman who I remind you is the wife of another colored man. I will simply say this. Do we the citizens of Loring that pay our taxes to the United States Goverment really want to send our womenfolks into a place where a colored man hangs around for no good purpose?

Furthermore I will say this. The colored man in question behaved in a very agresive maner when it was said to him that if he did not have bisiness to transact he should step aside in favor of one that did. I would not for one moment have hesitated to make him step aside was it not for the fact

that this was a public place and I did not want to cause con-
fusion there that might turn violent in the event that one of
our women or the Good Lord forbid a child should come in
and become swept up in the turmoll.

Leaving aside how it is that this situation could have
come to pass without action on the part of our civic leaders I
ask all good people of Loring is this the way we want things
to be or do we want to turn things around and take back the
institutions of our fair and lovelie town?

Sincerely
Terrell Andrew Payne

"Well?"

Leighton tried to give back the letter, but Tandy made no move to accept it. So Leighton folded the page twice, then reached out and tucked it into the space between two buttons on his brother's shirt.

"I suppose that means you don't like it?"

"First of all, it's illiterate—I'd be embarrassed to publish it for that reason alone. Second, it's incendiary. Loring's a peaceful place now. We don't have any troubles here with our colored folks, and I don't know why anybody'd want to start any, unless he was just somebody who liked to bring people grief. That woman hasn't done anything to you. But then, maybe that's the problem."

Tandy's features had always been soft: he lacked the pronounced chin that Leighton and their father had, and the skin on his cheekbones was actually a little bit flaccid. But his face now looked as if some type of hardening solution had been applied to it.

He actually hates me, Leighton realized. He didn't know why he'd never seen it before, but he hadn't. In a strange way, the hatred invested Tandy with added stature.

Without moving his eyes away from Leighton, Tandy

pulled the letter out of his shirtfront. He unfolded it and gently smoothed the creases. "One way or another," he said, "I'll get this circulated."

"Well, I suppose I can't stop you. But it won't be in my paper."

Tandy tipped his hat and started toward Main Street. Before he'd taken more than three or four steps, he stopped and turned around. "What you said a minute ago's not the truth. She did do something to me. And believe me, brother, it's a goddamn shame she didn't do it to you, too."

LEIGHTON entered the bathroom, intending to shave, not realizing anyone was inside. Sarah lay in the tub, her breasts jutting up through the suds. When she heard the door open and saw him standing there, unable to keep himself from staring at her, her face colored. She sat up and grabbed a piece of pumice, then doubled over and began scrubbing her feet.

Water sluiced down her back. She had a cyst near the base of her spine. Unsightly already, it had gotten bigger in the last two years, but she refused to see a doctor, for fear he'd tell her it would have to be cut out. This was her only physical imperfection, and the sight of it—coupled with the certainty that only he knew it existed—always drove Leighton half-mad with desire.

He walked over to the tub and knelt down to lay his hand over it.

"It's sore today," she said. She stopped scrubbing her feet but continued to sit there, bent over. He ran his hand up her back, over her shoulders. For the bath, she'd done her hair up in a bun. His fingers glided over the tightly wound strands. She sighed, then gripped the rim of the tub with one hand and pushed herself up.

Water dripped from her heavy breasts, running down her belly and over her thighs. She stood there facing him, letting him drink her in with his eyes, even as his face began to burn from embarrassment.

4 6

"We can go in the bedroom," she said. "If you want to."

She lay with her head between two pillows, her legs open just far enough for him to get inside her. Though he always promised himself that he'd keep silent until he'd finished, he began to whisper how much he loved her, how he treasured her body, how he walked around town all day thinking about doing this, wanting to be where he was right now. "Um-hmm," she murmured. "That's real sweet, Leighton." She kept her eyes closed all the while, her hands down by her sides, hips flat against the mattress.

He gasped and surged into her, then lay there wet and happy, not yet humiliated by his need and the words he'd said, though he knew all of that would come soon enough.

She raised her hand and patted him gently on the shoulder. "I'll have to go wash again," she said, glancing at the clock. "If we don't hurry, we'll be late. I was hoping for a seat near the stage."

Lying there alone, he heard her drawing yet another tubful of water, then listened to the sounds of her moving around the bathroom. He imagined her rubbing herself with the washcloth, scrubbing herself down there with a big bar of soap, and before long, he wanted her again.

He got up and walked over to the closet. He pulled his suit off the hanger, laid it out on the bed, then walked over to the window. The breeze coming in from the street was cool. He stood just to the side of the window and leaned his head against the wall, letting that soft breeze cool the sweat on his body.

By the time she returned, he was already dressed, poised at the mirror, carefully knotting his tie.

"OUR POSITION in the community," Seaborn said, "demands that we be present. Otherwise, every Negro in Loring will know we didn't want to watch another Negro make a fool of himself, and they'll feel bad because they *did* want to watch. At the same time, the white folks'll suspect we believed it was beneath us. So we're going. And I'll promise you this: listening to an idiot play 'Dixie' in two keys while he hums it in a third key may not thrill us, but it surely won't kill us. The joke, as always, will be on somebody else."

So they had come and now were sitting on a rough-hewn bench in the roped-off area along one side of the tent. The Negro section had been almost full when they arrived, but as if by common accord, people had left two empty spaces on the bench nearest the rope. When Seaborn saw that their spots had been reserved, he chuckled and whispered, "Put your best Negroes forward."

She could see Tandy Payne over in the white section, and, four or five rows in front of him, Leighton Payne and his wife and their son. Though the Payne boy looked a lot like his father had when he was that age, he was arrogant in a way his father never had been. A while back, his mother had sent him to the post office to mail some letters. After opening the door, he took one look at the big red-faced white man in muddy overalls who was waiting in line behind Mrs. Claiborne Gray, realized he was either a sharecropper or day laborer and marched right past. The man licked his lips and stared at the floor but never said a word.

That white man's name was Grover Beam, and he was here today, too, sitting at the rear of the tent, accompanied by his wife and three small children. Loda reminded herself once again to stay out of his way. Given that she'd witnessed his humiliation, he was dangerous.

THE STAGE, an improvised platform made of cypress boards resting on stacked concrete blocks, was barren except for the concert piano placed in its center. As the first sounds of impatience began to register, a tall man clad in a gray suit and matching hat strode through the crowd. He climbed a set of stairs and stood onstage, facing the audience. The noise began to die down.

The impresario was Boyce Hendricks, though he called himself Colonel Jameson. Every white person present probably believed what the circulars said—that he hailed from Savannah, Georgia, and had served in the Army of Tennessee under General John Bell Hood—but Loda happened to know he'd grown up in a small town in southern Ohio. Seaborn's cousin lived in that same town and had written them to say that Hendricks had purchased his main attraction's contract from a former Confederate cavalryman with money he made supplying bootleg whiskey to Cincinnati brothels.

"I'm Colonel John Dabney Jameson." He stepped closer to the edge of the stage. "Ladies and gentlemen, you are about to witness something so unusual, so utterly extra-ord-inary, that there's no name for it in any known language except for one which is spoken only in an obscure mountainous region of western Africa. The tribesmen there call the phenomenon in question *dumcumbanyala*."

Seaborn leaned over and whispered, "This fool might as well have *Bluff the yokels* scrawled across his forehead. I think I'm starting to like him."

"When a person is possessed of *dumcumbanyala,* he has the ability to do amazing things that he can neither understand nor explain because his mental faculties are badly impaired and he does not have the powers of rational speech.

"The man we know as Blind Bob was born in slavery, on a plantation in the Carolina Piedmont. He has never seen the light of day. Certain sounds—thunder, for instance, and also the lowing of cattle—are terrifying to him. The moment he hears them, he will invariably cower, covering his ears with his hands. He eats only potatoes and corn, will drink nothing but water and, strange as it may sound, blackberry balsam, which his system appears to regard as a dessert. Though he has the physique of a fully adult male, he has never shown any signs of sexual proclivity—he is not, in other words, dangerous to any of the fine ladies I see arrayed before me.

"He manifests *dumcumbanyala* in musical discourse. He has had no musical training, but his special skills, which will soon be on display, were discovered by his owner when Bob was a child of four. One day, Bob's master summoned Bob's mother, a house slave, into the room where his daughter was playing a minuet on the piano. For some reason, Bob was with his mother, tagging along behind her, hanging on to her skirt. While the master gave Bob's mother her orders for the day, the daughter got up and went outside. The next thing Bob's mother and her master knew, Bob had wandered over to the piano. He felt the keys a few times, running his fingers over them. Then, to his mother's horror and his master's mystification, he sat down on the bench. His fingers touched the keys, and he began to play the minuet as pretty as it had ever been played before or since.

"The master and Bob's mother stood there stunned. In no time, the master effected the return of his daughter. He made her sit back down at the piano and play another piece, a fragment of the *Moonlight* Sonata. When she finished, Bob sat down and played it back perfectly.

"Ladies and gentlemen, that was in the year 1858. Since that morning, Bob has played for three presidents, more than twenty governors, eight foreign heads of state, and Queen Victoria of England. The tales of his prowess are legion. Audiences large and small have watched him in pure awe.

"He loves applause. Applause, when he hears it, seems to stimulate his abilities. Therefore, please, if he delights you, let him know it. The noise of a delighted audience may be the only pleasure this poor benighted creature shall ever experience."

The colonel swept one hand back, and the curtain at the rear of the stage parted. His voice rose to a shout. "Ladies and gentlemen, please welcome him here today in Loring, Mississippi, the finest living example of the phenomenon of *dumcumbanyala,* the strange and amazing Blind Bob!"

THE MAN who walked onstage and sat on the piano bench was indeed blind, but he was neither an idiot nor without musical training. True, he'd played fluently before learning the meaning of the word *note* or the relationship of notes to scales or scales to chords. He'd received his training after the man who'd once been his master discovered he could play.

Today, to start things off, he played Chopin's Mazurka in C-sharp Minor, reveling in the barrage of sevenths that came at the end, disconcerted only slightly by the colonel's shouted commentary: "He hasn't the faintest idea what he's doing, ladies and gentlemen. He's never seen this piece written on the page, though he once heard it *en plein air* in Paris."

In fact, he'd heard it not in Paris, but in Prague, at the Estates Theatre, while sitting quietly behind a curtain in a box belonging to a countess who admired his playing. He had stayed at the lady's house back in the days before the colonel had purchased his contract. He had eaten at the table with her and her family, and her husband had taken him for a walk on a hill above the city on an icy December evening. The gentleman described for him the way the city looked spread out far below, how snow covered the rooftops and smoke billowed up from hundreds and thousands of chimneys, and while the gentleman would not have believed that he could see those rooftops, those chimneys, he had seen them, and he saw them again now and would show them to those who would see them.

Notes were sights, chords were pictures, melody was places and memories. Once, in a town in eastern Arkansas, a little girl had come to the stage and played a piece she'd composed, and the air in the tent had been heavy with the odor of chitterlings being boiled in a vat out back. The girl's song, which he still played, was the sense of that evening: the taste of the chitterlings the colonel had allowed him to eat after the performance, the feel of the child's nervous sweat on the keys. Though the song was not on today's program, he played it anyway, just as the girl had, and while playing, he wondered if the girl remembered him at all, if the countess or her husband did.

He wondered, too, how many of the people who were here today would remember him in ten years. Would they recall, as he would, that a train had rumbled through town just before the performance, that the air smelled of rain? These were the memories he'd hold on to, the ones he would play next month or next year, to a new audience in yet another town, wherever the colonel told him to sit on the bench.

He played another piece he loved—Listz's "Funeral Gondola," filled with eerie augmented fourths—and then, because it was time, he went through a few of his novelty routines, playing two melodies at the same time, plunking a swatch of this tune, a fragment of that one, "Yankee Doodle" on the left hand, "Dixie" on the right. After which, having felt Hendricks' palm come to rest on his shoulder, he got ready for the part of the performance that audiences loved most, when the colonel would invite various locals up to the piano to play their own compositions, which he, Blind Bob, would then repeat—though much improved—note for note.

. . .

"My momma can play the piano!" Will was on his feet. "My momma can! She makes up songs!"

The colonel smiled and extended his hand, beckoning her. She could feel her cheeks heating up. She wanted to mount the steps and take the stage, realized now she'd come here wanting to do that very thing, though she could not have said why. In any case, her position in the town—she was, after all, the mayor's wife—forbade her taking part in such spectacles.

She shook her head emphatically, but the colonel was persistent. He descended the steps, and as the audience roared, he reached down and took her hand. From behind, she heard Tandy's voice. "Yes, indeed. Let's hear it for the lady!"

Leighton sat on the far side of Will, staring straight ahead like he did every Sunday in church, as if he had nothing to hide from the Lord Himself. She could not have met God's gaze—too much already tucked away in a dark corner of her heart. Seeing one who could always left her stiff with envy.

Had Leighton leaned over and said *Don't*, she would've remained in her seat, but he did nothing, so she rose and, while the audience whooped, let the colonel lead her to the steps.

He smelled of cologne. "Ma'am," he whispered, "what would be your name?"

"Sarah. Mrs. Sarah Payne."

She stood near the piano. The colonel snapped his fingers, and a Negro boy ran onstage and laid a towel over Bob's bench. Bob himself sat on a stool at the rear of the stage, head lolling forward, eyes unfocused.

"Now, don't you worry about the keys," the colonel whispered. "I make sure Bob's hands are washed before he plays."

After she'd positioned herself on the bench, the colonel faced the audience. "Our first pianist is your own Mrs. Sarah Payne."

The audience applauded. She knew Tandy was watching

her. She looked her best in profile—he'd told her so just the other day. He stopped by most mornings, sitting down with her at the table and drinking coffee, paying her the occasional compliment. He told her of the places he'd been, of dangerous men he'd known in New Orleans. He'd played poker once with Charles Matranga, he said, and he would have beaten him had he not seen from the look in Matranga's eyes that it would probably cost him his life. He knew George and Peter Provenzano, the Matrangas' bitter rivals, and could've solved the mysterious murder of David Hennessy, the police chief, had the Provenzanos ever asked him. Instead, they had told him not to get involved, he said, because they knew more murders would follow.

No fool, she didn't believe half of what Tandy told her. She knew, furthermore, that he didn't expect her to, that he was only trying to entertain her, to take her ever so briefly away from these streets of mud and horse dung.

"Now, Miss Sarah, could you play us a little something you've composed yourself?"

"All right." She laid her hands on the keys.

"Before you play it," the colonel said, "could you tell us what it's called?"

She cleared her throat. "'The River Waltz.'"

FOR TANDY, the song summoned bitter recollections.

Of a morning in midsummer, the two of them sitting together on the dock out at the landing, water lapping softly at the pilings. His father had been dead for less than a month; the will had not been opened, since his father's lawyer was away in Memphis, but Tandy already knew it would bring no good news for him.

It was July of '88, the yellow fever scare. The previous week, a family from Jackson had attempted to escape the quarantine by sneaking through the Delta to reach relatives in Tennessee. South of the Deadening, they made camp. Around midnight, screams woke them. A panther had stolen into the camp and seized the baby, whereupon the father leapt up, grabbed his gun and fired a shot that missed its mark but attracted two more cats.

Hearing pandemonium, Leighton had tried to rouse his brother, but Tandy, who'd been drinking all day and into the evening, told him to go to hell. So Leighton alone mounted up and rode toward the screams. Upon reaching the clearing, he shot two of the animals and ran the other one off.

There was plenty of blood and carnage, but the father and one of the children had survived. Leighton became a hero, whereas Tandy's reputation had been mangled as badly as the fugitives' corpses.

Tandy had known as he sat there that morning beside Sarah that he would leave, that he could never live at the Deadening, with his brother playing the big-shot planter, while he was viewed as a no-account.

"When the will's opened," he said, "all of this"—he gestured at the river and the land on either side of it, at the broad fields of knee-high cotton spreading out as far as you could see—"is going to belong to my brother. And that's something I just can't live with."

"What makes you so sure Leighton'll get it all?"

"He's the kind of fellow that'll get up in the middle of the night to go shooting panthers, and I'm not. And my daddy, unfortunately, knew as much."

Sarah's father did, too. A contractor who built Queen Anne residences for the wealthy and soon-to-be, he would never give the hand of his daughter to a disinherited son. Tandy was eighteen, which surely was old enough to know some basic facts.

Sarah was eighteen, too, though she knew a lot less. She

began to hum a tune, one he'd never heard before, a soft-sounding melody in three-quarter time. He'd sat there that morning and listened, just as he was sitting here now and hearing it speak to him once again of things he couldn't have because he didn't know how to want them.

His fingers closed tightly on the edge of the bench. *That loony-looking idiot better play it right.*

"LUNATICS," Seaborn whispered. "The whole lot of them."

They were outside now, moving away from the tent, past a vendor in a striped shirt who was selling molasses candy, barking, "Hot pull! Hot pull!" as he twisted and kneaded the golden rope with hands dusted in flour. A second vendor stood at a booth, hawking hot dogs and corn on the cob.

"I didn't know they let Negroes into the Royal Conservatory," Seaborn said, "but I suspect that's where Blind Bob got his musical education. That or someplace like it." He shook his head. "White people are something, aren't they? It's all right for a Negro to play Chopin as long as he doesn't know he's doing it. A thumb and self-knowledge being all that separates man from ape, and Negroes undeniably possessing thumbs—well, you see my argument, I imagine."

She did indeed, and something else besides. Leighton Payne had pushed through the crowd and was heading toward them. Behind him, his wife was just turning away, looking at his brother as he approached, smiling and tipping his hat at every woman he passed.

Leighton didn't touch his hat, though he did nod when he said, "Hello, Loda."

"Hello, Mr. Payne."

Leighton glanced about, then lowered his voice. "Seaborn, could I have a word with you?"

Seaborn pulled off his bowler, clasping it to his chest as if

Leighton had just paid him an honor. "Why, sure enough, Mr. Mayor."

Left alone, Loda watched while they moved off. During the performance, the sun had come out and now glinted off Seaborn's bald head, which, as Leighton spoke to him, began to nod.

ONE OTHER person stood watching.

He'd seen the mayor stroll over and say hello to the postmistress, no matter that she was colored. The mayor had never spoken to him and wouldn't speak to his wife or children if he met them on the street, would just walk right by them. Now he'd walked off with the postmistress's husband. Most likely, they were talking business—after all, they both owned things. Grover never spent a dollar at Rosenthal's without noting that twenty cents would end up in a colored man's pocket.

Very little money had ever found its way into his pocket. He'd moved to the Delta five years ago from East Mississippi, bent on leading a decent life and earning an honest living. Over there in Webster County, folks knew he was half Choctaw and treated him like a goddamn Indian. Down here, they thought he was white, but they still treated him worse than a nigger.

He'd lived on the Stancill place for four years; then the overseer told him to move on because they needed the house, and he knew damn well who they'd moved in there. All over the Delta, they were placing ads in hill country papers, promising colored folks the moon and half the planets if they'd just move down here and pick that damn cotton. Soon they'd own the fields they were picking in. A few already did. Whereas he was living on the Stark place, tending a rich man's horses. And even that wouldn't last. This year or next or the one after,

Stark would send his overseer riding out to tell him they needed the house.

But sooner or later, folks around here would learn you could push a man only so far. There were a couple sons of bitches over in Webster County who might've testified to that, except for one thing: neither of the bastards was where he could talk.

His youngest boy tugged at his sleeve. "Pa? Can we get us some of them sausages that fellow's selling?"

"Them's not sausages. Them's hot dogs. And naw, you can't have none. I ain't got no money."

Seaborn Jackson was nodding his head now, coming to terms with the mayor, probably selling him something for his newspaper or agreeing to place an ad in it.

"Nope, I sure ain't got no money," Grover Beam said again, batting his son's hand away. "But at least I ain't a biggity nigger."

THE PETITION

S EABORN sat by the fire, warming his feet and perusing the new catalogue. On the back was a picture of the Sears, Roebuck Building in Chicago, one of the biggest commercial structures in the entire world, according to the caption; it fronted on four different streets—Fulton, North Desplaines, Waymon, Jefferson—and had an address on each one.

"Talk about big," Seaborn said out loud, but only to himself. The sound of his own voice had always calmed him, and it had the same effect on others. He had discovered his aptitude for oration at Cold River College and briefly considered a career as a minister. But his mentor, a former student of no less a personage than Booker T. Washington, had convinced him that business and trades offered the best opportunities. He almost became a mortician, but one week as an apprentice had quelled that ambition, though it led him to his chosen career.

Put simply, he could talk almost anybody into almost anything, and this had stood him in good stead as an insurance agent. "Mr. Jackson," a client had once told him, "you make me feel good about the prospect of dying." That was his skill, his gift: talking people into feeling good about the product he was selling, that product being, more often than not, a funeral. But not just a coffin. A decent burial. Interment with style and grace and no small amount of pomp. He gave people, in death, what had eluded almost all of them while they were alive.

They were poor, most of those he served, so dire that *poor* was hardly the right word. Seaborn hurt for them and, even though he wasn't a preacher, ministered to them. He led a life which announced, in all its outward manifestations, that something better was possible, that the key to a good life lay in education and abstinence, probity and perseverance. If he could be successful, he sought to say, so could they. And while he was not convinced this was necessarily true, he did believe that the message he was selling offered comfort to those sorely in need of it.

This was the knowledge, the belief, that had left him trembling in anger after his conversation with the mayor. All his achievements could come tumbling down around him, so tenuous was the foundation upon which he had built. When he was a student, the *Cold River Weekly* had published an article entitled "A Story from One of Our Boys." In this article, a Cold River student told of the day his father had been asked to butcher a huge deer shot by the plantation owner for whom he worked. Deciding to have some fun at the white man's expense, the student's father had said, "Now, sir, could I just go on and acts you one thing? When a deer get to be this big, if didn't nobody shoot it, would it go ahead and turn into a moose?" The white man had taken the question seriously, explaining with a laugh and a shake of his head that a moose was a moose and a deer was a deer. "Is there anything white folks won't believe?" the article asked in conclusion.

If there wasn't much some of them wouldn't believe, the rest certainly didn't enjoy having it pointed out to them. The legislature threatened to close the school; the president kept it open by promising to shut down the paper, but even that was not enough. During the following weeks, several students were abducted and beaten by groups of white men who wore bandannas over their faces. They cut the big toe off the young man who'd written the article, then bound him hand and foot, attached a note to his shirtfront, and deposited him on the steps of the school chapel.

> *We picked this nigger by the toe.*
> *We liked the way he hollered,*
> *So this time we'll let him go.*

There were other things Seaborn knew, which every Negro knew or surely ought to. His own father, a doctor who practiced in a two-county region that spread from Carrollton to Winona, had been present in the courtroom when the Carrollton Massacre occurred. Two Negroes had charged a white man with attempted murder. All Negroes in town had been warned not to attend the trial, but several, Seaborn's father included, chose to bear witness. A band of armed white men rode into town, stormed the courtroom and opened fire. Ten Negroes died, but his father was lucky. He jumped from a second-story window and, though he broke his leg in the fall, escaped in the back of a wagon driven by a white man who knew him. That evening, after swigging from a bottle of whiskey, he set his own broken leg.

Loda herself had told him stories of things that had happened right here in Loring—or nearby anyway. That those events were in the past didn't matter; people still remembered both the acts and their reactions, and they knew, or ought to, that if you shoved them hard enough, white people would do those same things again.

SHE WALKED into the living room, wearing her dressing gown, her hair let down for the night. With her hair that way, you could see—even if you hadn't known it from looking at her skin—that her momma had crossed the white line. He'd asked her who it had been, but she always said she didn't know, because by the time she was old enough to wonder, there were no men around of any color. Her momma had kept a shotgun propped against the door, she said, and everybody knew she would use it.

"Where'd your momma get that shotgun?" he'd asked her. She claimed not to know. "Must have taken some doing," he said. "Guns were hard for a Negro to come by then—unless some white man passed one on. But why would a white man want you and your momma to be so well protected?" By that point, she was staring at him with dark, silent eyes, so he knew that asking any more questions was, at least for the moment, unwise.

Seaborn laid the catalogue aside. "I think someday, probably not this year but maybe the next, we should take a trip to Chicago."

"Why?"

"Just to see it." He thumped the picture of the Sears, Roebuck Building. "They do things on a grander scale up there than we ever will down here. Sometimes I feel an urge to see a structure larger than the compress. There's something to be said for sheer size."

She gathered her gown about herself and sat down. She'd made a cup of tea; the cup and saucer stood on the small table next to her armchair. At Cold River College, it had been the way she drank tea that caught his eye. Most of the young women, and many of the young men, too, had been sent there by benevolent societies; they came from the families of freedmen, and unless their parents had served as house slaves, they usually possessed no social graces whatsoever. To put a teacup in their hands was the equivalent of giving a surgeon's scalpel to a blind man and telling him to operate: nothing save misfortune could result. They would grab the teacup with both hands and start slurping, or while attempting to insert an index finger through the small opening, they'd spill tea all over themselves. Stern Mrs. Matthison, who taught homemaking, would shake her head and mutter, "Once again, we shall be keeping the laundry open late."

She never shook her head at Loda. Loda had not been sent by a benevolent society. Nobody knew where the money for Loda had come from, who that silent, light-skinned young woman with the impeccable manners truly was. But everybody wanted to know. Especially the young men.

"Seaborn," she said now. "I'd like to talk about what happened the other day."

He shook his head. He did not wish to revisit the issue. He had reported, in a matter-of-fact manner, the warning he'd received. The mayor had said his brother was angry because a member of the laboring population—that was how the mayor had put it, so that was what he related—had refused to step aside in his favor. This incident had occurred in the lobby of the United States Post Office, in downtown Loring, in broad daylight. The mayor advanced no suppositions as to the motives of those members of the Negro community who had been involved, nor had he alleged that those individuals had been engaged in anything other than a business transaction at the time. That was all Seaborn had said and all he meant to say.

"Seaborn," she said again. "Don't shake your head, please. I said I wanted to discuss this."

"But it is impossible to have a discussion in which one party chooses not to participate. And I choose not to participate because I have nothing to say—except that, as I mentioned a moment ago, I believe we should visit Chicago."

"Yes, but I want you to know that he'd just come in to see

if he had any mail. That's all. I don't know why he didn't leave or step aside when Tandy Payne walked in. He probably doesn't know himself."

His pulse had begun to speed up, and he had that light-headed sensation he got when he was agitated. Which was why he tried not to get agitated. Because when your head was light, you couldn't think properly.

"Too much idle speculation about what mental processes might obtain inside the mind of that . . . that *flunky*," he said, "does not become a woman in your position."

She lifted her teacup and sipped from it, her grace and calm enraging him. He was not calm now—she had stolen it away from him—nor was he graceful. He was thirty-five years old, overweight and bald, and of late he felt run-down. Though she was unaware—at least he prayed to God she was— he had begun wearing an electric belt beneath his clothing. The ad for the belt, an 80-gauge Giant Power Heidelberg Special, had promised that the current would increase circu-lation of the blood throughout the body, providing greater stamina and staving off all manner of illness. It was Seaborn's intention to live a long life. A good life.

"What is my position, Seaborn?"

"What is your *position*? You're a federal employee and the wife of a dignified Negro."

"Sometimes I wonder if you don't mistake material success for dignity."

"*Mistake* it?" He truly could see spots before his eyes—they looked like wads of cotton, all soft and fuzzy. There were thousands of them. "There is no way I could mistake it. Because without material success, there is no dignity. Not for us, anyway." His voice, so low and sonorous, had begun to rise into the treble clef. "You think they mean to let you feel digni-fied if you're out there picking that cotton, pulling a sack or toting a basket from daylight till dark—*yes suh this* and *yes suh that, show nuf Mr. White suh, show do thank you for letting me tear my fingers on them cotton bolls, show do love the way that sweat feel when it run down my rumpus*–and then come sundown, you drag your own tired self into some little bitty old stinking hole and lay down on a thin little mat, and they can bust in on you if they take a notion, trickle meanness and white spite all over you? You think you'll feel dignified then?"

He could scarcely breathe. He sat there with his hands resting on his knees, taking one rapid breath after another, not getting much air from his efforts, for the most part just sucking in nothing. She continued drinking tea, her eyes on the fireplace, where the flames were beginning to flicker.

Within a few minutes, he had composed himself. He crossed his legs, leaned back in his armchair, locked his hands behind his head and allowed himself to yawn. "We really must visit Chicago," he said.

MISS Rosa Bates did not cook, but she ate frequently and well, which meant that Tandy did, too. He'd put on ten pounds since moving into the boardinghouse. If the truth be known, there had been times in the last few years when he'd had trouble putting food on the table or finding a dry place to lie down. Back in early August, right before he decided to come home, he'd spent two successive nights in the loft of a livery stable in Metairie. The liveryman had found him there one morning, covered by hay, and started him on his journey at the tip of a pitchfork.

"Want some more of them biscuits?"

"No, I do believe I better quit."

"Takes stamina," Rosa said, winking at him.

"What does?"

She speared a sausage and stuck it in her mouth. While her jaws went to work on it, she held her eyes on him; the little smile remained on her face.

She was wearing a silk dressing gown this morning, and he knew that underneath the gown there was nothing but Rosa. Fifteen minutes ago, she'd been on top of him, her face bright red and her eyes shut tight while she went all out. He'd never seen another woman who did it quite so hard. She'd raise herself up about a foot off the bed, then plunge down on him, knocking the wind out of him about every other time, moving faster and faster, breathing louder and louder. She sounded like a locomotive. He'd told her that once, and she thought it was the funniest thing she'd ever heard. She'd started calling herself "the Loring Cannonball."

She finally spoke. "You ain't commencing to fade on me, are you, Tandy? Not wanting something different?"

He was certainly starting to want a little less of what he had. The last few days, he'd taken several long walks around town. Their main purpose was to converse with folks about important matters, but every now and then he would just find a quiet place in an alley and sit down and shut his eyes, concentrating on something besides what went on in Rosa's bed. He felt like a hired hand. He'd had this feeling before, and for a while it was pleasant, offering confirmation that he could do one thing as well as any man. But sooner or later, it always got old. And it had gotten old now.

"Not hardly," he said.

"Thought maybe you wanted somebody a little more prim and proper."

"Prim and proper ain't my style."

"Well, there's a lot of men that prefer apple pie to pecan, but every now and then they get to hankering for nuts and Karo syrup. If you get my drift."

He got it but was not about to admit it. At least not till the pecan pie had been baked and set before him. "Apple pie," he said, "satisfies my every need."

"Good," she said. She lifted her coffee cup and sipped from it. "Because that's what I'm serving."

THE MEETING was set for ten o'clock that Saturday morning at Catchings Stark's house.

Catchings was a planter whose father had come to Loring County in 1853 with three slaves—each of whom, according to legend, had only one arm—and four old mules. The elder

Stark had homesteaded on Choctaw Creek, just a few miles from the settlement that would eventually become Loring. He'd begun clearing land that first year; by 1860, he owned a hundred slaves and six thousand acres. Now his son owned more than nine thousand acres. He lived in town in a big plantation-style manor that had a replica of the Liberty Bell in the front yard, a crack running through it in just the right place.

Tandy had talked to Stark first because he was probably the wealthiest man in the county, except for Percy Stancill, and unlike Stancill, Catchings was generally liked. Stancill never minced words: to Percy, a skunk was a goddamn skunk. Catchings would call a skunk "a small black mammal that, regrettably, needs to be exterminated." He had tact, in other words, though he could get things done, and it hadn't taken Tandy long to stir him up.

Provocation was something he'd always been good at. Once, on a riverboat he'd boarded in Paducah, he got into a game in which he recognized a sharper who'd cleaned him out three years earlier in Denver. Back then, the fellow had had red hair, talked with a lisp and worked with an old man who played a fancy violin. The fiddler, Tandy later realized with sickening hindsight, had been iteming the other players' hands by his choice of tunes. In the riverboat game, the fellow in question no longer had red hair or spoke with a lisp, but it was him, no doubt about it; there was that unsightly wart above his right eye, and when he scratched his nose, he still used his little finger. But he'd fallen a long way. Not much went on anymore on the river. The only professionals you'd find there were men like Tandy. Washouts.

That day on the river, Tandy decided it was the bartender who was in cahoots: he smoked one cigar after another, unusual enough in itself, because even bad cigars were expensive, and his smelled like good ones; every time he brought somebody a drink, he would return to the bar, light up and puff like mad.

Before long, Tandy had figured out the signals. He hung in until only he and the sharper were left, then hollered to the bartender for another shot. When the bartender came over with the bottle, Tandy made sure the man got a good look at his hand. As the bartender returned to his stool and lit another cigar, Tandy ran a couple of images through his mind: a picture of himself standing on a street in Denver, a cold rain falling while he looked in the window of a warm hotel that he didn't have the money to rent a room in; the sharper sitting on a velvet-covered sofa before the fireplace in that very same hotel, laughing and telling another sport how he'd fleeced this Southern rube.

Heart pounding, stomach muscles taut because he halfway expected a bullet to tear into them, he announced, "That would be three quick puffs on the cigar, followed by a long pause, and then another two puffs."

All three players who'd dropped out had remained in the lounge; they were the first to lay hands on the sharper, but not the last. A crowd of ten or twelve men pulled him from the lounge and out onto the deck. While Tandy sat at the table enjoying his drink, they pummeled his former adversary and threw him, unconscious and bleeding, into the Mississippi. The bartender managed to save himself by exiting through a service passage and leaping overboard.

When the mob returned, Tandy poured drinks all around. The others toasted his smarts, one proposing that they next hurl the captain overboard and let Tandy command the boat.

AT STARK's place, several saddle horses stood tied to the shade trees, and three or four buggies waited in the driveway. Assuming they belonged to the right folks, it was not a bad showing.

He jumped down off the bay, tied him to the porch railing and adjusted his new silken bow tie as he climbed the steps.

An old Negro wearing a dark suit opened the door. Tandy had seen this one before, but not here. He'd probably worked for somebody else, somebody whose house Tandy had visited when he was younger.

"Please come in, sir."

Tandy stepped into the foyer. The old man closed the door behind him.

"Right this way, sir."

Tandy lingered near the entrance. "Didn't you used to work for somebody else?"

"Oh, sir, I suspect I've worked for just about everybody else at one time or another. Excepting Mr. Percy Stancill in there—I've never worked for him. Though understand, sir, I'd be proud to serve him. Were I not so happy here."

Loud voices came from the living room. Tandy said, "You don't think he's a horse's ass?"

The old man was doing his best to usher him into the hall-way, but Tandy hung back. He was enjoying himself.

"Well, sir, I'm not sure who you mean."

"Percy Stancill. Don't you think he's a royal son of a bitch?"

The old man lifted a tray of shot glasses off a sideboard; the glasses had been filled with whiskey. "Would you care for one of these, sir?"

"I sure would." He plucked one from the tray. "But what about Percy?"

"Well now, sir, I personally consider Mr. Percy Stancill a fine, upstanding man. But of course I don't know him in the same ways I'm sure you do."

Tandy downed the whiskey, then set the glass on the sideboard. He stepped so close that the old Negro had to retreat until his back grazed the wall.

Tandy knew what that position felt like. It hadn't been two months since he himself had stood with his back against a brick wall, in a dark alley, and opened his mouth to receive the turd he'd promised to swallow so as to keep from losing his thumbs.

"You know what I once saw Mr. Stancill do?"

The old man's teeth were bright and perfectly straight. "No sir."

"It wasn't too pretty."

The old fool didn't even blink. Tandy had blinked. He'd blinked, and he'd begged, and he'd agreed that his mother was a bitch and his father was a bastard and his sister, though he didn't have one, was a whore who would do it with a broomstick if it was the only thing handy; and when he thought of all that now, he wanted to shove a big piece of shit right in the old bastard's mouth.

"It involved a fellow who'd be about the same age you are now, assuming he was still out and about and pursuing dusky pleasures."

"Well, sir, he may have been pursuing those pleasures too hard. That may be why Mr. Stancill did whatever it was he believed he had to do. Since I wasn't there, sir, I shan't venture any judgment."

Tandy heard footsteps in the hall. He grinned at the man, grabbed another glass and downed the whiskey, then turned around just as Sally Stark walked into the foyer.

"Why, Tandy," she said. "They were beginning to wonder if you were coming."

"You know me," he said, offering her his arm. "A day late, a dollar short."

"Now, OLD Stalebread Charley, he played—if you gentlemen can believe this—he played a fiddle made out of a goddamn

cigar box. Cajun played the French harp, Warm Gravy played
three or four different horns and whistles, and Chinee played
something that looked like a bull fiddle, though a friend of
mine told me it was actually a coffin with strings on it. They
called themselves the Spasm Band, and I first heard 'em . . .
well, if you gentlemen'll accept the fact that I was there on
business, I'll admit I first heard 'em back in '96 at the Star
Mansion."

There was laughter all around. "Now Tandy," Catchings
said, "what kind of business could you have been transacting
at the Star Mansion?"

"I'll wager it was octoroon business," Percy Stancill said.
"You been after that old dyed wool, Tandy?"

"Now, you gentlemen know me, you know my brother and
you knew my father. My heart's just as pure as long-staple
cotton."

"Even that cotton's got a few burrs," Robert Vaiden said.

"Madam Gertie still in business down there?" Stancill said.
"Reason I ask is, I used to know a fellow claimed he knew her.
He spoke right highly of some feats she performed."

"I myself know a fellow claims he knows her," Tandy said.
"And if he's to be believed, Percy, Madam Gertie's skills ain't
been diminished by her executive status."

Another round of laughter.

They were sitting in the living room, and the door to the
hallway was closed. Drinks all around. Tandy knew
everybody, had for years: Percy Stancill, Catchings Stark,
Robert Vaiden, A. H. Ellsbury, Charles Baskett, James Burth
and three or four others, including old man Newcomb
Teague, who everybody said had built the first plank residence in Loring County. Even Baker Stallings was there. He'd
lost a leg at Vicksburg, and folks said he'd been out of his
mind for fifteen or twenty years. He was propped up on the

sofa, with his eyes closed, brown spit staining his frizzy white beard.

"Speaking of wanton conduct," Catchings said, "I believe Tandy aims to apprise us of a potentially nettlesome situation."

Tandy had been sitting in an armchair. He stood and straightened his jacket. "I've already spoken to a couple of you gentlemen," he said, "and I know Catchings has had conversations with the rest of you. But before I say anything more, I think I ought to say this. When I was just a little boy out there on the Deadening, my daddy had a story he used to tell. He said he knew a fellow back in the hills of East Tennessee that took a notion to leave there about the same time he did. They decided to ride together. They got to the Sunflower River one day in late April of 1850. My daddy was twenty at the time, the other fellow a year or two older. Now, Mr. Teague over there, he was already here, had hisself a nice place built, though of course my daddy didn't know about it yet. All he could see when he looked around him was trees and swamps and snakes and mosquitoes. Daddy said the fellow he was with said, 'This here is without a doubt the scariest damn place I ever saw or hope to see, and I aim to put a lot of distance between it and me.'"

Tandy walked over to the window and pretended to be interested in something outside. Catchings had built a belvedere out back, and his kids were out there playing croquet in the shade of it, attended by an elderly Negro woman who sat on the steps, watching.

After a moment or two, he turned back to face the men. "Y'all know what my daddy said to that other fellow? He said, 'You can go on and go on.' That was it. Not another word. He just climbed down off his horse, pulled a hatchet out of his saddlebag and walked over to a tree and started cutting off dead branches to build hisself a fire. He said by the time he looked up again, the other fellow had ridden off.

"The place looked like hell, Daddy always said, but something in his character must of helped him see the heaven it could become. It was home, he said, from the very minute he laid eyes on it. He used to tell me and Leighton that, and I reckon with Leighton it took right off, and with me it didn't. Some folks learn faster than others is what I mean to say. It took me a while, but I'm here to stay, if y'all got a mind to let me."

"Aw, hell, son," old man Teague said. "Some folks just need to get out and rut around a bit."

"You one of us, Tandy," Percy Stancill said. "Your daddy he come in here and wrote y'all's name big. It's a Loring County name. Ain't nothing gone change that."

"I'm glad to hear you say that, Percy," Tandy said, and he meant it. For a moment, the emotion almost overcame him. He'd been a stranger for so long, in so many different places, that every place had come to seem strange.

Except here. Even with all the changes that had occurred over the last few years, he could still close his eyes and walk all around town. The same plank had been missing in the little footbridge over the bayou for the last twenty years; he knew as well as anybody how to avoid putting his foot into empty space.

"Now Tandy," Catchings said, thumping ashes into a brass tray, "what's this thing that happened the other day down at the post office?"

"Well, I went in there to mail a letter to some former business associates of mine down in New Orleans. Now, I knew y'all had a colored woman serving as postmistress, and whether or not that's a good idea—well, that ain't up to me to say, because I been gone."

"Ask me, it ain't a good idea," Charles Baskett said. "What's gone happen if every damn one of 'em starts wanting to work in town? You tell me who's gone pick that cotton. I sure as God don't aim to do it."

Old man Teague said, "She can read real good, can't she? Seem like somebody told me that."

"Yeah, she can read," James Burth said. "She talks like a white person, too."

A. H. Ellsbury said, "Looks about half white."

There was a moment of silence. Robert Vaiden leaned over and picked up his glass. He sipped his whiskey, held the glass up, studied the amber liquid for a moment, as if he meant to subject it to chemical analysis, then set the glass back down.

Finally, somebody coughed. Catchings shifted in his chair, making the legs creak. Baker Stallings started to snore. Old man Teague poked him in the ribs, and he shut up.

"Anyway, I go in there," Tandy said, "and she's standing behind the counter, talking to a nigger man."

"Wasn't her husband, was it? Old Biggity?"

"No sir, it was not her husband. It was a nigger named Blueford that used to work for my daddy. Used to be bad to put rocks in the sack."

"Way I look at it," Ellsbury said, "you got to just allow for that. What I do is, I tell my overseer to dock 'em four pounds every time they weigh up. Do that, you'll end up pretty much even."

"This ain't about weighing up even, A.H.," James Burth said. "This is about inappropriate behavior in a federal place."

"I don't like that word *federal,*" old man Teague said. "No sir, I sure don't."

Percy Stancill banged his cane on the floor. "Goddamn it, if there's one thing I hate, it's when folks keep busting in and fucking up a story. Go on, Tandy, and tell the goddamn thing."

So he told it, and as he told it, he stuck a lot closer to historical truth than he had thought he might. When you told a story, you never knew exactly what you'd have to alter until you saw your audience's expressions. In this instance, he didn't have to change too much. The mere fact that Blueford had remained in the post office, that he hadn't stepped aside, was enough. The only real change he made came in response to a question from Percy.

"What'd you do, boy, when that nigger kept standing there? If it'd been me . . ."

Percy didn't need to finish—everybody knew perfectly well what would have happened if it had been him. But he had struck a sore nerve. Though Tandy was a fairly big man, he'd never relished physical conflict. It wasn't pain he feared so much as that moment when things skewed out of control, that place where words were cast aside, the time for talk simply passed, and the only thing that could save you was a wild rush of blood. When he succumbed to rushing blood, it was preferably in the presence of a naked woman. And it was usually the things he had said, not anything he'd done, that had made her remove her clothes.

"Percy," he said, "I could've walked over to him and knocked the stuffing out of him, and I probably should have. But I'd seen a couple of kids hanging around outside eating ice cream, and I didn't want 'em gettin' hurt if things got out of hand."

"Probably just as well," Ellsbury said. "That nigger might have had a knife on him. Most of 'em do."

"Yours may," Percy said. "Mine don't. I catch one of mine with a knife on him, I'll whittle me an ebony trinket. And they know it."

"I'll confess I never thought we had a problem down at the post office," Catchings said, "but in retrospect, it probably wasn't wise to let them put her in there."

"Folks get packages there," James Burth said. "Hell, for that matter, I got some land up in Coahoma County, and my tenants pay me through the mail. There's a good bit of money and God knows what else passing through that woman's hands. I reckon I'd rest easier if they was the hands of a white man."

"She draws a pretty big salary as postmistress," Vaiden said. "Add her income to what old Biggity makes selling burial insurance, and they got a right good bit. Too much, you askin' me."

Everybody agreed it was a poor situation, and the behavior of Blueford Lucas was just one example of where it might lead.

"Looks to me like we got two things to deal with," Percy said. "The first one's the woman herself. We get her out of there and put in a white man. That part's easy." He looked at Tandy. "You got any pressing activities you need to pursue in the next year or two?"

"Eventually, I aim to get back to raising cotton, like Daddy. But I could hold off a little, I reckon, if y'all wanted."

"Your brother was good enough to step in and take over as mayor. If we's to put you forward as postmaster, is that something you could handle for a while?"

Tandy smiled. "I don't suppose anybody'd mind if from time to time I had me a little card game in the back?"

"You can count me in," Baskett said.

Old man Teague said, "Charles, you can't tell an ace from a strip of panty lace. You start playing cards with Tandy, he'll take the hairs right off your rump."

"Percy said we got two things to deal with," Ellsbury reminded them. "I reckon the second one's the nigger that acted smart to Tandy. What we gone do about him?"

Percy's fist closed around the marble knob on top of his cane. He was about to speak, but Tandy beat him to it.

"That part," he said, "is even easier."

. . .

HAVING laid so many problems to rest, they did what people always do in the Delta when worries have been dispensed with. Catchings summoned his hostler, a sullen-faced white man, and told him to go get the little steer from the lower pasture and kill it. A couple Negroes were called in to dig a pit in the backyard, which they filled with oak logs they then fired. They stretched hog wire over the pit, went to mix up a tub of barbecue sauce and, once the steer was skinned, they laid the carcass on the wire. One of the Negroes used a mop to spread the sauce on it.

"That thing'll be mighty good come morning," Catchings said. They all had pulled chairs up near the fire and they were out there now, in their jackets, with a case of good whiskey Catchings had bought in Memphis. This would be an all-night affair: they'd drink and tell stories until they fell asleep, and then in the morning they'd wake up and eat the barbecue.

Tandy felt better than he had in years. Some of these men had accents so strong and thick an outsider would never have been able to parse their vowels. But he understood them perfectly. And they him.

"I liked the way you took charge in there, boy," Percy Stancill said, clapping him on the knee. "Your daddy, he would've been pleased. He'd be proud of Leighton, too—we all are—but your brother's got some funny ideas."

"Aw, you know Leighton," old man Teague said. "He don't mean half of what he says. He's just got to say it."

"Sam Payne never did too much talking," Percy mused. "Seem like his boys got their own words and his, too."

ONE OF Sam Payne's boys was riding a single-footing mare along a country road.

He didn't come this way too often, though he tried to ride into every little hamlet in the county at least once a month, gathering news for the paper. Folks liked to read about themselves, and he tried to give folks what they wanted. Two-thirds of what he printed in the paper concerned events no more momentous than a visit from somebody's aunt who lived in Jackson, or a list of all the different pies that had been baked for a church fund-raiser. That was the way he liked it: for things to stay quiet and peaceful.

Things were peaceful enough now. There were a few hands in the field on his right picking cotton, dragging sacks toward a wagon that stood on the turnrow, a pair of oxen hitched to the double tree. Some of the women had brought their children to the field, and you could see them out there, running through the cotton, knocking bolls off with flying legs. In a year or two, these kids would be old enough to pick cotton, too, and they'd be out here in late September with sacks of their own. The colored schools never opened till the crop was in.

Leighton himself didn't like farming, wouldn't have taken it up again even if you'd given him every acre of black gumbo between here and the big river. But he couldn't help it—he loved fall, loved picking season, the bite in the air, the sight of all that cotton and, above all, the sound of those voices singing the old spirituals.

> *The trumpet sounds within my soul.*
> *I ain't got long to stay here.*
> *Steal away, steal away.*
> *Steal away to Jesus.*

They were out there now, singing that very song, his favorite one of all, because it promised that in the end, no matter how you'd suffered here, a better place lay waiting. Three or four women sang it together, their voices lifting toward him over the sound of hooves stamping along the dusty road.

> *Steal away, steal away home.*
> *I ain't got long to stay here.*

"RECKON I've stayed on too long," Ephraim Barnes said.

A big globe stood nearby, one of those fancy ones with ridges to indicate mountain ranges. Idly, as he spoke, Barnes spun the globe with his index finger. You couldn't exactly say that he was sitting on the couch, nor could you call what he was doing lying. He was just there: his surprisingly small feet propped up on the coffee table, his shoes still on, his socks mismatched. Stains streaked his shirtfront; a couple of buttons were missing.

"Seem like the first year or two, everything went right. Good crops. High prices. Don't know what went wrong after that. Guess I wasn't cut out for Delta planting. Couldn't get a woman that could stand the damn place. Your momma, she never did hate it here?"

"She liked it all right, I guess," Leighton said. "Got used to it anyway."

"Come from the outside, did she?"

"No sir, she was actually born close by. Over in Greenville. She was a good bit younger than my daddy."

Barnes burped. "How'd she meet her end? If you don't mind my asking."

It was a hard thing to talk about. "A moccasin bit her. She took sick and died."

"Happened here on the place, did it?"

"Out there in the backyard's where she got bitten. She died . . . well, sir, she died right here in this room."

She'd called it her sitting room. It had been neat, uncluttered, just a couple of chairs and a writing desk and a daybed. Now broken furniture was everywhere, papers strewn about. Cobwebs hung from the ceiling. The room stank of sweat and mildew.

"Been a lot of folks died around here?" Barnes said.

"Just her and my father. He had the yellow fever. That was back in '88."

"Reason I ask is, I've heard stories. Nigger narrations about all kind of folks being dead. You heard tell of anything like that?"

"I remember there were some shootings nearby. That was a long time ago, though."

A whiskey bottle stood on the coffee table, alongside a glass that looked as if it hadn't been washed in ten or fifteen years. Barnes lifted his feet off the table, leaned over to pour the glass full, then glanced up. "I'd offer you some, but I know you're opposed." He turned the glass up and drank about half of it, and when he set it back down, he burped again.

He wiped his mouth on the back of his hand. "Not to be inhospitable, but how come I'm enjoying the pleasure of your company? Being as you ain't been once since the day you sold me the place."

"I think back when you and I were negotiating the sale, I mentioned to you that I had a younger brother?"

Barnes chuckled. "Mr. Terrell Andrew Payne. Apparently, he don't cotton to his nickname. Leastways that's what he told me."

"So he's been out here to talk to you?"

"Oh, he's been out two or three times."

"I'd heard rumors to that effect. I was just wondering if they were true."

"There's a lot of folks that'd disagree with what I'm fixing to say, but I'll say it anyway. In my experience, when you hear a rumor, it generally *is* true—providing it's a bad rumor. If it's a good 'un, it's damn near always false."

Neither of them could find anything else to say for a couple minutes. Leighton sat there wishing he hadn't come. He'd promised himself years ago that he would never again cross the threshold of this house, that he'd never even set foot on any land that had belonged to his father. It was a promise that he should've stuck to.

Barnes said, "Seem like you and your brother must not be real close."

"Not especially."

"I got a brother myself," Barnes said, whirling the globe in a bluish blur. "He's the spitting image of my pa. And my pa, rest his soul, he started out life as a son of a bitch. I'm sad to say he ended it the same way. So, being as my brother reminds me of him—well, me and him ain't never been overly close, either."

Leighton said, "I heard Tandy might be trying to buy back the place."

"Best I can tell, he don't have no money."

"But I'm right about him being interested?"

For a while, Barnes did not reply. He sat staring at the bottle. You could tell he'd spent a lot of time staring at that bottle or one just like it. "I hate this place," he finally said, his chin beginning to quiver. "I been out yonder in back, son, and seen that graveyard where your ma and pa's buried. Them ain't the only graves I've come across. There's others, too. And don't nobody seem to want to talk about them, save one or two old niggers, and you know how they get to rollin' their eyes and bullshittin' about hobgoblins and whatnot. To hear them tell it, ain't nobody ever just been his own self—everybody's his own self and twenty-five somebody elses. Lord God, I'd hate to be a nigger. Always draggin' too much behind 'em."

He picked up the glass and finished his whiskey. "You wanting to know whether or not I'd be willing to sell?"

Leighton stood. "I was just wondering if my brother had expressed an interest. That's all I came out here to ask. I hope you'll forgive me, because it really wasn't any of my business."

Barnes's eyes were half-hidden beneath his ragged gray bangs. "I'll sell this place to your brother in a snake-bit minute if he can lay his hands on some money. Sell it for a whole lot less than I paid. Because between me and you, son, there's a hellacious bad smell hovering around. And I think you know what's doing the stinking."

THE PATCH of ground had never been cleared.

His father had bought it and two other parcels in the spring of '78 from one of the last remaining Negro landown-ers in the county, a former slave named Zollicoffer, who had briefly served in the state legislature and been an ally of James D. Lynch. Like a lot of black Republicans, Zollicoffer had decided that he might fare better farther north. He sold his property for next to nothing, loaded his family into a wagon and left Loring County in the middle of the night.

The ground was low, swampy in places, overgrown with

cypress and elm, hickory and honey locust. What his daddy
had meant to do with it was anybody's guess; he never moved
anybody into Zollicoffer's house or showed any desire to
make the land fit for farming. He might have bought it just to
keep someone else from getting it—he'd done things like that
before. The land joined his property on the east, between him
and town, so he had to pass it on his way into Loring; it
must've annoyed him to ride by there, knowing that the man
who owned it had risen all the way from servitude to the state
legislature. He'd suffered grievous wounds trying to make
sure nothing like that could ever happen. In buying Zollicoffer's land for a pittance, he could have claimed he was restor-
ing natural order.

Now all was quiet. The odor of rotting mulberries hung in
the air. No sunlight filtered through the dense canopy.
Leighton sat there on his horse, looking from one tree to
another, each tree a separate memory: a name, a voice, a face.

NEVER *be without work.* That was one thing her mother had told her. "You don't have work, you don't have yourself. You belong to them just as surely as if they held the papers on you."

You belonged to them, too, in a different sense, when you worked for them. She knew this and believed her mother had known it all too well. At least when you worked for them, you could hold a corner of yourself back—which was what she did. She held a corner back from them, and at times she even held a corner back from Seaborn. A corner here, a corner there. Sometimes she felt as if she had no middle, as if she were nothing but the fringes she kept hidden. Sometimes she didn't know how it all added up, who she really was, or would be, if you summed her.

That was another thing her mother had told her. *Never let them know you.*

So for all those reasons, and for others as well, it disconcerted her to discover that Tandy Payne knew what she did most weekdays at twelve o'clock, when she closed the post office for the noon break.

Most people, Seaborn included, surely thought she went home. After leaving the building, she turned the corner, walked straight past the newspaper office and on down the street, turned right on Loring Avenue and walked toward the tracks. At that point, anybody who'd taken an interest should have lost it, figuring she was headed for her house.

But she walked on past her house and crossed the tracks. The street narrowed into little more than a lane. The dogs got skinny and mean-looking, and the children playing in the muddy yards got skinny, too; a few of them would call, "Hey, Miz Jackson," but most paid her no mind.

The house she always went to was a couple blocks from the tracks. The front porch had collapsed the winter before, but that didn't matter so much, because the woman who lived there never went out. She lay in bed all day long, tended by a twelve-year-old girl who had a speech impediment. Nobody knew that Loda paid the girl's momma for her services. Not even Seaborn.

The girl was sitting in the tiny front room near the fireplace, a dishpan in her lap. The pan was full of water, and a jar of beans stood in it, upside down.

"Are you having trouble getting that top off?" Loda asked her.

The girl's lips began to move, but no sound came out. She set the tub on the floor and got up. Talking seemed to be easier for her if she stood. "Y-y-yes'm. M-momma, she say you be having trouble with one of them tops, just put it in hot w-w-water."

Loda leaned over, picked the jar up and placed it on the chair. She twisted the top, and the wax let go. "Here you are."

The girl just stood there.

"You can go on and eat. I'll be with Miss Bessie."

The girl took the jar, shrugged her coat on, and left the house. She never ate in Loda's presence. She always went out back and sat down on a bench near the outhouse and ate her meal there. Loda had objected once or twice, but it hadn't done any good. The girl just put off eating until she left.

In the back room, Miss Bessie lay in bed. "That poor girl," she said. "That girl try to say something, she sound like a Gatling gun. Tell me why the Lord give that child a voice if He never aim to let her use it? You ain't got no answer for that one, is you?"

Loda pulled a stool up beside the bed and sat down. "No, I don't guess I've got an answer."

"Naw, child, and you ain't gone have one. I tell you, though, who gone can give you a real good one. Give you five or six dandy ones if you need 'em. And that man's your own husband. *Mister* Seaborn P. Jackson."

It was the same every day. She had to go ahead and get this part out of the way. It never lasted long.

"What do that *P* stand for anyhow?"

The *P* had been added many years after Seaborn's birth. "Purcell," Loda said.

"And just who, pray tell, was Purcell?"

"A white man who once gave his father a ride in a wagon."

"Some white man pick his daddy up and take him down the road, and his daddy go and name a baby for him? If that don't say it all." Miss Bessie began to laugh. You could hear the rattling in her chest. The laughter turned to coughing, and the coughing lasted three or four minutes. By the time it ended, she was breathless. Spittle hung from her chin.

Loda picked a rag up off the bedside table, made sure it was clean, then wiped her chin dry.

"Oh me." Miss Bessie fell back against the pillow. "Tell me how I ever got to be so old. I ought to been dead twenty years ago."

Loda laid the rag aside and sat down. "You've got a long time to live yet," she said, though she knew that couldn't be true.

Miss Bessie didn't know exactly how old she was or even where she'd been born. She believed it was somewhere over in East Mississippi. She'd told Loda she remembered walking through red clay hills in the middle of winter, her feet wrapped in burlap. She was one of several children who'd traveled in a group with six adults—three men and three women—all of them driven like so many cattle by a man called Griswell. He'd worn a big hog-leg strapped to one thigh, and sometimes at night while they were all chained together, doing their best not to freeze, he would drink a lot of corn liquor and he'd blast off a few shots into the woods, aiming at nothing, and afterwards he'd cackle. The other thing he did at night, from time to time, was pull one of the women off into the woods, shove her face against a tree trunk and use her hard. The youngest of the women always moaned when he was doing her—*"Unh unh unh"*—but Miss Bessie's momma never made a sound. She told the younger woman that Griswell chose her so often because she let her pain show, but she never did learn to keep quiet.

Miss Bessie told Loda how the overseer on the first plantation she remembered living on, way over by the river, had loved to watch the children run backwards. He'd line them up and squeeze a shot off, and they'd run. If they moved too slowly he'd fire at their feet. Sooner or later, they'd run backwards into a tree or fall into a ditch, or sometimes spook a horse and get kicked halfway to kingdom come.

One day, a big soot-colored slave named Hervey got close enough to the overseer to grab his gun and shoot him in the back of the head. When they caught Hervey, Miss Bessie said, they hitched his feet to one team of horses and his arms to another and then whipped the horses, thinking they'd pull Hervey neatly in two. "Problem was," she said, "a person's arms just naturally weaker than their legs. Them arms just pulled loose from the rest of him. The horses running lickety-split, them big arms of Hervey's just a-bouncin' along behind, and everybody act surprise. Ain't a thing in the world Hervey can do but lay in the dust and holler and watch them arms of his till they done gone clean out of sight."

She told Loda things about her mother that she herself would never have mentioned. "This old coal black devil name Andrews try to buy your momma from Sam Payne back in '59. You didn't know they was no colored slave owners? They was. Maybe three in the whole world and him one of 'em. He come here from somewhere down around Natchez, say he own nine and looking for number ten, and your momma catches his eye. That man, that man . . . You know that damn old Sam Payne treat him just like he was white? Old Sam was living in that first house of his they burned during the war, and he lets Andrews walk right in the front door. Let him set down in the parlor, your momma said. Said he come to do business, and Sam know what kind of business, too. But he don't know who it is old Andrews aim to buy, and when he found out, he like to killed him on the spot. That devil Andrews took off from there like somebody dip his hindside in turpentine."

She'd told Loda that her mother walked off the plantation in June of '64, said she walked all the way to Memphis and lived there with a Jewish cotton trader through the following spring, when Ulysses Grant himself threatened to have the man shot if he didn't leave town. Loda knew General Grant could not have done that: by then, he was far away, in eastern Virginia, where he had Lee's army pinned down. But she listened anyway because certain truths belie fact, and she recognized that kind when she heard it.

"So your momma she lived hard for a while, lived hand to mouth, if you ask me, and she was living like that when but who do she see? See him on a street right there in Memphis, Tennessee. Had him a wife by then, too, but he fetched your momma home that summer."

"The summer of what year?"

"Child, don't ask me that. Summer's summer. You want, I can make up a year. Say '68, maybe '69."

"Did she come home big?"

"Come home tired. Hadn't of been tired, she wouldn't of come back. I knew her well enough to say that."

She knew her well enough to say a lot of things, and Loda had heard almost all of them, though every now and then Miss Bessie would remember something new. Not necessarily something about her mother. Sometimes the story was about Bell Irvin, the last man she'd lived with, or Blueford, whom she'd practically raised, or one of her own eight children. The one child she never mentioned—Markham—was the only one Loda had actually known. And neither of them could bear the thought of speaking his name again.

Today, Miss Bessie did not seem to be in a storytelling mood. Her joints ached, she said, her back hurt, and she'd spit up blood last night. Before Loda could suggest summoning Dr. Ormesby, Miss Bessie said, "Now don't send that fool over here with that damn carpetbag. He ain't got nothing in there can make me feel better. I ask what good is all them shiny tools and he puff hisself up and say they let him make 'the proper diagnosis.' He talk a lot like Seaborn. I told him, I say, 'You know they ain't nothing in the world wrong with me but I done live too long. Now get on away from here,' I say, 'and go cure you a ham.'"

Loda got up and went into the front room. She'd brought a sackful of potato peelings with her; she opened it and dumped the peelings onto the floor, then took up the broom and began sweeping. Finished in the front room, she pushed the peelings into Miss Bessie's room and swept it, too, then collected the whole mess in a dustpan and dumped it into the sack.

Miss Bessie watched with approval. "I'm the one taught your momma to do that. She was bad to take a sneezing fit when she swept the house, and I told her, I said, 'Dump you some potato peels on the floor before you sweep, and they'll keep that dust from rising.'"

Loda began collecting towels and washcloths and dirty bed linen. She stuffed them in a canvas bag, pulled the draw-string tight and carried the bag into the front room. Then she walked back into Miss Bessie's bedroom. "I'll have Johnnie Mae take those things to her mother and get them washed," she said. "Is there anything else you need right now?"

Miss Bessie had turned her face to the wall. "No, hon," she said, "not a thing I need." For a moment or two, she just lay there. Then she said, "Bell been round here again."

"Did he speak to you?" Loda asked.

"He don't never say nothing. Just stand by the bed. And you can't tell if it's him being dead that make him quiet or if it's just because he never like to say much anyway, even back when he was alive. You know, supposed to be that when they come back, the dead can't talk. Least that's what I always heard." She rolled over, raised her arm, pointed at the window. "He come in over yonder. Window go flat black for two or three seconds, then there he is." She let her arm fall back onto the bed. "Now it's another thing I've always heard—when a dead person come through the window, the window go all black. You know what I study on, though?"

"What?"

"Suppose the dead person white?" Miss Bessie said. "You reckon them windows turn black then, too?"

She started laughing again. This time, the whole bed shook.

NEARING the railroad tracks, she saw a tan-colored mongrel coupling with a little gray feist. The mongrel's legs were down in the road ditch. A high-pitched yipping came from the feist.

Loda never missed a step, didn't glance at the dogs for more than a second. But Tandy Payne had seen the glance, and a glance would do.

He stepped out from behind a tree just north of the tracks. "They going at it, ain't they?"

Her eyes scanned the road ahead. Empty. The first row of stores was a hundred yards away. Behind her, the closest building was a policy shop. She doubted anyone would be there now. From what she knew, they didn't start playing the numbers until late afternoon.

"Makes a person think," he said. "Don't it?"

"What does?"

"You know what."

"It doesn't make me think about anything."

"I believe you're lying, Loda." He looked over at the dogs and back at her, then grinned. "Old Biggity do it to you like that?"

Hatred, she'd heard, made most folks feel hot. But for her it was cold, an emotion that seized her heart in its icy hold, freezing her from the inside out.

"He don't, does he? Don't do it to you that way or any other. Not often enough to make a difference. You look to me like you're aching for a rut."

"With that one," her mother had said, "everything comes down to one thing. 'What is it that I don't have?'" But he wasn't like his daddy. He wouldn't just reach out and grab it; he never really believed it was there.

"I'm not going to let you lay a hand on me," she said. "Not willingly, anyway."

He reached out and placed his hand on her shoulder. In one fluid motion, she slapped his face so hard that his head snapped back and his hat flew off.

For a moment, his eyes lost all expression. She hoped and prayed he would cry. She'd seen him cry before. He'd been leaning against the wall of the smokehouse out on the Deadening, and she'd stood there and watched while his fist worked on his bone white member and desperate sobs shot from his throat. She had to watch him, he'd told her, or he'd say what he'd seen her do and who he'd seen her do it with. He'd first tried to make her do that same thing with him, but she said she'd let him kill her first, so in the end he agreed that she could just look on while he did it to himself.

A red band—the imprint of her hand—stretched across his cheek. He touched the skin there and laughed, then pulled a folded sheet of paper from his jacket pocket.

"This is what's called a petition," he said. "Being as you're a lot better educated than I am, you'll know what that is." He unfolded the sheet. "What it says is that the *undersigned*—ain't that a wonderful word, *undersigned*? Catchings Stark wrote this, by the way. So, these undersigned demand your immediate resignation from the office of postmistress, due to the recent event that *occurred*—now that's another nice word, always reminds me of a honeycomb for some reason—the recent event that occurred *involving*—and let's face it, ya'll been involved before—one individual *colored man*—Catchings is so damn polite—named Blueford Lucas. Signed, the *undersigned*."

He handed her the petition. Then he bent over, picked up his hat, dusted it off and set it on his head.

"That paper," he said, "will be the least of your problems, bitch."

BLUEFORD loved the odor of roasting coffee beans, and he loved the drink that came from them. Every morning, Miss Bessie used to make coffee so rich, so black and so sweet that he sometimes poured it over hoecakes as if it were molasses.

He'd built the roaster himself. A cast-iron bin with a removable hood and a firebox under the oven, the contraption stood on four iron legs he'd attached castors to so it could be rolled. It was outside now, on the sidewalk in front of Rosenthal's, and he had a good fire going. As soon as he put the beans on, people would flock to the store. They came, Rosenthal said, because they also liked the smell.

Rosenthal talked a lot about smells—about all he missed from his past life, it seemed. When he and Blueford were alone, in the mornings before the store opened and in the evenings after it closed, he'd tell Blueford about the smell of pickled herring or gefilte fish, the tangy odor of stewed cabbage, the sweet, yeasty aroma of challah bread. To hear him go on like that, you'd think he'd never tasted anything. Just sniffed it.

Blueford filled a pan with beans. He wrapped a rag around his hand, lifted the hood off the oven and set the pan inside. He replaced the hood, then took up the long metal spoon he used for stirring. He could have sat down on a stool, but he remained standing. Nobody had told him he ought to. He just knew.

A lot of Italians had moved into the Delta in recent years; most of them worked shares on the big plantations, but a couple owned businesses. One of them, a man named Bartelli, who sold bananas and oranges, sometimes came to the store with his wife. One day, Blueford had heard Mr. Percy Stancill ask Bartelli what the difference was between an Italian and a dago. Bartelli said, "The Italian, he got around three hundred dollars. The dago don't got nothing but himself." A Negro, Blueford understood, was a colored man who remained on his feet. The second he took a seat, he became, in the eyes of white folks, something else.

Insofar as he could do so without any loss of dignity, Blueford was willing to be a Negro. The moment standing became demeaning, he would sit down in the middle of Main Street. He'd lived too long and seen too many things to spend his life worrying about what white folks thought of him. He knew what he thought of himself. That was enough.

The beans began roasting. Before long, the odor wafted up, and folks started streaming into the store. The mayor came with his wife and their son. "Hey, there, Blueford. Sure smells good this morning."

The mayor always spoke to him. Unlike most white folks— who'd give him any name they felt like, most frequently "Butch"—the mayor got his name right. Of course, the mayor had known him most of his life.

"Yes sir," Blueford said. "This gone be a real good batch."

"Are those the ten-cent beans or the fifteen-cent ones?"

"Well, sir, just between you and me, they ain't really no difference in the ten-cent beans and the fifteen-cent beans. Just depend on what bin we put 'em in."

"That's something I've long suspected. I'll stick with the ten-cent batch from now on."

The mayor's son and his wife went inside, though he lingered. He was tall and powerful-looking, a man nobody would want to mess with in a fight. And that was a good thing for the mayor. Because he was not, and never had been, a fighter.

He stood close to Blueford now. Closer than white folks normally would stand. "Anybody been trying to give you a hard time lately, Blueford?"

They hadn't, but they would—Blueford knew that much from Loda. She'd told him about the petition and warned him to watch out, and he'd promised her he would. When he asked her what she aimed to do, she said she didn't know.

"No sir," he told the mayor. "Ain't nobody been bothering me."

"Anybody does, you let me know. You hear?"

Blueford raised the hood and stirred the beans. They popped and crackled. Brown smoke rose from the grate. "Yes sir. I sure will."

"We're not going to have any disorder in this town," the mayor said. "Not as long as I've got anything to say about it."

He smiled at a woman who was leaving the store, then turned and went inside.

MISS BESSIE had always been able to tell first thing in the morning whether or not she'd lay eyes on a snake that day. "Snake coming today," she might say. Sometimes she'd say, "Gone be a *two*-snake day." Before the sun set, she would've seen however many snakes she'd predicted. Blueford never knew if the snakes just came along naturally or if, having foreseen their presence, she made sure to come across them. In the end, he reckoned, it didn't matter. A snake was a snake and could not be ignored. Likewise, in the end, it didn't matter whether he'd been watched because he realized he might be or whether he'd realized he might be watched because he was already being watched. The point was, they had him in their sights.

He laid his broom down that evening, washed up and said good-bye to Rosenthal, who was sitting at his desk totaling the day's receipts. Rosenthal reached into the cash box, pulled out a silver dollar and handed it to Blueford. "A bonus."

"Sir?"

Rosenthal looked up at him and smiled. "Those beans, they smelled wonderful today. They smell wonderful every day, Blueford. I'll tell you something. I have watched you roast the beans, and I been out there myself and tried. My beans, they smell like I took something from the cow pasture and set it on fire. I think you have a special talent."

He would say things like that, old Rosenthal. The other thing he would do was talk to Blueford about the village he'd grown up in, a place called Mlawa, which he said was not too far from Warsaw. It was a fine place, he told Blueford, to be gone from. Once, when he was a small boy, another boy about the same age had disappeared. The boy was a Gentile, the son of the town's only attorney. He'd been seen playing out behind his father's office; an hour later, he was gone. They mounted a search of the surrounding area but found nothing. Not even a footprint.

"And that night what happens? Those people, Blueford, they go crazy. A roundup they staged—like with cattle. They drag away my uncle, they drag away Elo the baker, and they gonna drag my father, but he was in the city buying thread for his looms. They drag them into the field, and there they do to them things which I don't say. And then the next day, a ped-dler brings the missing boy back. He's gone to sleep in some-body's wagon, and they've taken him on to other places and done their business in those places, then they bring him back. And my father, he comes home and he hears what's been done, and he cries for my uncle and he cries for Elo, too, and everybody says there won't be no bread worth eating for a long time, and they're right. And then my father, he wipes his eyes and he says, 'Well, there's stuff to unload.' *Stuff to unload!* But for me, I say, in a silent way, I'll unload that stuff today, but when I'm old enough, what I'm gonna do is unload myself from this place.

"But you know what, Blueford? What I say today is everybody on the face of the earth has got his own personal Mlawa. Every single person that ever lived."

When Rosenthal said that, Blueford had nodded and said, "Yes sir, I guess so." What he didn't say was that for some folks, every place was Mlawa.

He told Rosenthal he appreciated the bonus—it was a third of a week's salary—then he opened the door and stepped outside. The night was chilly and perfectly dark. A wind had sprung up in late afternoon, and dry leaves swirled in the air. Others crunched beneath his feet as he walked along the bank of the bayou. He'd taken this route home every night for more than four years and still looked forward to it.

He thought a lot while he was walking. He didn't think about the past or envision the future. He never imagined far-away places or saw himself living like a white man. Instead, he thought pictures: bright shapes and colors that did not add up to images of anything existing in this world. He would start with a single color—blue, say, a deeper, darker blue than the sky on a clear day—and he would think it into a shape. Then, around the borders of that shape, he would add another color—maybe burnt orange—and then he'd peel part of that color band away from the blue and fill the space with another color. Before he got home, he'd have something. He didn't know what to call it, but it was there in his mind, and he could summon up the same set of shapes and colors again a week later or a year later if he chose to—and sometimes, just to prove it to himself, he did. He must have had several hundred of these pictures in his mind, each different from all the others, yet all of them his and his alone.

The one he was working on that night started with a big sunburst orange box; then the shape got squeezed and lengthened. In the middle of it, he put a small purple square, which he squeezed into the same form as the outer figure. He laced a band of white around both the inner and outer shapes; then he placed the whole thing against a black background, which he instantly began to contract.

He was doing that when he became aware of a rustling in the weeds along the bayou. "Somebody out yonder?" he said, turning, then gasping as something—a length of clothesline, it felt like—tightened around his neck.

The ground rose up to the back of his head. He saw new shapes in his mind—stars, mostly—and they began to spin. When somebody stepped on his face, he could smell shit on the sole of the boot that tromped him.

"This is one dreamy nigger," a white voice said. "They generally pretty hard to slip up on."

"Damn near ever one of 'em got some Indian blood."

He heard a thunk as bone struck bone, and somebody groaned.

"You got a problem with Indians," the first voice said, "you'd do real good to keep it to yourself. Tie his durn feet up."

He did his best to roll free, but whoever the stinking boot belonged to stomped his face so hard that three or four of his teeth let go. He began to choke on teeth and blood. He opened his mouth to holler, but again the boot bashed him.

Somebody wrapped a rope around his ankles and pulled it tight. The first voice said, "Now get his hands."

They rolled him over. The boot was applied to the back of his head, grinding his face into the dirt.

They tied his hands, too, and rolled him back over, and somebody stuffed a rag in his mouth and draped a burlap sack over his head. And then somebody began to undo his pants.

No, Lord. No, Jesus.

They pulled his pants down around his calves and he lay there on the ground and waited for the cold blade to strike, to tear through the single piece of flesh they could not forgive for being. But the blade tore not through flesh but through the fabric.

"Now get his shoes off."

They unlaced his shoes and pulled them off, then lifted him to his feet. They cut his jacket and tore it off, ripped the buttons from his shirt and tore that off.

The first voice spoke. "This here's a warning—that's what I been told—but I imagine that before too long I'll be sending your black soul wherever a black soul goes. Seem to me you a mighty wayward nigger. I doubt learning lessons is what you do good."

Somebody drove his fist into Blueford's belly. While he was doubled over, trying to suck air in through the burlap, the first voice said, "Now bring that goddamn roan."

IF LEIGHTON hadn't overslept, he might have been the one who'd come down Main Street at the break of dawn and discovered the horse tied up in front of the post office and seen the burden on its back. If he'd been the first one there, he would have led the animal away before anyone else could see it; and nobody, save for those who'd done the deed and the one they'd done it to, would've been any the wiser. But he'd overslept, so someone else had found the horse.

By the time he got there, it was nearly seven o'clock. A crowd had gathered, though he couldn't tell what they'd clustered around. Then somebody moved, and he saw the horse's legs.

The men in the crowd were almost all day laborers or sharecroppers. He didn't know their names, but he knew who and what they were because of the way they were dressed. As he walked toward them, he wondered what they were doing in town, at seven on a weekday morning, with cotton still in the field.

"You reckon the hair around his bayhacker's like barbed wire? That's what I've always heard."

"Don't know. Can't see it and don't aim to touch it."

"The horse might could tell us."

"The horse don't want to think about it."

One of them saw Leighton and whispered something to the others. They began to step aside.

The body tied to the horse was only slightly darker than the horse itself. Somebody had draped a burlap sack over the man's head and painted a white stripe up his back, beginning just above the buttocks and ending at the base of the neck.

At first, breaking into a run, Leighton assumed the Negro was dead. But when he got closer, he saw the note—pinned to the man's rib cage with a big darning needle. Though the paper was streaked with blood, you could still read the words.

This white line is where we will devide his black carcase next time he forgets that the Good Lord saw fit to put the mark of Cain upon him

It would only strike Leighton later—much later—that he hadn't been shocked someone had stripped a man naked, bound him to a horse and stuck a six-inch needle through his skin. Instead, he was surprised they'd stopped at that. And while his first impulse that morning was to apologize to Blueford Lucas for what they'd done to him, he knew the worst thing he could do was speak to him on the street, where he lay strapped to the horse, with a bag over his head.

Leighton pulled his own coat off and threw it over Blueford, leaving only his legs and feet bare. If Blueford didn't end up with pneumonia, it would be a wonder. Overnight, the temperature had dipped into the thirties.

Leighton walked around to the hitching rail and untied the horse. He pulled the reins, and the big roan turned.

"You reckon he's any smarter this morning, Mr. Mayor," somebody said, "after spending an evening at the school for ill-mannered niggers?"

The fellow who'd spoken was a heavyset man in a pair of apron overalls. He had a reddish face and thick black eyebrows. Leighton had been seeing him around town for two or three years.

He could tell the man had Indian blood—quite a bit of it. Leighton had some himself, and so did Sarah. Lots of folks did. They had that kind of blood and other kinds, too. But nobody ever talked about blood. That was something you just didn't do.

He paused in front of the man. "Judging from the looks of you," he said, "there're places not too far away where you'd be held in about the same kind of regard you hold this man in."

He walked on past them then, leading the horse into the street. Before he'd gone far, a voice rang out behind him.

"Ain't careful, you liable to find yourself tied up, too."

AFTERWARDS, he would claim he hadn't seen them, but he had. One of his clients who lived on the Panther Burn Plantation had passed away during the night, and he was on his way to pick the hackney up so he could go to offer solace, sympathy and sustenance. Loda had baked a sweet potato pie, and he carried it with him, one plate overturned atop another and a warm towel wrapped around the two.

He saw them as soon as he turned onto Second Street: the mayor, head held high, one hand clamped around the reins, eyes trained on something only he could see; the big roan following behind. Black legs protruded from beneath the mayor's coat; black arms clasped the roan's neck.

Jesus God in Heaven.

He inched backwards, then ducked into an alley. For an instant, he cowered there near a pile of rotting garbage. A stray dog was nosing through the refuse; spotting Seaborn, he bolted to the far side of the alley and lingered, watching to see if Seaborn meant to hurl something at him.

Which Seaborn had no intention of doing. Providing charity to the neediest creature within earshot suddenly seemed important.

He composed himself. "Here, boy," he whispered. "Here, boy." He pulled the towel off, lifted the top plate and dumped the steaming pie onto the ground. "You hungry, ain't you, boy? Come on and get it, son. This here's a good pie—it's a fine pie."

The dog looked at him as if he'd lost his mind.

"You want it, you got it. Come on, son. Slink along to Seaborn." He stepped away a few feet, then squatted and smiled at the dog.

The allure of the pie proved strong enough. The dog crept across the alley, looking as if he expected Seaborn to jump up any minute and deliver a kick.

Burying his nose in the pie, the dog began feeding noisily. He was still working on it when Seaborn, after straightening his suit, slipped across Second Street into another alley and, for reasons he would never quite fathom, set off after the mayor.

BLUEFORD's legs had turned to ice. At some point during the night, he'd lost all feeling in them. He'd never quite lost the feeling in his hands and arms, though, nor in his side. He felt as if they'd stuck a sword in him.

"Easy," the mayor said. "Just rest easy for a spell."

Blueford couldn't tell whether the mayor was talking to him or to the horse. It didn't much matter. Over the course of this ordeal, he'd become one with the horse. They'd bound his arms tightly around the animal's neck, not leaving him much room to wiggle, but still he'd managed to caress the horse with his forearms. He'd made a gentle humming sound for it, too. He felt bad that it had to stand out there all night long with no blanket on, but told himself that at least he was providing it a little warmth, even as the horse was granting him some. In his loins he could feel its flanks rise and fall, and before long he was breathing right along with it.

It was a good horse. A patient horse. A horse that—

depending how you saw these things—might have made a marvelous Negro.

"We're almost there now," the mayor said. "Won't be but just another minute. There's not a soul within shouting distance, nobody watching. Everybody's way back yonder."

Gravel crunched beneath the horse's hooves. Something brittle—a falling leaf, Blueford bet—grazed his arm.

"I'll get you down from there. Just a second."

Hinges creaked, and the horse ducked its head. The hinges creaked again.

The mayor lifted off the burlap sack. They were in some kind of dark shed. Blueford could see shelves along the walls, where paint cans and various tools were arranged: hammers, screwdrivers, drill bits. The place smelled of chemicals and sawdust.

The mayor's eyes never met Blueford's as he pulled a knife from his pocket and cut the ropes that bound his hands and arms and ankles. "I'll go in and get you some clothes," he said. "Then we'll get you inside and call the doctor."

Blueford sat up straight. The coat slipped off his shoulders, but he managed to catch it before it hit the ground. He handed it to the mayor, who still refused to look at him.

"Who did this to you, Blueford?"

"Somebody." He slid down off the horse. The moment his feet hit the hard earth, streaks of fire shot up his calves. He braced himself against the animal.

"You don't have any idea who it was?"

"Could of been anybody. Could of been you."

"It wasn't me."

"Well, seem to me like *was* can be a funny word. *Wasn't* can, too. If what you mean to say is you wasn't there and that if you had been you wouldn't of tied me up—well, I reckon the first one's true and the second one might be."

He looked down, with no more than passing curiosity, at

his right side. He could see it was a needle they'd stuck him with.

"The doctor'll pull that thing out and bandage you up," the mayor said, his face as red as if he'd been standing over a forge. "Let's not try to mess with it ourselves."

Blueford reached down and pulled the needle out. It burned, but not that much. The note fluttered to the ground.

The mayor said, "I'll go get those clothes now." He walked back over to the door and shoved it open.

There, framed in cold sunlight against a backdrop of falling leaves, stood the dark-suited figure of Seaborn P. Jackson.

BLUEFORD was skinnier than Seaborn had always supposed.

He'd spent no small amount of time conjuring the man's body, convincing himself that underneath those baggy clothes was a mass of rippling muscle. But Blueford's arms, compared to Seaborn's own, looked like pencils; it was hard to imagine how he could ever lift a sack of hog shorts.

"Clothes," Seaborn said, stepping into the shed. In his disturbance, he forgot himself. "My God, man, let's get some clothes on this nigger."

Blueford said, "Mayor gone bring me something."

For the first time in many years, Seaborn and Blueford were face-to-face.

As if he knew that he was an unwelcome guest here in the storage shed behind his own house, the mayor departed.

After a distant door slammed, Seaborn said, "Who did it?"

"Can't say."

"Can't say—or won't?"

"Can't. And most likely wouldn't if I could."

"Seems like they behaved fairly mildly. In some ways."

"Yeah, in some."

"Though in others not hardly." While he stood there, Seaborn was careful to keep his gaze at eye level. From this morning on, he would associate the smell of sawdust with embarrassment and humiliation. "Must've been cold out. Almost froze, I suppose?"

"Just about."

"I have business associates down in Jackson."

A corner of Blueford's mouth curled in disdain. "No thank you."

"I could advance you funds for travel."

"I ain't studying funds for travel. I wanted to travel, I could get up on this horse here and do it."

"There's something to be said," Seaborn ventured, "for remaining constantly mobile."

Again they heard the door slam, and Seaborn turned to see the mayor hurrying toward them. He carried a pair of shoes, an old suit, a white shirt and a black tie. Evidently, he intended to dress Blueford for church.

"We'll just get these on you," the mayor said. "They're mine, so they'll be a little bit big."

Behind the mayor, at an upstairs window, his wife's face appeared. She looked down at Seaborn. Then past him.

Her gaze lingered there for several moments before the window went empty.

THE MIRROR on the old dresser he and Scheider had brought home from the dump was cracked in five or six places.

So it was not just a scarecrow that stared back at him when he got home that morning, but a scarecrow bent and broken. The sleeves of the coat hung down past his fingertips, making it look like he had no hands. His arms skewed off in various directions. Shards ran through him.

To satisfy a curious nature, he raised his right arm and bent it sharply. The elbow split in two; the forearm separated from the biceps.

Next he stuck his leg out at an angle. It splintered.

He was in many pieces now. He wished he owned a camera.

N O O N E knew she owned the revolver.

She'd found it in a big trunk, under a bunch of old clothes, the day after her mother was buried. It had been loaded then, and it was loaded now. She kept it in a metal box she'd shoved under the house.

Retrieving it was not pleasant—the ground in the crawl space was like ice, and some chickens had spread their droppings under the house—but she felt a lot better when her fingers grazed the box.

She lay there for a moment, fingertips resting on the metal lid. Then she pulled it open.

The revolver was a .36-caliber Patterson with a nickel-plated finish. Even in the scant light under the house, the barrel gleamed. She had half a mind to place it in her mouth.

Then, suddenly, she was of one mind. She lifted the gun, opened her mouth and laid the barrel on her tongue. When she put it in there, she meant to pull the trigger, and for the rest of her life she believed she would have done it had it not been for one thing: the gun barrel tasted like garlic. It tasted like garlic, and she had always loved the taste of garlic, loved it when you mixed garlic up in lard and smeared it all on a slice of hot bread. She loved other tastes as well, and not all of them were gone from this world.

The gun was on the ground. You should never lay a gun on the ground. She tasted salt; her cheeks felt damp.

She rolled onto her back. Above her ran a floor joist. She raised and closed her hand on a rough timber, a splinter working its way into her palm. She squeezed harder, hurting. Her other hand slipped up under the coarse sweater she wore, up under her blouse, the camisole. Her teeth ground down.

She lay there on the dirt. As one day, in blessed promise, the dirt would lie on her.

"TAKE out from here," Miss Bessie said. "It was me, I'd light out from here so fast, my feet burn a hole in the road." As if she meant to show just how convicted she felt, she swung her legs out of bed. For the first time in two or three years, she sat up under her own power. "Tell me what in the world it is holdin' you back. And don't you say it's me, because like I done told you, I supposed to be dead. Fixing to be, too, and that's how come I don't need you. You hear me talking to you, girl?"

Loda pulled fresh sheets from the bag. "Since you're already up," she said, "we'll go on and change the bed."

She reached for Miss Bessie's elbow, but the old woman pushed her hand away. "It's that Seaborn P. Jackson. He got business to attend to. Yes sir, he got local commerce. You mark my words—that man gone get you killed. He gone get you killed dead, or he gone get you killed but make you live, and that's twice as bad. He don't want y'all to leave town, ain't that right?"

She and Seaborn had not even discussed the possibility. He'd come home yesterday morning and told her what he claimed another Negro had told him: how they'd tied Blueford up naked on a horse and painted a stripe down his back and attached a note to his side with a big needle. How they'd left him in front of the post office, where the whole town could see him.

"It's regrettable," Seaborn had said. "Very regrettable." She was standing with her back to him. He laid his hands on her shoulders. They felt strange, those hands of his. So big, so soft, so capable. So helpless. "They're like children," he said. "Give them what they want, and the next thing you know, they've forgotten they ever wanted it. And when they've forgotten, everything can go back to being the way it was. Only better. Because you've seen right through them, and they can't even see you. They want you to resign, so you resign. I've got a plan or two in mind. Much as we've got saved, we'll lay around a little while, say *yes suh* every time we can find anybody to say it to, and after we've said *yes suh* till we can say it backwards in our sleep, you know what we'll do?" He chuckled. "We'll buy them. Lock, stock and booty. We're going to open ourselves a savings bank. I'll secure backers in no time."

Keep your clothes clean, keep your hands washed, brush those teeth till they gleam since they're the one thing on you that's whiter than anything they've got. Keep good books, make every dollar count. Buy this—and before too long you'll own that, too.

She stepped to the foot of Miss Bessie's bed and lifted up a corner of the coverlet.

"What you aim to do? Pull the cover off with me settin' on it?"

"What else can I do if you won't let me help you up?"

The question enraged the old woman. "Well, Jesus Lord have mercy I ain't never." A cane stood propped against the bedside table; she hadn't used it in ages. Now she put her hand out, grasping, but the bowed handle lay just beyond her reach. She lurched. Before Loda could react, she sprawled upon the floor.

Johnnie Mae bounded in from the front room. When she saw Miss Bessie there, with Loda bending over her, she began to stutter. "La-la-la . . ."

"What that child doin'?" Miss Bessie rasped. "Trying to sing the doe-ray-me?"

"Johnnie Mae, it's all right," Loda said, doing her best to wrap her arms around Miss Bessie. "Could you come over here and help me?"

But Johnnie Mae stood rooted. Slowly, she raised her hand. Her mouth had fallen open, and she was staring at a spot just above Miss Bessie's head.

The window was there. Loda thought maybe somebody had walked into the backyard, but all she could see was the outhouse. "What is it?"

Miss Bessie's voice sounded stronger than it had in a long time. "Bell Irvin. He must of seed me fall. He just look in to see if I was ready."

"Seaborn would, too," Loda said. "If he'd passed on and it was me down on the floor there instead of you."

"Yes, I 'spect he would," Miss Bessie said. Her eyes burned. Her breath was hot, too. "So just to stay on the safe side, to make sure you got you an angel when you need one, why don't you tell your husband, Mr. Seaborn *P.* Jackson, to go on ahead and drop dead right this minute?"

The Postmaster General
The Department of the Post Office
Washington, D.C.

October 15, 1902

Dear Sir:
Owing to circumstances sundry and various, I shall no longer be able to continue in my present position as Post-mistress at the Loring, Mississippi post office. I am grateful for the opportunity afforded me some years ago by the

McKinley administration, and were it not for events which have recently come to pass, I should certainly have served out my term with great pleasure.

He made a couple of circuits through the room while she wrote, but was doing his best not to hover. Now, however, as she held the pen in her hand, staring at the little dome lamp on her desk, he said, "I'll turn on the electric light."

"I don't want electric light."

He reached for the string.

"Seaborn, I said I don't *want* electric light."

He padded heavily from the room. In a moment, the door on the kitchen stove creaked open. He tossed another log in. The stove door closed. She heard him set the kettle on the pig iron.

I liked my work. I took pride in doing it well. Nevertheless, I must bow to the will of certain citizens of this town, for to ignore it, I am afraid, would cause misfortune, not only for my husband and me but for the entire Negro community. An event such as the one which occurred here two evenings ago, in which an innocent member of my race was accosted and humiliated before the whole of the town, can only be taken by the rest of the Negro citizens of Loring as a warning.

Therefore, please allow me to tender my resignation, effective immediately, from the position of Postmistress at the United States Post Office in Loring, Mississippi.

Respectfully,

Loda Jackson

HE WANTED to accompany her, but she told him no, and this time he did not insist. She put on her warm coat. She picked up her purse, which contained the pistol, and left the house. Walking across the yard, she looked back; his face was pressed to the window.

The streets downtown were empty. She pulled the key from her purse and unlocked the door, then stepped inside and locked the door behind her. For a moment, she stood there in the dark. She recalled the first time she had come here. She was with her mother. The building, back then one of only four structures on Main Street, was so new you could still smell the odor of freshly cut cypress.

The postmaster was a white man whose nose was long and hooked. He never said a single word to anybody unless a business transaction required one or two.

Six cents.

One pound, eight ounces.

Bound printed matter.

Special standard B.

He'd reduced himself, in her mind and in everybody else's, to a series of phrases, the tools of his trade. And he had seen himself, she felt sure now, in precisely the same way that everyone else had. He had thought of himself not as Samuel Scroggins but as "the postmaster."

Upon accepting the position, she had remembered him and promised herself that she would never define herself as "the postmistress," yet she had come to do so. At work, she had shown no more of herself than Samuel Scroggins had done before her.

Thirty-one cents, please, sir.

First-class, ma'am?

Aside from the occasional encounter with Blueford, or

those rare moments when Rosenthal, having posted a letter to a foreign address, remained at the counter long enough to ask her how her tomatoes or cantaloupes were doing, she allowed herself no banter. She displayed a straight face to the world.

She had been the postmistress, but now was only herself. And it was wrong, almost maddening, to find that being yourself suddenly meant so little. As if she were standing on a platform at the station, waiting for another self to come along.

She did not bother to switch the light on. She knew her way around. She walked over to the counter, stepped behind it, lifted the rubber stamp and postmarked her letter. Then she opened the canvas sack, dropped the letter inside it and pulled the drawstring tight.

Leaving, she locked the door. She propped the sack against it and laid the key on top of the sack.

A ROCK AND
A KNIFE

EHIND the counter, in the part of the place you never saw when you walked in and mailed a letter, Tandy found several ledgers. They lay in a stack on a desk near the mail slots. Opening the first ledger, he discovered two neat rows of credits and debits.

He learned that she had paid Loring Light, Ice and Coal eight dollars and forty-nine cents for fuel during the month of October. Colter Moody, "yeoman," had received two dollars and ninety cents for shoring up sagging floorboards. The C & G had charged her four dollars and twelve cents for delivering seven copper-coated letter-box plates, which she'd custom-ordered for various individuals, including his brother and Catchings Stark. Otherwise, she hadn't spent a penny of government money in the last three months.

Most days, the receipts totaled no more than ten or twelve dollars. It looked like people bought more stamps on Mondays and Wednesdays than at any other time. Going back into 1901, he saw that the week leading up to Christmas had been especially busy; on the twenty-first of December alone, she'd recorded receipts of $161.77. If he got into a situation where he needed to skim a little bit off, it might be easier near the end of the year.

Though he was not officially the postmaster, he would be soon enough. When Catchings gave him the key, he'd told Tandy that he'd spoken personally with Senator Hale over in

Greenville, and the senator had assured him he would urge the administration to act swiftly on Tandy's nomination. The president was coming down to the Delta to hunt bear, the senator said, and he would present it to T.R. then. In the meantime, Tandy should just go ahead and assume all relevant duties.

He'd gotten up early this morning, come down and fired up the stove in the lobby. A lot of mail had accumulated; he meant to sort it and get it out before any customers showed up. The first stack contained a large number of magazines and circulars, which he threw in a pile on the floor. He could already see that it would take forever to put junk like that out, so he decided to initiate a new practice: he'd stick all that crap in a big box, put the box in the lobby and let folks who really wanted the stuff paw through it themselves.

The letters, it turned out, were an even bigger pain. A lot of the handwriting was indecipherable to begin with, and sometimes the ink had run. The lowest mail slots were no more than a foot above the damn floorboards, and he was bending over so often he got a cramp in his back. Until now, he'd never done any real work, because he'd always felt he was destined for something bigger. Of that he was no longer certain, but he could see one thing for sure: work was work, and he'd been wise to avoid it as long as he could.

Then something happened to brighten his morning. He came across a letter addressed to Catchings Stark, bearing a Memphis postmark, with the word *Private* written across the flap and underlined twice. Despite having promised himself that at least in the beginning he would play it straight, he managed to open the envelope without damaging the flap too badly. Inside was a single sheet of paper, folded in quarters, on which a graceful hand had written:

Dear Sir,
I am as I have previously related in straitened condition. I
would not for all the world bother you but for that. But my
dear sir I do need aid. I beg you to come to me at my own
address or failing that send someone who can provide for me
a little succor. I have not nor will I ever be so bold or trouble-
some as to come upon you in your own town where as I
understand you are a respected man. But as I have said
before I only make such request when for weeks at a time the
sun does not shine—if you, sir, know what I mean.

Yours as ever so sincerely,
xxx

Catchings would surely know what the anonymous correspondent meant, and so did Tandy. He chuckled, put the letter back in the envelope, then licked the flap and stuck the
envelope in Catchings' mail slot. He made a mental note to
watch the outgoing mail, see if Catchings sent anything to
Memphis.

Even though his back had stiffened up and his knees were
starting to hurt, he almost felt lighthearted after opening the
letter. He'd known, of course, that he was not the only man in
Loring, Mississippi, who'd ever made a mistake; but since he
couldn't walk the streets without bumping into his brother
and seeing that look of disapproval on his face, it was nice to
be reminded.

He bet a few more envelopes might contain some news
about some other folks, too.

HE FINISHED putting out the mail a few minutes before
nine, wiped his hands off, then walked over and unlocked the
door.

By nine-thirty, he'd served three customers, old ladies all. Every single one had skin fit for making halters or buggy tops, but he'd told each of them how young she looked, how little she'd changed since he was a boy. The first two glowed at the compliments, batting their eyes and fluttering their lashes. But the last—Miss Lena Grider—reached out, rapped his knuckles and snarled, "Don't be making up to me like that, you blackguard."

He was still smarting from her rebuke when Sarah walked in. "What a pleasant surprise," he said.

"It's no surprise at all. You knew I'd be in this morning."

She pulled off her gloves. Her fingers were long and thin, much whiter than he'd ever noticed.

"You look funny back there," she said.

"Funny how?"

"I don't know. I guess I always thought if I ever saw your face in a post office, it would be on a wanted poster."

"Anybody can straighten up."

"Anybody but you."

A gold chain of woven wire dangled from her neck, the pendant hidden beneath her collar. He knew what was just beyond the pendant.

"Have you opened my mail yet?" she said.

"Certainly not."

"Do I have any mail?"

"Not this morning."

"See? That's why you didn't open it. So, whose did you open?"

"Nobody's."

"You're lying. But at least you're discreet."

"I'm about as discreet a body as you'll ever come across," he said. Then, because candor, if strictly limited, sometimes proved more effective than lies, he added, "When you've got as many bones in your attic as I have, you do well to be discreet."

"You don't have any attic to put all those bones in."

"I'll have one soon enough. I mean to get my own place."

"Does Rosa know about that?"

"I imagine so. She's not as stupid as most folks think."

"I don't think she's stupid at all. I've lived in the same town with her all my life, and letting you move in on her's the only stupid thing I ever saw her do."

He knew, from the color in her cheeks, that she had not come here to insult him—or at least not only to do that. Sometime between now and the last time he'd seen her, the ground had shifted.

This was a game he'd played more times than he could count. Unlike all the other games, it was one at which he rarely lost. "Know what's back here?" he said.

"Where?"

"Behind the mailboxes."

Easing down to the end of the counter, he tripped the latch on the gate and held it open. "Let me show you," he said.

Without moving, she looked him full in the face. "I saw what they did to that colored man. Leighton brought him home on a horse."

"Yeah, I know he did. And it didn't make a real good impression on folks, I'm sorry to say. There's been talk."

"What kind of talk?"

He shrugged. "Just talk." He stepped aside, inviting her.

He walked her along the row of mail slots, pointing at names written in ink beside numbers. "Yonder's James Burth's. And that one there's A.H.'s. Course you know where yours is. And this one here, it's old man Teague's."

Certain of herself out front, she now seemed tentative,

ready to feign interest in something of interest to no one. She moved awkwardly, rather than flowing as she had learned to at the finishing school in Mobile. Once or twice, she ducked her head.

The storage room in back was full of hardware—he didn't know what any of it was doing there. Several wedge-plate hammers, chisels and gouges, a ratchet-bit brace, a whole set of Champion screwdrivers and an old Acme Princess coke stove identical to the one out front.

"I think I'll get rid of that stove," he said. "It ain't here for any good purpose. I believe it's warm enough already." When he slipped his arm around her waist and pulled her closer, she offered no resistance.

"You just came to stir up trouble," she said.

He felt her breath, warm and moist, on his cheek. "I'd like to stir some up with you."

"You're turning people against Leighton. That means you're turning them against me."

"Now how do you figure that?"

"What am I but an extension of my husband?"

"Plenty, if you don't only want to be that."

"Who says I don't want to?"

Her bitterness surprised him, and he was no stranger to bitterness.

Pulling away, she walked over to the stove and stood with her back to him. Her finger traced the fluting on the oven door. "You had a chance with me," she said. "But you ran off to St. Louis."

"I wish I hadn't. If I had it to do over—believe me, I'd stay with you."

Turning, she laughed. "Oh, Tandy, no you wouldn't. You've never even stayed with yourself."

Even though he knew she was probably right, he told himself that he was capable of wanting some things, and she was one of them. He was about to tell her so when he heard the front door open.

"Just a minute," he whispered. "Let me tend to whatever fool that is."

Out front, he found himself eyeball-to-eyeball with his brother.

Leighton set a cardbox box down on the counter. "This is a striking bag I ordered for Will," he said. "I'm sending it back."

"He wasn't feeling pugilistic?"

"First time he hit it solid, the bladder busted."

"Good for him. I reckon that's proof positive he's a Payne."

"Yeah. I guess so." For a moment, Leighton observed his brother as if he were a poor specimen for gainful employment. "Send it COD," he finally said. "They're the ones that made a defective product."

"Can't let 'em off scot-free then, can we?" Tandy said. He was about to lift the box when he heard a footfall.

His brother looked past him, then stiffened. Whey-faced.

It was a wonderful moment, a terrible moment, the kind of moment Tandy had experienced too seldom and too often.

"Your brother," Sarah said, "was just showing me around."

THERE wasn't much to do but sit inside and look out. A blanket of gray had spread itself over everything. The trees were barren, the grass dead. Though it no longer seemed like fall, it wasn't winter just yet.

Seaborn, decked out in his business regalia, lingered longer this morning. He'd drunk two cups of coffee rather than one, and he'd commented already on a wide array of events and nonevents.

"Greenville paper says there'll be high water come spring. They've already had three or four feet of snow up in the Dakotas, and every last bit of that's got to come right past the Greenville Landing. Stein's Grocery's expecting a shipment of ten thousand navel oranges this Christmas. That's enough to make me take a trip over to Greenville, though you know I don't like going to Greenville. And my goodness—would you listen to this? Says that over in Paris, France, three brothers that had been born on the same day in 1833 all died on the same day last month. The first one had a heart attack, about two hours later the second one had a stroke, and then the third one found out about the first two and he went and jumped out a high window. Stuff's popping, left and right."

He lifted his satchel, walked over to the couch where she was sitting and patted her on the head as if she were a bird dog. "I'll go make my rounds, and this evening perhaps we'll eat an early supper and then go over to Dr. Ormesby's and play a few hands of bridge with him and Matilda. How does that sound?"

She glanced at him over her shoulder and did her best to smile. "It sounds like the kind of activity you could be expected to propose if you meant to get me out and about."

"Far be it from Seaborn P. Jackson to lapse into inconsistency."

"You might want to try it one day."

"Whatever for?"

"For the sake of variety, maybe?"

"How might I go about it?"

"I don't know. You might just let yourself go a little crazy."

She could see his reflection in the windowpane. She didn't hear him sigh, but she saw his shoulders fall.

"People who live between a rock and a hard place can afford to go—as you put it—a little crazy. But we live between a rock and a knife." This time, instead of patting her head, he touched her briefly on the shoulder.

The floorboards creaked. The door opened and closed.

HIS ABILITY to negotiate the space between rock and knife was once what had proved so fetching.

She recalled an excursion during her second year of college. Thirty-five or forty young men and women, watched over by Mrs. Matthison and Dean Williams, had booked a steamboat for a Saturday on the Cold River. They'd picnicked on the water, eating ham, potato salad, baked beans and cole-slaw, washing it all down with iced tea and lemonade.

Everyone had worn Sunday clothes and practiced good etiquette in such matters as grammar and posture. Thus they resembled mannequins in the window of a Negro dry-goods

store, stiff and stylized, having collectively deluded themselves into believing that if you looked like a mannequin and
smelled like a pharmacy, you would be treated like a human
being.

Seaborn had come to stand beside her at the railing. For
months, each of them had been glancing the other one's way
as they crossed the courtyard between classes. Unlike so
many of the others, he never walked with his head down,
never shuffled along or engaged in shrill horseplay. He
earned the highest marks in every class he took. Rumor had it
he would deliver the valedictory address.

"It is a beautiful afternoon," he said.

"Indeed."

"You come from the Delta, I hear."

"Yes."

"From up in Loring County."

"That's right."

"I myself hail from Carrollton."

"It's near Greenwood?"

"That's correct."

The walking beam was rocking like a seesaw, the cylinders
hissing steam. The river itself lay quiet. Sweet gum and locust
formed an impenetrable wall on the bank they stood facing.

"And do you plan to return to Carrollton?"

"Not necessarily. I believe that a man, if he is to venture
into the world to any great effect, must endeavor to maintain
his options."

"And what options do you wish to maintain?"

He allowed himself a faint smile. "Any and all."

A rent appeared in the wall.

"I have considered a ministerial career," he was saying, "but
Dean Williams, while acknowledging the importance of the
clergyman, speaks against it. He believes that the Negro com-

munity is sorely lacking skilled artisans and businessmen and that the greatest contributions might be made in those realms."

A little white man stepped out of the trees, wobbling as if his knees were about to buckle. He righted himself, then wiped his mouth on the back of his hand and laughed silently.

He was followed from the woods by a copy of himself. Both men wore brown pants, black vests too tight for their bulging little bellies, and tall black stovepipe hats. Each of them carried a weapon that looked for all the world like a blunderbuss.

"The dean has spoken with a mortician, who may offer me an apprenticeship."

The first little man made eye contact with her. He dug his elbow into the ribs of his double, then pointed at her and Seaborn.

"The gentleman operates a funeral home in Vicksburg. And while Vicksburg is not necessarily a city in which I would elect to live, I might be prepared to spend some months there learning the trade."

The little men resembled characters in a Washington Irving tale, a couple of tipplers who'd stayed too long at the village tavern and would do well to make it back home before they passed out.

The first one raised his weapon; the second followed.

"Though as of yet I've made no commitments, the thought of working with the dead does not unnerve me, for, as Reverend Hamilton noted in his homily last Sunday, the righteous pass from death unto life. The souls which once lived in those ruined bodies will have taken up residence in a far grander place."

The first blast hit the gunwale and sent people diving to the deck. The second shattered a window in the wheelhouse.

Ever so calmly, Seaborn gripped her elbow. "It would be

best," he said, "not to become overly exercised. We fourth-year men are studying physiology this quarter. Putting undue stress on the heart is never wise."

Her legs were trembling, her breath coming hard. She let him lead her to the leeward side.

"The river," he said, "is perhaps best viewed from this prospect."

THERE WERE no more shots.

Apparently, only she had seen the little men. Seaborn himself said he hadn't noticed anybody and that the entire episode should simply be forgotten.

People rose from the deck and brushed themselves off. Within moments, as if they all realized that much more was at stake than an outing on the river, they began to converse again, though she noticed that Dean Williams kept his head below the railing.

As the party proceeded downriver, she remained at Seaborn's side, listening to that calm, stolid voice as it spoke of the opportunities awaiting those who would seek them. He never succumbed to the fear the others had given into. She herself had acknowledged fear too often in her life and felt it had cut her to the quick one time too many.

She believed, as she stood beside him on the steamboat, that she needed a palliative. She suffered from an excess of feeling. This peculiar disease clearly did not afflict Seaborn P. Jackson. His veins, she decided, contained some substance with anesthetic properties, and she longed for this herself. What she sought was a certain numbness.

But now, as she sat on her own couch looking out the window at a landscape bereft of color, she marveled once again at the human capacity for self-deception. You could deaden nerves with ether. But to keep them dead, you always had to kill them.

. . .

SHE WAS still sitting there when she heard a knock at the door. Her purse stood on a table nearby, and the purse contained the pistol. Though it was within easy reach, she didn't take it out, nor did she consider the possibility that the knock should go unanswered.

She unlocked and opened the door, and there stood a small chubby-cheeked white man in an ill-fitting suit, holding a leather cabinet bag. He sniffled as if he had a cold. In a thin but determined voice, he said, "Mrs. Loda Jackson?"

MR. HENRY Wheeler Meadows, chief postal inspector for the fourth U.S. region, comprising all of Mississippi, Alabama and Arkansas, as well as parts of Louisiana and Tennessee, carried with him the odor of Purple Jack. She could not figure out why that odor would cling to him now, unless he'd discovered a way to raise tomatoes after first frost.

Neither could she figure out why he was sitting here in her living room, where no white man had ever sat before, nor why he'd rested his cabinet bag on her coffee table and was, at this moment, snapping the locks to open it. He had made mention of the departmental handbook, of "Section Six, Article Three, point one," which, according to him, stated that "barring due and just exigencies, departmental personnel may be relieved of said duties, subsequent to their having tendered, to the appropriate superior, in writing, a clearly stated request to that effect."

The notion that he had come to reprimand her for negligence, or perhaps to charge her with dereliction of duties, was appalling. "I don't understand," she said. "Perhaps my resignation was not received? I submitted it two weeks ago. I would have thought that by now—"

"Oh no, ma'am, it's been received. It most certainly has. See, that's what I'm trying to tell you, Mrs. Jackson. There's—"

"Please, sir, don't address me in that manner. I assure you

that were someone to hear you referring to me as *Mrs.* Jackson, it would not serve me well."

He withdrew a leather portfolio from the bag. "Well, first of all," he said as he opened the portfolio, "nobody's hearing it but us. And second, it's departmental policy. Section Two, Article Two, point two. 'All departmental personnel are entitled to be addressed with proper forms of respect.' The proper form, in this case, being *Mrs.*"

Officious little men were not her favorite kind. "Mr. Meadows, I understand that you're not from here. But locally—"

"Oh, I'm from near enough to here. I was born in Meridian and lived there till September of last year. But my point of origin doesn't absolve me of performing my responsibilities in a responsible way. So between you and me, you're Mrs. Jackson, shall we say? If I have need to address you in public, which I trust won't be the case, I'll employ some kind of circumlocution."

He pulled a cream-colored envelope from the portfolio. "The key phrase in all that rigamarole about how to resign and be relieved of your duties is the bit about 'due and just exigencies.' What you and I have to deal with is the fact that we're facing a set of exigencies so due and so just that folks in high places have taken note."

He handed her the envelope. When she turned it over and saw the blue seal, she said, "Mr. Meadows, you must be joking."

"No ma'am. I assure you I'm not."

Don't ever let them see they've unnerved you—her mother had said that, too. Nonetheless, her fingers shook as she opened the envelope.

October 28, 1902

Mrs. Loda Jackson
Postmistress, Loring Post Office
Loring, Mississippi

Dear Mrs. Jackson:

Your request to resign your duties as Postmistress of the United States Post Office in Loring, Mississippi was duly forwarded to me by the Postmaster General. He informed me that he was seriously concerned about some of the statements you made in your letter. Sharing, as I did, those concerns, I instantly commissioned an inquiry into the matter. The results of that inquiry, which was conducted by Mr. Henry Wheeler Meadows, whom by now you will have met, were presented to me by Mr. Meadows two days ago here in Washington. After reviewing the matter and discussing our options with various members of my administration, and with one very prominent Negro leader whose opinion I hold in the highest regard, I have decided to ask that you rescind your resignation and serve out your term in office, which at present is scheduled to conclude in March 1904.

Federal officeholders must never be subjected to threats or intimidation; once attempts to intimidate officeholders have been made, they must be dealt with swiftly. For you to leave your office now, after having discharged your duties with distinction for many years, would only encourage the ruthless among us. I realize that I am asking you to make certain personal sacrifices. But I wish to assure you that under no circumstances will acts of violence or harassment against you, your husband or other members of your race be condoned. The rule of law must and will be maintained; of that, you have my personal assurances. You may call upon me personally; and you may treat Mr. Meadows as my personal representative in this matter.

I shall be visiting your state in a very few days. It is my hope that by the time I reach the area, you will once more be fulfilling your duties as Postmistress, as you have done so capably in the past. Perhaps when I am in Mississippi, you and I may have an opportunity to meet.

In the meantime I remain respectfully yours—

> *Theodore Roosevelt,*
> *President of the United States of America*

Her first thought, ludicrous as it would come to seem, was that Seaborn would want to publicize the letter, that he would carry it over to Dr. Ormesby's and show it to him and Matilda, that it might well become an item in his sales pitch when he went to court new clients. Within seconds, though, she realized Seaborn would be no more pleased than she to learn of the letter.

"As you can see," Mr. Meadows said, "the president's behind you."

She laid the letter on the coffee table. "I believe I made clear my desire to resign."

Meadows sneezed. "Excuse me." He drew a handkerchief from his pocket and polished the tip of his nose. "When the weather changes, I suffer." He folded the handkerchief and put it back in his pocket.

Having done so, he leaned forward. "Mrs. Jackson, let's be perfectly candid with each other. You've done your job unusually well. In more than five years, you never missed a day. I went over both reports my predecessor submitted on you. If somebody had praised me like that, I would've framed 'em and put 'em on the wall.

"Now, I know all about what happened to that colored man. I know the mayor and his brother are behind this, and I know that the brother's just a small-time gambler, whose main skill seems to be an ability to hoodwink lonely women into feeding him and giving him a bed to sleep in. If he hadn't left New Orleans when he did, he'd be dead by now, though it's hard to see why anybody would think him worth the price of a bullet.

"You used to live out on the place the Payne brothers' father owned. Something bad happened out there about twenty years ago, but I can't find out what it was. I don't suppose there's anything you could tell me about that?"

Her beaver shawl was draped over the arm of the couch; she reached for it and pulled it around her shoulders. She was not cold, but she did feel exposed. "I don't know anything about it," she said.

"Seems like nobody does. But being college-educated, you probably do know about Bishop Berkeley's famous question: When we turn our backs on the tree, is it really still there? Seems like folks around here are historical empiricists. Turn your back and nothing ever happened."

"Sometimes," she said, "it's best to turn one's back."

"Well, ma'am, that's one point of view. Another way of looking at it's that when you turn your back, you present the fellow slinking along behind you with a great big old bull's-eye."

"If he intends to shoot you, Mr. Meadows, it doesn't make a lot of difference whether he discharges his weapon from the front or the rear. The bullet will achieve the same basic effect."

Like most of them, he expected his word to become law. The notion that his efforts might be rebuffed was not one he had entertained. "See here, ma'am, the president of the United

States does not intend to see a decent, hardworking individual like yourself thrown out on the street."

She waved her arm around the room, calling attention to such features as the floor, the walls, the ceiling. "I'm not on the streets, sir. I'm sitting on the couch in my living room. My husband and I possess the wherewithal to continue our lives as we choose."

Henry Meadows began to perspire. His ears, naturally flat on top and very large, turned the color of an autumn sunset. "Ma'am, I'm going to tell you a story," he said. "It hasn't been five years since I was down in Cuba, lying on the grass at the base of Kettle Hill. My father was the captain of the Meridian Rifles, and he'd sent me to the front with a message. I had my face pressed right into the dirt. Those Spaniards were shooting their Mausers—oh Lord, were they shooting.

"I heard somebody yelling at me. Looked up, and there was this khaki-clad rider with a droopy mustache and thick spectacles, sitting on a big white horse and waving a pistol at me, hollering something about doing my duty.

"Now, you may think I'm fixing to tell you that I got up and charged up that hill like he wanted me to, but I was so scared I couldn't breathe, let alone run. So that rider—and I don't think I need to tell you who it was—he shook his head and rode off and left me to wallow in my own shame." He paused for a moment to let the import of his story sink in. "If you walk off this job right now, Mrs. Jackson—well, I've got a sneaking feeling that one day you'll be ashamed, too."

"You've got a sneaking *feeling*?" she said. "An actual *feeling* has crept up on you?" She stood, and the shawl slipped from her shoulders. It seemed as if the floor had tilted, that she might sweep down on this little man and cast him aside. "Why can't you just leave us alone?" she said. "You think we're balloons you can blow up with whatever hot air's giving you your indigestion?"

His face glistening, Henry Wheeler Meadows glanced around the room as would a soldier determined to take cover.

WALKING the streets, he held his head low.

People who saw him might not have taken notice but for the fact that his cabinet bag was open, dangling from his hand, the contents in danger of spilling out. Most people probably thought he was a drummer, one of the itinerants who showed up and spent a night or two at Miss Rosa's or the Loring Hotel. Later on, the few folks who remembered having talked to him recalled only that he'd said his name was Meadows, that he hadn't talked too much, just asked the kinds of questions any visitor might if he was sitting beside you at a lunch counter and wanted to be polite.

The only citizen who could have tipped them off ahead of time didn't. The operator at the Western Union, a fellow named Gaylen Hitt, he doubled on Saturday night as a barber at Your Brother-in-Law's Barbershop. He never said a word about the telegram Meadows sent, nor the one he received. Gaylen Hitt was quiet to begin with, even when cutting hair. That was one reason certain customers sought him out. Some folks like to sit back and relax with a hot towel over their faces without having to listen to a steady stream of gab.

THE STREETS oozed mud, but Tandy did his best to skirt the puddles. He'd bought himself a brand-new pair of patent-leather oxfords and meant to keep them clean; they went nicely with his new suit. As he walked, he tested the air from time to time with his cane, which was made of ebony and had a gold-plated headstock.

He went to work looking every bit the gentleman. Since taking over as acting postmaster, he'd seen every woman in town. Correspondence, he knew, was at an all-time high.

"Seem like every time I go down Main Street," Rosa had said this morning, "the post office lobby looks like a meeting of the Women's Civic Club's in progress. You reckon any of them's got more than a passing interest, Tandy?"

"Oh, I don't hardly think so," he'd said. "They just want to get caught up."

"Caught up on what?"

"Conversation."

"Every damn one of them gals is married. But their husbands probably don't do much talking, not that I'd blame 'em for that, not when the wives don't have the sense God gave a cocklebur. Nor the spunk of a potato."

He'd been working on his mustache, clipping it with a pair of tailor's points. He could see her face in the mirror. She didn't look too good. She'd drunk five or six glasses of whiskey the previous night—big glasses, filled to the brim—and this morning her cheeks showed a fair amount of sag.

"I'll grant you, most of the ladies ain't candidates for no inventor's contest," he said, "but they can't all lack the get-up-and-go."

"Depends on where you want 'em goin' to, I reckon."

Her mood was not exactly sunshiny, and he foresaw no improvement anytime soon, so he finished his grooming and left.

Now, as he rounded the corner at First and Main, he could see that it was a good thing Rosa was safely at home. Sally Stark, Gracelyn Ellsbury and Floyce Baskett were all waiting for him, clustered about the door like a bunch of sows shouldering up to the trough.

"Mornin', ladies." He tipped his hat. "Just let me open the door, and we'll be set for business." He pulled out his keys.

"Oh, Tandy," Sally said. "Look at this poster."

They stepped aside to let him see it.

BY ORDER OF THE PRESIDENT

The Loring Post Office
Is Closed Until Further Notice
A meeting to discuss the situation
will be held next Monday in the
Loring Town Hall at 7:00 P.M.

For a moment he thought it was a joke, the kind Uncle Billy Heath liked to play. Then he glanced down at the door and saw that the lock had been changed.

He stood there looking at the bronze knob, feeling in his heart that he must have known this scheme would fail like all the others. While some folks might straighten up, Sarah had told the truth: he never would. Fate would not allow it. He might be living in an era of progress, but for him, possibility was merely a remnant of the past. His family's past, for God's sake. Tandy himself, six months from now, would be fighting stray dogs for alley space in Memphis or Cincinnati, just looking for a spot to lie down.

He entertained such darkening thoughts for several seconds. Then he looked back at the poster, at BY ORDER OF THE PRESIDENT, and realized that these words from Washington—big, bold and black—were presenting him the greatest opportunity of his life.

SEABORN popped the matched blacks with the buggy quirt, hollering, "Step out there, sah! Step out!"

They were a few miles north of town now, bouncing all over the road. He'd come home sweating, the armpits of his dark suit soaked. "We must go now," he'd told her. "Got to go." He grabbed her wrist, squeezed it—twisted it, almost—and in her shock, she acquiesced. He'd never touched her before with such determination. It was not altogether unpleasant.

The buggy flew by a house teeming with poor whites. Five or six men were out in the yard now. A skinned hog hung from a crosspole, its stomach cavity gaping open above a steaming pile of entrails.

"What am I telling you?" Seaborn said. "What am I saying? I'm gonna tell you what I'm telling you. I'm gonna say what I've been saying."

Were it not for his frenzied motions, she might have entertained the notion that he'd suffered a stroke. As it was, she knew he'd simply opened his eyes. Or someone else had opened them for him.

"That Blueford," he said. "That boy about town. That boy don't know the Lord made him brown? That nigger never looked in a mirror?"

Reaching under the dashboard, he came across an empty bottle of tooth powder. He drew his arm back and hurled the bottle at the horses. "Faster, sah!" Glass crunched beneath the wheels.

Up ahead, on the right, lived a man named Loyal Taylor. He still owned his own land, but he had quit farming cotton and raised only what he needed to feed himself and his wife and children. He never went into town anymore.

Smoke rose from their chimney. A mule waited in the front yard, hitched to a corner post. A dog—a well-fed mongrel with a glossy coat—stood watching them, its tail taut as a trip wire.

Seaborn, she feared, would drive until either he or the horses dropped dead of exhaustion, if left to his own panic. "Turn in there," she said. "At the Taylors'."

"What for? Can they help us stir up any more trouble?"

But he did as she said, hauling back on the reins. "Whoa there!"

NICEY Taylor was making hominy, so Loda fed ears of corn into the hopper while Nicey turned the crank. She said she liked to soak the corn in water overnight to soften it and make it swell, then put it in the washpot with water and a sack of hardwood ashes and boil it until the skins separated from the kernels. Next, she'd drain off the lye water, wash the corn in plain water and skim off the husks.

"I use pepper and salt," she said, "but I ain't never seed the use in no meat seasoning. Don't set right, seem like."

Loyal came through the back door. He'd let his beard grow since the last time they'd seen him; his whiskers were snow-white, rich enough for a rug. He pulled a turpentine bottle from the pocket of his overalls. "Just exactly what you need," he told Seaborn. He walked over and offered him the bottle.

"Turpentine?"

"Naw, it's regular moonshine, but I leave a drop or two of turpentine in there to add a little extra flavor."

Seaborn pursed his lips, sniffed. "If this kills me," he said, "I'm doubly discommoded. I carry my own burial insurance." He breathed deeply, then took a swallow. Tears ran from his eyes. "This," he said, "makes me want to utter swearwords."

"Go on and take you another little jolt," Loyal said. "You already lookin' calmer."

This time, he took a bigger swallow. Afterwards, he licked his lips. "What are the ingredients?"

"Put corn in there, some rye and barley malt, add some yeast and then you cook it all up and let it mature a little. Understand, I don't sell it, I just make it and drink it. You want that bottle, you can have it."

Seaborn did not say he wanted it, but neither did he refuse. He said, "We find ourselves, Loda and I, in an unfortunate position."

Loyal laughed. "I been in an unfortunate position all my life. And I'm fortunate to be in it."

"Perhaps you heard about the ceremonial neutering of Blueford Lucas?"

"Heard they stripped him off buck naked and tied him to a horse. Didn't know they had no ceremony, too."

"What I'm saying," Seaborn said, eyeing the bottle again, "is that this was the starting point. This was, as it were, the tip of the white iceberg."

He recounted how Blueford had entered the post office and become embroiled in a verbal altercation with Tandy Payne.

Loyal whistled. "That's that younger one. Years ago, I was riding along out there by the Deadening, and I saw this little colt batting it down the road, dragging that boy by the stirrup. And I said to myself right then, I said, 'Go, little colt, thin out them Payne ranks.' But that horse wasn't up to the job."

Seaborn said, "Mind you, I'm not saying I approve of this," and tipped the bottle up once more. He was starting to glow. He looked healthy.

He walked them through it, step by step, explaining to Loyal and Nicey how Tandy had stirred everybody up, how they'd grabbed Blueford and done him wrong—Loda's ears noted the sincerity with which he used that word—and then how Loda had gone on and done as they asked and resigned. And then some little man had come to see her and told her that the president himself wanted her to stay in office, and she'd said her resignation still stood. And now they'd closed the post office entirely.

"Every Negro who can vote votes Republican," Seaborn said. "Evidently, the folks up in Washington think it'll help them pick up those votes if they're perceived as supporting Negro rights. But in the meantime, the folks in Loring aren't going to stand for having no post office. It may be that Loda needs to rescind her resignation. Or that she needs to let it stand. But we need to figure that out. Because the way things are—my goodness, I'm afraid we'll be run out of town."

"Being run out of town ain't so bad," Loyal said.

"Not that town anyway," Nicey said. "That town got some folks make a cottonmouth look downright winsome."

"That's how come you don't see us there no more," Loyal said. "See, they won't let me try on a coat before I buy it, so you know what I do? I make my own coat—make it out of rags if I have to, so's I don't have to go buy no material. They let my cotton stand out in the rain while everybody else's go in the compress, so I quit growing cotton altogether. They don't need me, I don't need them. When they craving sport, I live too far off for them to fool with.

"That trash down the road there—they don't bother me. Ever now and then, they get to wanting something good to drink and come up here, and I tell them what I told you. Tell 'em I don't sell it, I just make it and drink it and they welcome to a little bit if they want it. And they do. But now them folks that live in Loring, they ain't nothing but trouble. Going way back."

"We've lived our entire adult lives there," Seaborn said. "We have our own place. Loda's got her garden out back. All the Negroes are depending on me to see them through sickness and death. We've done our best to get along. Now we're afraid to go home."

Loyal looked at Nicey. She shook her head as if to say that while such foolishness was hard to understand, it would have to be indulged. So he turned a ladder-back chair around and straddled it. "Seem to me like what y'all gone have to do if you just bound and determined to stay there," he told Seaborn, "is help the white folks decide what they mean for you to do. And then you gone have to hurry up and do it, without letting them figure out you helped make up their minds.

"See, I know y'all know this, except you in a position where your brains all shoveled up and you ain't thinking straight. But the fact is, white folks never more dangerous than when they confused. They get confused, they can't see red, can't see yellow, can't see gray nor green nor blue—can't see nothing in the world but black and white. White's them. Black's you.

"So it's to your own advantage for them to have clear vision. Because the problem ain't y'all, it's a separate set of white folks, and that's the hardest thing in the world for them to accept. So you got to let them know you willing to go along. Let 'em see that if they want you to dance—well, you got your dancing shoes shined. Want you to sweep the floor, you got a broom made of magic bristles. Soon's they hear you humming that same old tune, they liable to start seeing straight again. And then you can just go on about your business. Same as always."

"Yes, but what if they don't start seeing straight again?"

Loyal reached into his pocket and withdrew another bottle, identical to the first. He pulled the cork but did not drink. "Well, if that come to pass," he said, "y'all probably gone wish you'd went ahead and relocated."

GOING home that night, she handled the horses.

Once or twice, Seaborn's head lolled off to the side. He rode with the bottle clamped between his knees. "I am so tired," he said. "It's like being in one of those plays we staged back in college. Do you recall the time I played Julius Caesar? For weeks, I walked around acting the part. And it took its toll on me. I began to think of myself as a man whose sole duty was to live until that moment when they pulled out the knives.

"Playing Seaborn P. Jackson takes its toll on me, too. I feel as if I'm parading the streets in blackface. But the black *is* my face. It won't wash off. Isn't that strange? That it's real but feels as if it isn't? You don't suppose they ever feel like that, do you?"

She didn't suppose so, but she knew there were times when they felt out of sorts. The difference was that if you were she and Seaborn, you had to deal with their disturbances, their misfortunes, but they never had to worry about yours. You had one overriding misfortune, as far as they were concerned, and they figured it was always on your mind. Because if they had been you, they believed, that single misfortune would have been the only thing on their minds.

"I'm not sure what they feel," she said. "I just know I'd like to quit worrying about it."

"So would I. So would I." He yawned. "My goodness, I'm sleepy."

"We're almost home."

"No sign of a lynch party?"

"No sign of any party. There's nobody out."

"Where will we leave the horses?"

"Don't worry. I'll take care of them."

She helped him into the house, then went back out and drove to the livery stable. A sleepy young Negro, whose name she could never remember, came out and accepted the reins, and she gave him a nickel and wished him good night and walked through the dark streets home.

Seaborn was already sleeping, but when she lay down beside him, he opened his eyes. He smelled strongly of rye. "I did what you said I ought to," he told her. "I went just a little bit crazy."

"I know you did."

"I suppose it's all right for one evening. But I daresay I'll regret it tomorrow."

Be ye not free with the indefinite pronoun—that had been a cardinal rule of Rhetoric and Discourse, as taught at Cold River College by the Reverend Stephen Hamilton. But just as Seaborn might regret *it*, she had suddenly felt it. And indefinite it was and ever would be.

She touched him.

He whispered, "Dear Loda."

THE DOUGH lay on the table, ready to be rolled. Her rolling pin was the fancy kind. Made of hardwood, it would leave a dozen different impressions when you rolled it across a sheet of dough. After baking, you could cut the dough into individual cakes. One would bear the image of crossed sheaves, another the image of a milk can or barrel churn. But the dough was just dough until she rolled it. If she rolled it.

Which she had one less reason for doing now. Traditionally, Sally Stark threw a special quilting party whenever a young woman from Loring's elite became engaged. Sally and Floyce and Gracelyn and Sarah prepared the refreshments, and each girlfriend of the young woman who'd just gotten engaged brought a piece of material with her own initials embroidered on it. After all of the pieces had been sewn together into a quilt to be given the newly engaged girl and her fiancé, everyone would stand. Sally would fling her big cat, Bloomers, onto the quilt. Whichever girl stood closest to the spot where the cat came off was said to be next in line for marriage.

Sarah had participated in more of these quilting parties than she could count, the first one having followed her own engagement to Leighton. But Sally had thrown one yesterday, to which she had not been invited; she'd learned of it only when Norah Minton, mother of the young woman in whose honor the party had been held, stopped her on the street and thanked her for all her efforts.

No one had to tell her why she'd been excluded, just as no one had to tell her why she'd ever been included in the first place. You were your last name, with all its attendant strengths and liabilities. Hers had just been devalued because her husband had led a naked Negro through the streets of Loring on a horse, then clothed him in his own suit and insisted on driving him home in the same buggy she and her son rode in. He had not thought to ask her in advance how she felt about the matter, nor had he chosen to discuss it with her later, except to say, "I'm sorry you had to see that. Try to forget it ever happened."

The ability to forget had been his own balm, and he believed it could be hers. But he was wrong. Even if her memory had been as selective as his, the collective memory of her social circle wasn't. Some things were harder to live down than he imagined.

He entered the kitchen now, stooping when he passed through the door. He'd never hit his head before, and he never would, but it was part of his overall prudence, she supposed, to behave as if he might.

"Making cookies?"

"I guess so."

He observed her from a distance. "By the way, did Will do a halfway decent job on his schoolwork?"

She nodded. "Halfway. But not much more."

"Did you see the mark he got on his Latin the other day?"

"Yes, I talked to him about it."

"I heard him moving around last night at about eleven or eleven-thirty. I went up there to see what was going on. Found him in bed reading *The Wilderness Hunter*. I'm glad he likes books, but that's one reason he's not doing better in school. He's too busy reading for pleasure to pay attention to what they're trying to teach him."

"I guess he gets that from you."

"The reading? Or the inability to learn a lesson?"

He'd offered an opening for a discussion, but she chose to close it. "The reading."

He pulled out his pocket watch. "Guess I better be going. There's a meeting tonight. Due to start in fifteen minutes." On his way out, he touched her shoulder.

She sat there staring at the dough, which would be dough and nothing more until she rolled it. If she rolled it.

ROSENTHAL rolled the bicycle out of the back room. He knew that Blueford must have seen it back there—he could not have failed to—but he hadn't said a word about it. He hadn't said a word about anything. When Rosenthal spoke to him, he'd only nod or shake his head, once or twice managing a tight smile, as if trying to let Rosenthal know he wasn't just being surly.

Rosenthal understood this all too well. After the goyim came and dragged his uncle to the field and cut his fingers off and made him eat them until he choked on his own bones, his aunt never said another word. She was not exactly dead herself, but neither could you say that she was living.

"Blueford," he said, "might I ask you come to me?"

Blueford was in the corner sweeping up, doing it just as thoroughly as he always had. Rosenthal had thought it best to shield him from the public eye—for his own good as well as Blueford's, various individuals having indicated to him that they were surprised and affronted by his unwillingness to fire the Negro—but Blueford seemed bent on taking care of daily business. Just yesterday, he'd walked into the street and unloaded a hot-air incubator all by himself.

When Rosenthal called him, he leaned the broom against a shelf and walked over.

"This bicycle," Rosenthal said. "Blueford, I want you to have it. It just came here straight from the factory. This thing will really ride. You going to take it outside and go. A dark blur you'll be, too fast to see. You'll ride it out the back door, not walk home on those streets out there no more. Is this agreeable to you, Blueford? This bicycle free of charge?"

Blueford laid his hand on the saddle.

"That saddle there," Rosenthal said, "it's top-notch. Fully padded."

"That horse they strapped me onto, it was padded, too."

Rosenthal's eyes stung. "Blueford, they got some kind of meeting tonight. Walking home—this is no longer all right. You going to have to pick you up some speed with your movements. You need to roll like the river." He meant to keep his voice steady, but he heard something in it that he couldn't control. "Like *Wisla* you'll be, Blueford. You ever hear of this river? They call it the Vistula here, those who know about it. It's a river that runs near that town I told you about, the one I'm cursed to call my hometown. My uncle, his name was Jakub, too. He never had no bike."

WALKING down Main Street, Leighton saw Tandy coming toward him. His brother was wearing a new suit and carrying his cane; in the glow of the gaslight, the headstock glittered.

Ever since the other day, when he discovered Sarah in the back room of the post office, Leighton had felt as if almost every breath he took required conscious effort. Sometimes, when he was setting type or composing copy, he could forget about the episode for several moments, or even for an hour, but sooner or later he'd remember it again. He found himself wishing that she hadn't showed herself, that she'd just stayed back there and waited till he left; then he would have been none the wiser. But she had wanted him to wonder, though he couldn't imagine why.

He and Tandy met at the corner. The odor of pomade and hair tonic coming off Tandy was strong, but not enough to hide the smell of whiskey. A cool flame burned in his eyes. "Brother." He tipped his fedora.

Leighton said, "Got another new hat, I see."

Tandy pulled the hat off and turned it over, admiring it. "Nutria. You ought to get you one."

"Yeah, I guess so. I guess that's just what I need."

Tandy tapped the sidewalk with his cane. "Going to the meeting?"

"Yeah. In fact, I aim to run it."

He said it as a challenge, and when Tandy's eyes flashed, he could tell his brother had taken it that way. He'd run scared when there was no reason to, and he'd run scared when there was.

For an instant, Leighton saw Tandy racing away through a thicket; he felt a piece of cold steel in the palm of his own hand and heard his father's acid voice speak again. *Do excuse my worthless offspring for fleeing from your plight. Notice that my elder son and I stand witness to your suffering. Don't worry about forgiving us for what we've done, because me and him's both so proud that we could piss our britches.*

"I'm the mayor," Leighton said, to himself as well as Tandy. "This is still my town. Did you think I meant to sit by and watch you work folks up to tear it down?"

Tandy put the fur hat back on, tucked the cane beneath his arm and shook his head. "I just feel so bad," he said. "You've never understood how damn bad I feel. Just look at all the trouble you and Daddy make me go to."

IN THE wings, Seaborn waited.

It was drafty backstage, as the window wasn't well sealed. To make matters worse, a scuttle stood nearby; the cold air seeping in stirred up the coal dust, making him sneeze. He put his palm over his nose to muffle the sound.

He heard them coming, boots drumming on the floorboards, chair legs scraping hardwood. He could see them even with his eyes shut: a veritable corps of gray men, led by Mr. Percy Stancill.

Seaborn carried in each pocket a letter that Loda had written. The presence of dual missives on his person was no small cause of concern. He didn't know which one he would need, wouldn't know until later, when he'd heard enough to decide. He'd devised a code to keep them straight in his mind. The one on the left was the give-up letter, in which she acceded to their new demands and agreed to return. The one on the right was the one in which she said she knew she'd made the proper decision in resigning her position and would not change her mind, her own wishes coinciding with the wishes of the citizens of Loring, Mississippi.

Left like Lee, Robert Edward, who surrendered his army when he ran out of bacon. Left wasn't any problem. Right like what? Right like Roosevelt, who, if this turned out to be the proper letter, would be wrong, and *wrong* started with the same sound as *right,* if he could just remember.

"You listen real careful to what's being said," the mayor had told him. "You're a pretty sharp fellow—you'll pick up on the way things are going. That's the main thing, Seaborn. You stay on edge back there, and I believe we'll get out of this just fine."

"On edge," he'd said, beginning to hate the mayor, just as Loda had always hated him. "I certainly shall stay on edge, Mr. Payne. I shall stay sharp as a razor."

Was it his imagination, or did a tremor pass through the man?

"Seaborn," the mayor said. "When you're out there talking to them? Maybe you could try not to sound so—"

"Articulate?" Seaborn said. "Don't worry, sir. I can drop my *g*'s and slur my vowels as well as any Negro alive."

IN THE absence of a gavel, Leighton banged his fist on the podium. "Y'all hush up now," he said.

They sat there before him, forty-five or fifty men, almost all of whom he'd known his entire life. The two exceptions were the postal inspector, Mr. Henry Wheeler Meadows, and a thin, almost frail-looking man with snow-white hair, who wore a double-breasted cardigan and sat to one side, a notebook open in his lap. Leighton meant to approach him after the meeting and find out why he was taking notes.

"Everybody knows why we're here," he began. "We're here because—"

Percy Stancill banged the floor with his cane. "We're here because the goddamn federal government's tried to piss in our trough."

A loud chorus of assenting voices.

"Now Percy," Leighton said, "you know as well as I do that the United States Post Office is a federal office. It's not administered by the state, and it's sure not administered by the municipality."

"I ain't talking about the municipality," Percy said. "I'm talking about Loring, Mississippi."

Leighton stepped away from the lectern, moving slightly to the side. One thing he'd learned from his father was how a big man could quiet an unruly group with his size alone. Of course, his father had more than bulk on his side. "Percy," he said, "it's not up to you or me or anybody else in this room— except maybe Mr. Meadows, though I'm not clear on exactly what his responsibilities are, either—to confirm federal officials or, for that matter, to solicit their resignations. What we're here for tonight, it seems to me, is to listen to Mr. Meadows present the administration's position—so we can find out what it's going to take to get our mail service restored."

He nodded at Meadows, offering him the chance to address the assembly.

HENRY Meadows rose to face the angry and belligerent crowd, which numbered upwards of 250 men, many of whom appeared to be armed, the correspondent for the *Chicago Tribune* would write in his hotel room that evening, amazed at having stumbled onto a story much better than the one he'd been sent to write about the rumored acquisition of the C & G by the Illinois Central. *One could only imagine that the man had nerves of steel. And indeed, one was to learn, Meadows is no stranger to open conflict, having served in the trenches during the recent war with Spain under the command of the Rough Rider himself.*

Meadows informed the mob in no uncertain terms that the only acceptable solution, from the point of view of the administration, was for the Negress Loda Jackson to return as postmistress and serve out her term. Otherwise, he said, the Roosevelt administration would have no recourse but to keep the Loring Post Office closed.

The hooligans greeted this last bit of information with curses and angry gestures. Yet Postal Inspector Meadows stood his ground with stern resolve.

HENRY Wheeler Meadows' knees were shaking. No words could have expressed the resentment he felt at being put in this position. He'd felt similar resentment four years earlier when his father sent him forward with that damn stupid message, risking the life of his only son, and back then the same damn man who'd made him stand here this evening had almost gotten him killed. He hated foolhardy fellows, the ones who craved confrontation, who were never content to leave trouble alone. He hated them even when they were right—and in this case, the man whom he represented was right. You couldn't let riffraff force a decent woman out of her job just because she happened to look different. He knew a thing or two about being different.

"Why the hell does that son of a bitch care who puts out our mail? What damn business is it of his? If he wants to eat supper with niggers, we don't give a damn—leastways I don't, though I sure wouldn't eat supper with one myself—but he needs to know there's things we'll put up with and things we won't, and this thing's one of the latter."

The man who was on his feet, shouting at him, had gotten so red in the face that he looked as if at any minute blood might spurt from his cheeks. As he spoke, he waved what appeared to be a Bible, though he made no reference to it.

The mayor rose and strode to the rostrum. Meadows was so grateful for his hulking presence that he almost embraced him. Certainly it struck him that the mayor might not be a bad man to have on your side.

"Sit down, Charles," the mayor said. "Everybody just get quiet. Y'all contain yourselves. Please."

THE MAYOR of the town, Leighton Payne, is in the peculiar position of being both a civic official and editor of the town's only newspaper, which critics say is little more than a mouthpiece for the local planters and their interests. Reluctantly, the mayor returned to the podium and made a halfhearted appeal for order on behalf of the beleaguered but unbowed Meadows.

ON HIS feet now, with his stomach in his throat and mayhem in his heart, Tandy faced his brother. There were ten or twelve heads between him and Leighton, and that was how he saw them: as heads with no bodies attached, no personalities. Heads without histories. In this moment, he could redefine them all, as well as his relationship to them. It was stunning how a man made himself up day by day. Everybody was really just telling his own story. That the world, or a portion thereof, should lie at the feet of a natural-born liar thus seemed right and proper.

"If my father were here today," Tandy intoned, "I feel sure that that good man would groan. Maybe he lies groaning in his grave."

Poetry—a faceless figure in prospector's boots—was stalking him tonight.

"He used to show us his wounds," he said, moving into the aisle, preaching now, wishing he could borrow the Bible Charles Baskett had been waving earlier. "In his side, right under his rib cage. A wound in his leg, too—he took that one at Corinth. His kneecap had been blown around onto the side of his leg. The last twenty-five years of his life, he walked stiff-legged.

"His blood flowed all over the battlefields of Tennessee, North Mississippi and northern Georgia. And it flowed, gentlemen, to wash away scum, like the scum which faces us here this evening."

"Oh brother," Leighton said, shaking his head.

"Yes, I am your brother. That's why this saddens me like it would Daddy. To see you stand there and defend this vile little encroachist."

"*Encroachist* is not a word."

Percy Stancill banged his cane on the floor. "Let him talk, Leighton. You don't hold the rights to the whole damn English language."

Tandy pointed a finger at Meadows. He'd seen little men like him before, little men with soft skin and plump forearms and peculiar tastes—men who'd sometimes pay for certain pleasures, if you ever sank so low as to covet the odd patron. He shuddered. "This little man talks like he's one of us, but he's not. Nor is the man that sent him here. When Teddy Roosevelt comes south, he likes to tell how his uncle on his momma's side fought aboard the *Alabama,* but there's something else he don't tell. And that's how when he was a little boy living in London, England, he started a fistfight with Jeff Davis's son. I reckon y'all know who won."

The laughter had a nasty edge to it. He was preaching hard now, and his congregation was ready to roll down the aisle, flattening any obstacle that got in their way.

"He don't say 'take that nigger woman back' and make us do it! No sir. We don't let any asthmatic son of a bitch from New York City, New York, send some little *cyst* into town to tell us what's what. My daddy didn't give his blood, he didn't bear the sorry *cross* which was that war they forced us to fight against our own sovereign will and stately testament—he didn't do them lustrous deeds which I just *listed* so you and me could be *bested* by prissy flits that fash and fawn!"

Percy Stancill was standing now. "You tell that son of a bitch Roosevelt he better not show his face down here," he said. "Because if he does, we liable to take a notion to hunt us some bear, too."

He leveled his cane, pointing it at the rostrum, though whether at Meadows or Leighton, or both of them together, was hard to tell. "And then you tell him that if he's trying to hang on to the nigger vote, he needs to remember one basic fact: a fucking corpse can't mark a ballot."

IN WHAT appeared to be a carefully orchestrated move, the brother of the mayor, who sources say the mayor and local planters attempted to install in place of Loda Jackson, got to his feet and, in the guise of disputing his own brother's appeal for calm, incited the crowd to issue vicious threats against the physical well-being of President Roosevelt!

WITH HIS heart sinking, Seaborn looked on. He remembered the day his father knocked the horse out.

This was the same horse his father rode to visit his patients, who were scattered all over two counties. He'd just filled the horse's bin with oats. Most days, he carried an apple, too, or a carrot or sometimes a handful of sugar. He would hold it out and let the horse take it. But on this particular day, he'd gone empty-handed, and as soon as he turned his back, the horse bent down and took a plug out of his butt.

A farrier's hammer lay nearby; Seaborn's daddy grabbed it, spun around and hit the horse squarely on the head. Before it pitched over sideways, Seaborn saw the look on its face: though the animal might have been dumb, it had sense enough to be surprised.

Seaborn Jackson was not without self-knowledge. He bet that if he could have seen his own face right now, it would have resembled the horse's. The difference was that he hadn't bitten the butt of the man who fed him, because no man fed him. But he certainly felt as if he'd carried a heavy rider on his back.

He put one hand in each pocket, pulled out both letters and ripped them to bits, one page at a time.

THE
DEADENING

THE MEN in the band wore straw boaters, striped shirts and armbands. It was too cold to be out in shirt-sleeves, but there they were, their instruments poised on their shoulders. Spit dripped from the tuba player's mouthpiece.

Leighton hugged the wall, doing his best to go unnoticed. He hadn't seen anybody he recognized, except for a couple journalists and Senator Hale, and Senator Hale didn't know him. The senator was standing with the welcoming commit-tee—eight or ten men with fat red faces and bulging bellies, planters like the senator himself, if their appearance was any indication. Probably not a Republican in the pack.

A couple hundred people milled about on the platform, including a bunch of kids who'd been let out of school. An old man with a pushcart sold parched peanuts and fresh hon-eycomb; a woman moved along beside him, kneading a strip of molasses candy, her tongue protruding through a gap in her teeth. Two bootleggers canvassed the crowd, seeking out the thirsty, then directing them to a wagon waiting at the far end of the platform, where two city policemen looked on, hot for their cut.

The train was an hour late. When it finally pulled in, the senator bellowed and waved his arms at the crowd as if it were a herd of cattle, even though nobody had approached the tracks. "Y'all get back now, you hear me? Y'all get back!"

At a nod from the welcoming committee, two Negroes began to toss a roll of red-white-and-blue ribbon back and forth over the train, starting at the engine and working their way toward the caboose. One of them would throw the roll, and the other one would catch it, snip the ribbon and throw the roll back, and then the first one would catch it and run down to the next car, and the process would start over. But there was a wind this afternoon, and the ribbon began to blow back over the train, furling itself as it came.

"Goddamn it," the senator sputtered. "Pay peanuts, you get monkeys every time." Disgusted, he spun around and gestured at the band. The conductor raised his baton.

You could tell they meant to play "Hail to the Chief." They stumbled across the melody several times but always managed to wander off again. Just when Leighton had begun to think their agony would never end, the door on one of the cars slid open. Three men in dark suits and black derbies stepped out.

The men looked almost as if they were triplets. The same size, they all had small eyes and sharp noses; except for the fact that one of them wore a bushy red mustache, each could have passed for the others.

The mustachioed one scanned the crowd, then looked back up the steps into the car and said something to somebody Leighton couldn't see.

On the top step, a leg appeared, trembled briefly; then the other leg followed and a whole man emerged.

The image Leighton would carry away was one of frailty: the president was shorter and thinner than he'd expected him to be, and his hair and mustache were shot through with gray. He'd been hurt a few months earlier in a carriage accident. Word was, they'd almost had to amputate a leg.

He looked nothing like the heroic figure Leighton had always imagined—but this, in a strange way, only made him seem more heroic. Everything Leighton had ever heard about

him confirmed that Theodore Roosevelt never shirked responsibility, no matter how much trouble entered his own life. The
president's first wife and his mother had both died within
twenty-four hours of the birth of his daughter, yet the following week he'd returned to Albany and resumed his duties in
the state legislature. Here was a man who held his own grief
private.

He stood there on the steps as if waiting for something
unusual to happen, but for the longest time, nothing did. The
band played on. The kids in the crowd continued to run wild,
bumping into grown folks and hollering at one another.

Then the conductor cut the air with his baton, and the
music died away.

Senator Hale stepped forward. He handed the president a
cavalry hat and shouted, "Welcome, Mr. President, to the great
state of Mississippi!"

Leighton had inched his way through the crowd, which
grew quiet now, anticipating a speech. He could see folks
moving around in the train compartment—a couple more
dark-suited men. One of them opened a window. Perhaps
because Leighton stood half a head taller than anybody else,
the man's eyes lit on him.

The speech never came. The president turned the hat over
in his hands, admiring it, smiling as if the sight of it brought
back old memories. Then he tucked it under his arm, leaned
down and whispered something to the senator, who laughed
loudly. Finally, the three men in derbies began to elbow folks
away, and the senator cried, "Get back now, y'all! Get on back!"

Surrounded by his bodyguards and the welcoming committee, the president crossed the platform and climbed into a
coach.

By that time, Leighton was close, just a few feet away. He
raised his right hand. "Excuse me," he said, to no one in particular.

The last of the bodyguards—the same one who'd eyed him from the train—pushed past, knocking him off balance.

"Excuse me," Leighton said again, but the man just kept going. He jumped onto the running board as the driver shook the reins.

THE PRESIDENT was staying at the Edison Hotel, on Washington Avenue, right at the foot of the levee. The lobby was busy when Leighton got there, but not packed.

At the desk, he asked whom he'd have to talk to about seeing President Roosevelt. The desk clerk told him the travel secretary was upstairs and had a telephone in his room, but that he'd left instructions not to be disturbed. "About all I can tell you is the secretary's a tall fellow with gray hair, and he's got some kind of rash on his neck. You're welcome to hang around and see if he comes down."

Leighton thanked him and gave him a tip. He walked across the lobby and sat down in a chair that offered a clear view of the stairs and the elevator.

The men in the dark suits had removed their hats. Two of them stood on opposite sides of the lobby. A third—the man with the red mustache—had positioned himself at the top of the stairs, where he stood perfectly still, his hands in his pockets, his eyes moving back and forth over the lobby, lighting every few seconds on Leighton.

Fifteen or twenty minutes passed. Then one of the bodyguards walked over. "Sir? Are you waiting for somebody?"

Leighton preferred to be on his feet during conversation, but something told him that, in this instance, standing up too fast might not be smart. Like a lot of journalists, he'd written an angry piece criticizing presidential bodyguards for letting Czolgosz get close to McKinley. He'd heard that the new protocols gave Secret Service agents leeway to act as they saw fit.

They'd already roughed up a few folks when T.R. was out on the stump.

"I was hoping I could talk to the president's travel secretary."

"And why would you need to do that? You making travel plans?"

The man stood five seven, at most. He had thick arms, a broad chest, short legs. He smelled of onions and spoke with a Northern accent. Leighton could imagine him resting his elbows on a bar somewhere in Georgetown, enthralling a bunch of drunks with loud, elaborate lies.

"No sir, I'm not planning any travel. I'm from over in Loring. I edit the local newspaper, and I'm mayor of the town. The president closed our post office down. I realize he's here for pleasure rather than business, but I was hoping the travel secretary might arrange for me to speak with the president for just a minute, so I might bring a few facts to his attention."

The man pulled a pencil and a small notebook from his breast pocket. "Name?"

"Leighton Payne."

"That's L-a-y—"

"L-e-i-g-h-t-o-n. Payne. P-a-y-n-e."

"And what's the name of your town?"

"Loring. L-o-r-i-n-g."

The man wrote the information down, then looked at Leighton. "My father fought against a Confederate general named Loring. That who the town's named after?"

"Yes sir, it is. What unit did your father fight in?"

"The Twenty-third New York. He fought and died in it." The man stuck the pencil back in his pocket, turned and walked away.

While waiting, Leighton went over what he would say. He'd tell the president that the town was full of good folks, that things had just gotten blown out of proportion, that if need be, Loda Jackson was ready to resume her duties. He'd say, too, that he believed folks would take her back if the president himself made a request of them, as he had made a request of her. Having it shoved down their throats was what they didn't like. They'd stood a lot of changes in recent years, and sometimes change brought out the worst in folks; they got scared things were moving too fast, maybe leaving them behind.

He'd say he had complete faith in the president's judgment, that he hoped he might be pardoned for this imposition during a vacation. But each and every place had its own set of peculiarities, and he believed he could speak to Loring's better than most folks.

He was set to say all of this and more. When the bodyguard approached him again, he rose.

"I've got a message for you, ah—" the man flipped open the notebook and glanced at the first page—"Mr. Payne. And it's not from the travel secretary, but from the president himself. He says that if there's anything you want to tell him, you need to go through the proper channels, and that the proper channel in this case is Mr. Henry Wheeler Meadows. He says, furthermore, that he is at present mighty ill-disposed toward the citizenry of Loring, Mississippi, a place he'd never heard of until a few days ago, and that he's especially ill-disposed toward you and your brother. Lastly, he asks me to inform you, so you can inform other people in this town of yours, that he hopes you've got good train connections over there, so the local people can easily travel around and see their friends and relations, since they won't be receiving letters from them anytime soon."

The man tucked the notebook into his pocket. He stepped closer—so close that Leighton could see the individual bits of stubble on his cheeks. "I don't like niggers myself," he said. "Never have liked 'em. I wouldn't want one handling my mail, and I doubt anybody else in my hometown would, either. But you people brought your problems on yourself. Personally, I think the whole South, nigger and white both, stinks worse than a mound of skunk shit.

"Now I'd like you to get out of this lobby, and I'd like you to do it right this minute. Because you're making my boss nervous, and you're making me nervous, and you've got me asking myself where my father's bones are and whether or not maybe your father wasn't the one that killed him."

The coldness came creeping into Leighton's arms and legs, set him to wondering if it was fair, after all, to call himself a warm-blooded creature.

"Maybe he did," he said.

A few days later, along with the rest of the world, he saw the picture and read the story.

In the photograph, the president and two other white men stood some distance to the left of the bear, which lay on the ground, its paws tied with rope. Two Negroes stood off to the right, one of them holding a dog by the scruff of its neck.

In the center of the picture, Senator Hale strode toward the bear. His hand gripped a hunting knife.

You could not describe the look on the president's face as one of disgust. You couldn't actually say what kind of look it was—whether it indicated revulsion or dismay or plain old-fashioned surprise—even if you knew that he had just turned down a chance to shoot the bear or do what the senator was about to do with the knife, or that he and the senator were becoming bitter enemies because of a post office in a town hardly anyone had heard of until a few days ago.

Of the incident involving the senator and the bear, President Roosevelt said, "I just don't need to kill anything that badly."

A BRITTLE crust of ice lay on the road this morning. Tandy liked the sound the ice made when the hooves crunched it. Since the horse would not have been here but for him, the sound acknowledged his own presence, his effect on the natural environment.

"Break the ice, break the ice, break the ice up nice." He sang the words to a tune he remembered hearing the old Spasm Band play. They'd been playing the tune inside the Star Mansion, while outside, in the alley, Tandy helped another man set a horse on fire.

The horse had belonged to a fellow named Big Broussard, and he owed money to the folks Tandy and the mulatto with the gasoline can worked for. Tandy owed those folks money, too, which was why he'd found himself crouching in the alley that night, keeping watch as the other fellow sloshed fuel on the animal.

You could tell the horse knew something was up—its eyes were big and round and white, and together they probably covered about three hundred degrees' worth of angle. The horse snorted and pawed the ground and kicked its rear legs out, though there was nothing back there for it to kick.

"Gone get this over as quick as we can," said the mulatto, handing Tandy the empty container. "I ain't saying I like it, no. You, you're gone be sorry Big Broussard ever rode you, and you not doing nothing but what a normal horse do. But me and this worthless white man, we got to set your hide on fire to save our own ass."

When the match struck the horse, the animal tore its reins loose from the post and raced from the alley like Satan's steed, flames blazing out behind. Street Negroes scattered, moaning, some beseeching gods seldom heard of.

Rather than run, as caution and good sense dictated, Tandy crawled under the stairs and got sick. He spent the night there, on his hands and knees among the garbage, looking out between the steps as Big Broussard stood and cursed and fired a bayonet revolver into the sky, calling out his intended targets one by one: "For you, Father. And you, Jesus. Take that one, Holy Mother, for letting 'em do me this way. Look out, John. Duck and crawl, Saint Paul."

Tandy had saved his own life that night by taking part in the burning, but it was months before the odor of roasting horse flesh cleared itself from his nostrils. As for the tune, he'd never forget it.

Break the ice, break the ice, break the ice up nice.

AT A TIME when no word tasted sweeter on the American tongue than *progress*, he'd come up with his own personal definition. Progress occurred when you put your hand out and money fell into it. All too often, when he'd put his hand out in the past, money had disappeared from it—plucked away, it seemed, by fate itself. He didn't put his current good fortune down to his own efforts. He'd come to believe that effort was worthless, that the world operated by no set laws, that some men could go out and cut down trees and burn them like his daddy had and see the big house rise up, while others could cut down trees and burn them and all they'd get for their efforts would be malaria and a coffin.

He knew damn well he'd end up in a coffin, too, but the

hole it would go in looked a lot farther off than it had four months ago. Then he'd been perched right on the edge, whereas now he was standing on a hillside and the hole was down in the valley. He'd finally blundered across the one thing he'd always lacked: an enemy secure and stable, one that wouldn't change from game to game. He'd set down across the table from the federal government.

His first stop this morning was Fairway, a crossroads with two stores on kitty-corners. The settlement was big enough to have a post office that operated in the spring and fall from one of the stores and in winter and summer from the other.

The folks who owned the stores hated one another's guts. The Strickland and Aycock families each operated cotton wagons that circulated through the community, picking up Negroes and poor whites and bringing them in to shop. Crossing over from one store to the other was not recommended.

Percy Stancill had decent relations with both sides, so he'd negotiated the terms of the meeting. Since this was November and the Stricklands had the post office, and the topic at hand pertained to the mail, they would host the event. But neither store would be allowed to sell anything while the meeting went on. And nobody could bring onto the premises any weapon more dangerous than a pocketknife.

They were waiting on him when he got there: Ira Strickland, Jack Aycock and three of his grown offshoots, Pick Flemming, Moody Bystrom, Fincher Smith and his oldest son, and enough white trash to fuel a fire that would burn all month. They sat on stiff-backed chairs, on wooden packing crates, on overturned cedar buckets and galvanized washtubs, and they sat, every single one of them, so that you could tell without any trouble whose side they were on.

"Here's Tandy," Jack Aycock said, rising and tucking his thumbs into the straps of his overalls.

"Who's runnin' this meetin'?" Ira Strickland said. "You or me?"

"Gone be Tandy, I reckon."

"Yeah, but who's gone introduce him?"

"Don't nobody need to introduce him. Everybody here knows who he is."

"You can't have no meetin' that way."

"How come?"

"That just ain't what a meetin' is."

"It ain't up to you to say what is or ain't a meetin'."

Strickland leapt up. "And it ain't up to you, by God, to say what's up to me."

"Gentlemen, gentlemen," Tandy said. "You know who'd just love to feast their eyes on this fracas?"

Aycock and Strickland were both breathing hard, and their supporters had begun to shift around and look at the front door, trying to gauge how long it would take them to get back to their spring buggies, where they'd no doubt secreted their squirrel guns.

"I'll tell you who'd just love this." Tandy walked to the counter and stood near the cash register, resting his elbow on the top ledge. "Mr. Theodore Roosevelt would love to see you folks fussing with each other. And old Booker T. Washington, he'd smile, too. For y'all to come to blows or take up arms— why, gentlemen, they'd be rolling in the White House aisles."

That quieted them. Both men sat down, and Tandy straightened his lapels and began his spiel. He said that he knew Percy Stancill had told Strickland and Aycock the bare facts, but he wanted to fill them in on the details. The Loring Post Office had been closed, he said, because townspeople had the audacity to think it was their right to keep a nigger woman from going through their mail. The president of the United States couldn't find anything better to do than poke his nose in and disagree. He'd written the damn woman a letter, telling her he supported Negro rights and begging her to come visit him at the White House.

"Now, if you believe Teddy Roosevelt gives half a damn about *knee-grow* rights," he said, "then I got forty acres over in the great state of Confusion that I'd love to sell you cheap. No sir, he don't care no more for their rights than me or you do. What he's got his eye on, gentlemen, is their votes. I daresay y'all have heard of Senator Mark Hanna, from up in Ohio? He's neck and neck with Roosevelt among the Republicans, and Teddy thinks some chocolate candy'll carry the day.

"Well, if you think it's all right for folks to play politics with your mail—to keep an elderly grandmother from hearing from her grandbabies, or prevent somebody that's tortured by rheumatism from getting their monthly supply of Dr. Bricker's— then you can just turn your back on Loring in her hour of need. But if you don't like it, and if you know you wouldn't want it to happen here, then we're asking you to help us out."

Strickland cleared his throat. "Naw, I don't like it," he said. "Me, I wouldn't want a nigger handling my mail. Be worse than having the Aycocks do it."

"Now, you listen here," Aycock said, "I ain't handled your mail. You don't never seem to get none when the office is at our place."

"I tell folks not to correspond with me in winter and summer. Whatever it is, it can just wait. My uncle Alton that lives over in Tutwiler? He's all the time complaining to me about a certain manly function he can't perform no more. And you don't need to know a thing about it."

"You goddamn fool—you just told me."

They were about to jump up again, so Tandy walked over and stood between them. He'd rarely felt like he could control volatile situations, but he knew he could manage this one. He had the whole world in his hands—or at least he had the Stricklands and the Aycocks.

"What we're asking y'all to do," he said, "is to chip in and help us establish an independent postal service. Folks in Loring would tell their kinfolks and friends to write to 'em at a box we'd rent from a regular post office—maybe Delain or Garrison, someplace close by—and we'd have our independent service come and pick it up and we'd take it back to Loring and distribute it. There's nothing in the world Teddy can do to prevent it. We just need some help paying for it. And the folks in Loring asked me to assure y'all that if you'll help us out, we'll never let you down if ever you're in need."

They didn't take long to respond. Aycock looked at Strickland, who looked back. "You gone say something, or you want me to?"

"Naw, you can say it. Seem to me we're like-minded."

So Aycock stood and glanced down at the floor. "Where's that spithole at?" he said.

"If you ain't been in here before, how come you to know about my spithole?"

"Jimmy D. told me about it. You remember that time him and Henry crawled up under here and let the bees loose on y'all?"

"Hell yes I remember. One of 'em flew up my pants leg and made a little honey out of one of my biscuits. That damn spithole's over yonder."

Following Strickland's finger, Aycock stepped over close to a cracker barrel and shot a stream of tobacco juice through the hole in the floor. Then he drew himself up and addressed the group. "I can't talk like Tandy can. Ask me, he's the kind of fellow ought to be in politics."

"You got that right."

"But what I'm gone say today is let's help him and let's help them."

"Yes sir."

"I'm gone give what I can. Now, I ain't as well off as the Stricklands, because I try to stay within the bounds of the law, but I ain't gone claim I'm broke, neither. And ain't none of y'all broke, so be men and admit it."

He reached into his pocket and pulled out several silver dollars and handed them to Tandy. Strickland already had his hand in his own pocket.

BY THE time the meeting concluded, Tandy had collected close to forty dollars. Standing with Strickland and Aycock on the porch while the other men climbed onto their horses or drove off in their buggies, he said, "If ya'll don't mind my asking, what caused this ill feeling between your families?"

"You want to tell him," Aycock said, "or you want me to?"

"I don't feel like talking about it. You say."

"I don't feel like talking about it, neither. And don't you be issuing me orders."

"You son of a bitch. I'm trying to act polite—and you jump on your high horse and give in to mean umbrage."

Tandy climbed into the saddle and rode off. Looking back over his shoulder, he saw Aycock running across the road toward his store.

OVER THE next four days he collected almost eight hundred dollars from folks in Loring, Sunflower, Coahoma and Bolivar counties. He gave the same basic speech each time, tailoring it to local conditions as the need arose.

A sense of purpose had arisen in him; he'd convinced himself that it really would have bothered him if a Negro woman were to handle his mail and that he truly was outraged at Theodore Roosevelt and the government of the United States. He'd begun to make wild assertions—they came to him on the spot, little gifts of inspiration. In Drew, he announced that he'd been a gambling man, something everybody there already knew, and that he'd been a drinking man, too. With tears in his eyes, he said it pained him to pass on such news about another, but he had it on sound authority that T.R. himself had been seen sot-drunk in a San Antonio brothel the night before the First Volunteer Cavalry left for Florida; granted, he hadn't been president at the time, but he had been a husband and a father. In Garrison, he told a large gathering that Booker T. Washington and Jim Hill had been spotted in Loring the previous week, leaving the home of Seaborn and Loda Jackson. They were grinning, he said, and speaking what other Negroes recognized as Nigerian.

When he saw a caramel-colored whore parading her wares on the edge of the quarters in Cleveland, he resisted the urge to ride over and inquire about prices. If he played it straight a little longer, he could have ten like her—even twenty or thirty, if he wanted them, which he hoped he wouldn't.

Lord, help me stay interested in civics, he prayed, though something told him that God wouldn't hear him.

S EABORN said, "I'm not sure I understand. Are you unhappy with the service?"

"By no means, sir," Fowler said. "The service has been, on all counts, superb. Every month I reach into my pocket, pull a dollar out and offer it to you, and you take it. You've never refused it, and you've never dropped it. And while that's all the service I've needed thus far, I feel sure that if I'd had the sad luck to die, you would have presided over my one-hundred-dollar funeral with all the dignity that any man, be he either white or colored, could ever demand."

They were standing just inside the door to Fowler's house. The house was really a single room, spotlessly clean, with only an iron bedstead, a small table and a chair in the way of furniture.

Fowler had already donned his sash and frock coat. He was Catchings Stark's butler. He also did Stark's bookkeeping, though few people knew it, nor did they know he owned a five percent interest in Heath's Livery.

"So if you're pleased with my service," Seaborn said, "why cancel your policy?"

"Well, Mr. Jackson, I'm canceling my policy because I no longer deem it advisable to continue it."

Being terminated by someone whose grammar and manners were as impeccable as his own annoyed Seaborn beyond all reason. A little bit of stuttering, some hem-hawing and a few butchered verb forms were his due. He felt a strong urge to put his hands around Fowler's throat.

Yet there was no one among his policyholders whom he respected more. Born a slave, Fowler had managed Newcomb Teague's plantation right after the war. And it had done better when he was in charge than it ever had for Teague himself.

"Your current employer," Seaborn said. "I take it he's indicated that continuing your business dealings with me might not be wise?"

"No sir," Fowler said. "He most certainly has not. Like you, Mr. Jackson, I pride myself on seeing ahead. When Mr. Stark thinks to ask me whether or not I have my burial insurance with you—which you and I both know he eventually will do— I'll be able to tell him that I discontinued it some time ago. I will express both bafflement and outrage at the scurrilous behavior of you and your wife. And it's my hope that by having done so, I'll make it much less likely that I'll actually need that burial insurance anytime soon."

"You're a forward-thinking man, Mr. Fowler."

"I'm an elderly man, Mr. Jackson. And I did not get to be an elderly man by giving in to sentiment. Personally, I admire both you and your wife. But I must say that I think your future lies elsewhere."

By EVENING, he'd lost three longtime clients, including his and Loda's bridge partners, Dr. Ormesby and his wife, Matilda, as well as Reverend Rice. Every well-educated Negro in town. The best had been the first to let him down.

Reverend Rice had leaned back in his chair, locked his hands behind his head and said, "We'll all have to try to stay alive until this passes over, Mr. Jackson, so that you can give each and every one of us the funeral we all deserve."

ON THE street, white people used to look right through her, as if she were only so much air. Seaborn had always considered this a good sign, a safe sign, air being transparent.

"When we seem solid to them," he'd always said, "then it's time to worry."

If his analyses could be trusted—and she knew that in many instances they could be—she had cause for concern.

At the corner of Second and Loring, while she waited to cross, Miss Lavinia Ashby's carriage appeared. Miss Lavinia was being driven by Scheider, the elderly Negro who lived with Blueford. Other Negroes often called Scheider "Spider Brain," believing he was touched, but Loda had always treated him with respect. As long as he wasn't drinking, he returned it.

Spotting Loda, Miss Lavinia checked to make sure she had her gloves on, then reached out and tapped Scheider on the shoulder. He drew rein. The carriage halted.

"You-all have made a wretched mistake," Miss Lavinia informed Loda. "Perfectly wretched." A fold of fat dangled off the tip of her chin; she looked like an old turkey. "You used to have the respect of all the people about town. Didn't we let you buy land on this side of the tracks? We sent our children to you to mail letters and never once worried about their welfare. And this is how you pay that confidence back."

"Miss Lavinia," Loda began, but Miss Lavinia raised her hand.

"It's too late now for sweet words and smiled lies. Everybody knows what they know. Take Scheider here."

Scheider rolled his eyes toward the sky, as if to ask the Lord to absolve him for whatever sin he was about to commit. If need be, Loda knew, he'd commit murder. Both Scheider and the Lord knew it, too.

"Do you think it's right, Scheider, for the colored to say what's what?"

Scheider looked straight ahead now, squinting as if he were trying to see all the way to Arkansas. "No ma'am. Colored folks don't know what's what—so how they gone be supposed to say it?"

"How indeed. How indeed."

Loda glanced both ways, then stepped behind the carriage and started across the street.

"I'm not through with you!" Miss Lavinia shrieked.

Loda kept walking.

"Did you ever see the likes of that?" Miss Lavinia asked Scheider.

"No ma'am, not hardly. But these young ones," Scheider said, shaking the reins, "they half-juba, Miss Lavinia. Show is. What these niggers coming to's a mystery for me to ponder."

DRY JOHNSONGRASS rustled in a cold wind that blew down off the northern prairies. Her breath smoked. Sitting on the ditch bank, hidden by the grass, she watched the clouds of smoke rise. They offered irrefutable evidence that someone—some*one*—was here. Anybody who wanted to find out more could draw near.

Nobody did. A couple wagons rumbled by, headed for town, but if the drivers saw the smoky clouds, they paid them no mind. Once she heard a horse and saw a derby bouncing along above the tall grass and thought that perhaps it was Seaborn. He traveled fast these days and never let night catch him in the open.

She'd come to let it catch her, and she'd come to catch it. She sat with her arms wrapped around her knees. The coldness from the ground stole up through her hips and into her spine. The coldness of death.

Her mother lay buried only a few miles away, not far from the house Sam Payne had lived in. Some said the yellow fever had killed him, that his death had been sudden, but she knew better. She'd seen him standing over the grave, seen him standing there at all hours of the day and night, dying all the time. She'd watched him without his knowing she could see him. And she'd watched him when he did know.

"What are you doing looking at me?" he'd said to her once.

"I don't like you looking at me when I'm trying to have a minute to myself."

"I don't care what you like," she'd told him.

"I could hurt you bad, girl. You know it."

She had stepped into the clearing—stepped right to the foot of the unmarked grave, faced him like the half fact she knew herself to be.

"You're the last person in the world who could hurt me," she said. "When I'm near you, I have no feeling. Look." She pulled a straight razor from her coat pocket, held her hand up and drew the blade across her palm. "I don't feel it," she said, and it was true. She held her hand over the grave, let the drops fall on the ground her mother lay beneath.

"You'd bleed yourself dry, wouldn't you, girl?"

She stared at him. She was, and would remain, the single dark indictment of all his earthly works.

"Ain't that a brimstone bitch?" he said. "To get rid of me, you got to get rid of yourself." He laughed. "Stupid girl. You think the blood taints you? Everybody's tainted. The most basic urge in the world is to take what ain't yours. That's what *come unto me*'s all about. Gathering in. To take. And take again."

She had waited there that evening until he shook his head and walked away. And she waited here in the twilight—the coldness creeping farther, up into her shoulder blades, into her neck and down her arms—until finally she heard the sound of wind hissing through wire-swagged spokes.

AT FIRST, as she stepped out of the grass and onto the road, she believed her vision had played a trick on her. Then, when he got closer, she could tell that it hadn't. He was riding the bicycle with his eyes shut.

His legs churned in a smooth, stroking motion; his hands gripped the handlebars loosely. He sat straight in the saddle, but not rigid: the picture of calmness and relaxation. She hated to call out to him, for when she did, she believed, he would open those eyes and all the calm would drain from his body, so ugly was the world through which he rode.

"Blueford."

To her surprise, he did not immediately open his eyes. He reversed the pedals. The coaster brake engaged, and the bike slowed. When it stopped rolling, he looked at her.

She'd never seen a ghost before.

Miss Bessie and her mother and most of the Negroes she'd known on the Deadening said they'd seen plenty of them, but ghosts had not been recognized on the campus of Cold River College, so even if somebody had encountered one, he or she would not have been quick to admit it. Seaborn scoffed at the notion of visible spirits. She had never belittled those who claimed they'd seen them, but she'd always had her doubts.

But Blueford was a ghost—if by ghost you meant the remnant of a self.

"Yes?" he said.

Even his voice sounded different. She stepped closer, then reached her hand to his cheek. It was ice-cold. "I'm sorry."

"For what?"

"For everything that's happened. And everything that hasn't."

He looked at her as if he were trying to remember when and where he'd known her. "Loda?"

"Yes."

"Where you been?"

"The same old place."

"I been someplace else," he said.

"I can see that."

"I'm gone go there again."

"We all will."

"Soon, I imagine."

"Blueford? Didn't you tell me you had an aunt who lived in Vicksburg?"

"I might of said that."

"Why don't you go stay with her?"

"Too far to pedal. Plus, it ain't worth the trouble."

"I'll give you money for a horse," she said, then closed her eyes, hating herself for having said the word.

"Me?" he said. "I ain't wanting no horse."

He reached out and laid his hand on her arm, touching her for the first time in more than twenty years. His fingertips were warm; she took solace from that fact.

"Don't you worry yourself about me none," he said. "There's nothing they can do they ain't already done."

His feet left the ground they'd come to rest on for a time, and the bicycle rolled off down the road.

SHE STOOD there in the cold wind until her hands lost all feeling and her arms and legs grew stiff. She was starting to freeze. From a sense of duty, more than anything else, she stepped back into the road and headed for home.

The wind was blowing harder now. Gusts rattled a sheet of loose siding on a shack as she passed, and a tin can bounced into the ditch. Overhead, dark shapes writhed in the tops of tall trees.

THE WASHTUB had a bad dent in it, so somebody had thrown it away. One of them had seen it, going through the garbage at the dump, then picked it up and brought it with him to the alley. They liked throwing in a little sawdust and a few sticks and pitching in a match.

Most nights, four or five of them squatted down there, rocking back and forth on their heels, passing around a jar of moonshine whiskey when they had any. It was cold now, so cold you'd freeze, even with that whiskey burning inside you. Having the fire was nice.

People knew where they were. You could see into the alley from several rooms in the Loring Hotel, and the fellow who owned the Feed and Grain couldn't step out back in the morning without seeing traces of the previous night's fire. But nobody ever discussed their presence. Even the night marshal left them alone.

They said things to one another they would never have said to anyone else, speaking in low, dull voices.

"Ain't no way to make a crop and a living, too. I might as well just tell old Percy Stancill he can go on and brand my ass. Being as he owns me and all I call mine."

"I wouldn't tell old Percy that. He liable to take a notion to do it. Used to brand his niggers."

"How come him to brand his niggers? Cow got enough sense to run off, but the nigger just stay put."

"Back when he done it, nigger had more sense."

"You seen that newest wife of old Percy's? You can look in that woman's eyes and tell she come from some mighty bad blood."

"Percy ain't got her for the eyes."

"Seem like ever time you see that woman, she's gritting her teeth."

"You'd grit yours, too, son, if he putting to you what he putting to her."

"He put worse than that to me. And it done got mighty old."

On those evenings, they nodded their heads from time to time in a show of sympathy. But they never acknowledged one another if they happened to cross paths on the streets during the day. Being in town during the daytime was never pleasant. They'd usually come in to receive another piece of bad news—from the bank, or Rosenthal, or one of the people who owned the land that most recently had broken their backs.

THOSE men were on the mind of Mr. Henry Wheeler Meadows as he sat across the desk from Leighton. Meadows had been admitted where Leighton had not; he said he'd talked to the president again the previous week, before he returned to Washington.

"He really means business," Meadows said. "If you-all had just given in and asked the woman to come back, none of this would have happened. You wouldn't be seeing your names and the reputation of your town dragged through the dirt."

Leighton had already seen his name in three Northern newspapers, including the *Washington Star*, a copy of which a friend who worked for the *Memphis Sentinel* had sent him yesterday, along with a penciled note: *Look what came on the*

*afternoon train! We'll probably do an article on the controversy
down there. Any comment? It looks like you're one of the bad guys!*

According to the *Star*, the suspension of service at the Loring Post Office had come up for debate on the floor of the
U.S. Senate. Senator Hale had accused the president of dicta-
torial tactics, and Senator Farnsworth of Wisconsin had replied
that "the honorable senator from Mississippi, along with the
despicable denizens of that little mud hole in the swamps,"
needed to remember who it was who'd lost the war.

He'd made the mistake of taking the paper home that
night in his briefcase, which Will had opened, looking for
some pencils Leighton had promised to bring him, and then
he'd pulled the paper out and left it lying on a table in the
hall.

When Leighton walked into the bedroom, Sarah was sitting up in bed, reading the article. "In this paper from Washington," she said, "they call you a defender of the status quo. I
guess you could sue them for libel."

"I could do what?"

She had color in her cheeks where lately there had been
none. "Sue them for libel. It's illegal to print lies in the paper,
isn't it? Defending the status quo would mean defending the
interests of the townspeople, which, it seems to me, you're
doing everything but."

"There are lots of people in town, not just Percy and
Catchings." The image of her walking out of the back room at
the post office surfaced again. "Not just Tandy, either. And
anyhow, sometimes folks don't realize where their real interest lies."

"I don't think you give them enough credit." She laid the
paper down. The collar of her gown, normally buttoned to
her neck, had come undone, letting him see the cleft between
her breasts. When she realized what he was looking at, she
reached up to fasten the collar.

The bitterness rose into his throat; in a moment, if he kept his mouth shut, he would choke. "You needn't worry," he said. "I'm not touching you tonight."

Her eyes flashed. "When did I ever say you couldn't touch me?" she said. "I *never* did. You do it whenever you like. And what do I get back for all that touching? People avoid me. Gracelyn Ellsbury hid from me yesterday at Tucker's Dry Goods. Behind a bolt of fabric. Like I had leprosy or something."

"You do," he said. "We've all got it."

She shook her head slowly. "You're losing your mind."

He walked into the hallway, opened the door on one of the bookcases, and pulled out Burnam and Gower's *Popular Encyclopedia.* Stepping back into the bedroom, he flipped pages until he came to the one he wanted.

"'Leprosy,'" he read. "'A chronic disease caused by the bacillus *Mycobacterium leprae,* first identified in 1874. Characterized by loss of sensation . . . deterioration . . . the eventual appearance of various deformities.'"

He shut the book. "That pretty much describes my condition. Wouldn't you say it's also a fair description of a good many folks around town?" He tossed the book onto the bed and then, without another word, he turned and left. For hours, he walked the streets, stirring up all the dogs and ruining a pair of good shoes.

Now one of the outsiders responsible for a fair amount of the trouble that had been deposited on his doorstep was sitting across the desk from him, warning him that things might get out of hand. For Leighton not to laugh in the little man's face took all the good manners he could muster.

"Your brother's running around the countryside collecting money and working folks up," Meadows said. "The administration's digging its heels in. And I'm hearing bad talk."

"What kind of bad talk?"

"From folks."

"That's almost always who does the bad talk around here. Our animals are too well behaved."

If the sarcasm offended Meadows, he didn't let on. The radiator in his room at the hotel was about to kill him, he said; the knobs on it didn't work, and it stayed so damn hot in there he had to sleep with his clothes off, even though being naked made him mighty self-conscious. He complained, but nobody cared a jot about his comfort.

"The truth is, they'd like me to move out, and God knows I'd love to be gone from this place, but my orders are to remain present to report on what's happening. The only way I can stand it at night is to open the window a little and let some air in. And when I open the window, I hear those men."

He said he didn't mean to imply that they spent all their time down there talking about Loda Jackson and the scandal. They'd only mentioned the subject a time or two. He remembered one man complaining the pitcher-pump spout he'd ordered from Sears, Roebuck hadn't come because they'd closed the post office, so he'd had to buy the damn thing from Rosenthal at double the price. And then, according to Meadows, another man said, "That nigger bitch's hide'd look good on one of them footballs."

That was all. After that remark, they'd gone on to some other topic.

"But that's actually what scares me," Meadows said. "The offhandedness of it." He adjusted his spectacles. "You weren't down there in Cuba, were you?"

"No."

"You wouldn't believe what I've seen folks do in the most matter-of-fact way." Meadows shivered. "Jesus God. I once saw a man ram a bayonet into a captured Spaniard while two other fellows held his legs apart. He twisted the blade a few times, then pulled it out with the man's entrails wrapped around it. He glanced at them and threw 'em off to the side, where they caught on a tree branch and hung there oozing blood and shit. He pulled a rag out of his pocket and began to wipe the bayonet clean. And while he was wiping it, you know what he did? He looked down at the Spaniard and told him he knew it must've hurt and he was sorry about that, but they'd done the same to one of his fellows, so he had to do it to one of theirs, and it just happened to be him. Can you believe such a thing?"

"Yes," Leighton said, "I can."

He meant to stop right there. Later on, he would wonder what madness made him continue, thereby unwrapping the bandage on a wound that had been festering for more than half his life. No explanation he came up with would ever suffice. He knew it had something to do with his and Sarah's conversation the night before, and with the story Meadows had just told him. But it had even more to do with something the man had not told him—something about Meadows himself—though Leighton would go to his grave without ever knowing what it was.

"You might not believe," he said, "what I saw some folks do just a few miles from where we're sitting."

IN THE summer of 1880, the woods were full of ticks. The horses got infested. At night, you'd hear a lot of banging in the stables; the next morning, when you went out, you'd find clumps of hair where the stock had tried scratching themselves on sharp corners. They all were losing weight. It was a sorry sight to see.

His father came in cursing one day. "Next thing you know," he said, "ever goddamn animal on the place'll be worthless. You can't even sell their hides—they're missing too much hair for the tannery."

He ordered old Bessie to tell Markham he needed to see him fast. Markham showed up a few minutes later. Leighton heard his father tell him to get a couple other Negroes and dig a pit six feet deep and fifteen feet long. "Slope one end," he said.

Leighton went along to help. His father liked to see him working, getting down in the dirt and sweating, but that wasn't why he did it. His mother had died the previous year, and ever since then, he'd had a hard time staying inside.

She was buried out behind the house. Neither Tandy nor his father ever went back there. The only people he'd ever seen near the grave were old Bessie and the girl's mother: he'd seen them both out there one day, the girl's mother hacking down weeds with a bush hook, while Bessie stood a few feet away and told her what a damn fool she was. "You think she'd keep the weeds off of you? Child, she'd mess where you lay dead."

Leighton had wanted to tell Bessie that it wasn't true, that his mother would have stood over the other woman's grave and cleared it of weeds herself. But if it had been the other woman who'd died, no weeds would have grown there. His father surely would've seen to that.

AFTER choosing a spot across the road from the house, in the corral they'd built some years earlier, Markham handed Leighton a shovel, and he began to dig. While they worked, one of the others, a boy just a couple years older than Leighton, asked Markham what the pit was for.

"Mr. Sam ain't told me that." Markham shook his head. "Tell you something, Blueford. Mr. Sam say dig a hole, what you gone do is dig a hole. Best not to worry too much about its uses."

Markham would say things like that when Leighton was around, but Leighton had noticed he never said them in front of Tandy. But then, by and large, Tandy was not around. At least not if there was work to be done.

The four of them spent all morning digging the pit. Markham hummed a strange-sounding melody, a bunch of long, drawn-out tones, and even though you could tell he was making up the tune as he went, the other two joined in. After a while, they could match him note for note; even their digging took on a certain rhythm; Markham's blade would bite the earth, and about the time he lifted it, Blueford's would strike, then the other young man's and, as the last one lifted a shovelful, Markham's would strike again. Leighton's own rhythm was erratic. He tried to fall in between the third Negro and Markham, but he'd be too quick one time, too slow the next.

At one point, through his sweat, he saw the girl standing at the edge of the road, shading her eyes and watching them dig. She had on a new dress, and you could tell, even if you knew no more about dresses than he did, that it was store-bought. Her mother's clothes were store-bought, too.

Sometimes, when he came across a group of Negro boys lying around on a riverbank in the shade of a cypress, their cane poles propped up with rocks, he could tell they'd been talking about the girl and her mother, about their clothes and the other stuff you'd sometimes see them with—the girl's nethersole bracelet, a silver pendant that dangled from her mother's neck, the books you'd see them reading if you walked by their neat little place and happened to peek through the curtains. But always, once he appeared, the conversations would stop. One of the Negroes would say, "Mr. Leighton, you wantin' to fish this hole? Us'll move on down the bank."

When she saw him looking back at her that day, the girl did not drop her head and shuffle away like any other girl on the Deadening would have. She'd never dropped her head in her whole life, and she'd never shuffled, either, and you could see she didn't mean to start now. She stood there and stared back at him until his face grew hotter than the sun could ever make it. He looked down at the shovel, stepped on it and turned up a few more clods. He knew as well as she did who'd drawn her attention. And it was not and would never be him.

Sam Payne never said whether they'd done a good job or a bad job, just gestured with his thumb at the woods along the river. "Y'all get over yonder and cut down enough of that bitter pecan to build me a good-sized squeeze chute." So they felled a couple trees and constructed the chute, bolstering the walls with willow poles they'd cut down in a slough.

The following morning, all the Negroes on the place except the girl and her mother were ordered to tote water from the river to the newly dug pit. They carried it in cedar buckets, stable pails and pump cans, in slop jars, wash boilers and stove pots. Anything that could hold liquid, they filled up. Leighton saw old Bessie filling a coal hod, but so much water sloshed over the rim that by the time she reached the pit, the container was almost empty. She must have made fifteen or twenty trips like that, her face scrunched up, feigning effort. She never did arrive at the pit with more than a few drops.

Most of them would act as if they liked doing the work his father ordered, or were at least grateful for the chance to do it, but Bessie always let his father know she hated it. Leighton had even heard her talk back to him. His father would tell her to do something, and before she went ahead and did it, she'd say, "You want it done, why don't you do it your own self?" Four times out of five, his father would just act as if he hadn't heard her. The fifth time, he'd slap her face or grab a handful of her hair and twist it.

"One day," he'd heard his father say, "I'm gone probably have to kill you."

"Go on and do it. Don't, me and you both gone have to put up with me acting upright, and you tell me what advantage that leaves either of us."

His father cast a glance or two her way that day when they were filling the pit, but he didn't let on if he noticed she was undermining her own efforts.

By ten o'clock, the water level was right at the rim. His father told a few of the younger Negroes to start unloading the wagon; he'd driven it to town the previous afternoon and brought it back loaded down with a bunch of one-gallon cans and several bundles wrapped in burlap.

The cans contained creosote, which his father told Markham to empty into the pit. Then, while Leighton and Blueford and several others went and got the horses, two old men used brooms to stir the reeking mixture.

Everybody had gathered, anticipating the show. Leighton

led his father's stallion up to the chute. The horse raised one leg and put it back down, then started backing up.

His father elbowed him aside. He stepped close to the horse, drew back one arm and brought his fist down on the stallion's hindquarters. "Get up there!" he bellowed.

Startled, the stallion tossed his head and surged into the pit. He came out the shallow end, blowing water, wild-eyed. He made two fast circuits of the corral, his head bobbing up and down, then threw himself on the ground and rolled over and over in the dirt.

A few of the Negro children began to imitate the horse. They ran around in circles, shaking their heads and making neighing sounds.

Markham said, "Bet that bath gone cure that horse's itching."

"May not cure it," another said, "but sure done got his mind on somethin' else."

They brought them up one at a time. His father never touched another one of the horses—he didn't have to. Markham took over, getting in behind them and shouting, whacking them on the rump. "Get in there," he hollered, and the horses bolted into the pit and came up dripping and shaking their heads.

"Like a baptizing," one of the Negroes said when the last horse had emerged. "Them ticks like sins. Done been washed away."

Leighton didn't know whether or not anybody else heard old Bessie. "Sin don't wash away," she said. "Two things a person can't get rid of without getting rid of hisself. One of 'em's sin. The other one's skin."

It was then that his father raised his voice: "Now you niggers pull your clothes off and jump in there."

. . .

FOR A MOMENT, nobody moved. His father stood with his hands resting on his hips, waiting for his word to be obeyed.

Markham wiped the sweat from his eyes. "Mr. Sam?" he said. "Sir, that stuff gone burn people bad."

"Not nearly as bad as it burns them ticks. Y'all carry the young'uns in there. Let it come up to their necks, but keep it out of their eyes. They ain't got sense enough to close 'em."

That more than ninety Negroes—men, women and children—began to peel off their clothes was a measure of the fear Sam Payne could still inspire. They piled the clothes beside the pit, where they would be set afire and new ones issued from the bundles that lay on the wagon.

Most of the adults jumped into the pit and crawled right out the other side. But the children began to wail the second the foul liquid touched their bodies. One little girl wiggled loose from her mother and went under, and when her mother pulled her out, she began clawing at her eyes. "Cane see!" she screamed. "Cane see cane see cane see!"

The only one who didn't strip off was old Bessie. She stood there not moving, hardly even breathing, until Sam Payne walked over, grasped the front of her brown shift and tore it in two. Then he grabbed her by the hair, dragged her over to the pit and shoved her in.

FOLKS said Dr. Sellers first appeared over close to the river. Some said the original sighting was in Beulah; others said Garner's Point. Some claimed it was farther down, closer to Estill or Glen Allan.

People said he'd fought for the Union army, that he'd marched with Grant and Sherman, but soon the story changed: that he hadn't fought at all, that he was just some dark-skinned huckster who'd run whores around New York City and had a hand in setting off the draft riots. Later on, certain people remembered having seen him, in the summer of '78, helping stir up the Exodusters, the group of Negroes who fled the state for Kansas. He drove a wagon of them up the river road, and they crossed on a ferry north of Memphis. He took them out to Kansas and just left them, folks said, and at least half of their number were killed by cattlemen and wheat farmers who didn't want them around.

Now, two years later, he was riding through the country-side promising the Negroes that in a place called Liberia they could set up their own government; they would own their own land, make their own laws, come and go whenever they wanted. Nobody would be treated like livestock.

Leighton had heard his father say he'd take care of Dr. Sellers if he dared venture onto the Deadening. He told Percy Stancill as much a week or two after the episode at the dipping pit; they were sitting their horses on opposite sides of the muddy lane that formed the boundary between their plantations.

"Tell you what," Percy said. "He comes onto your place, you call me and let me in on the sport. He comes over here, I'll call you. We'll make a big event out of it. It'll beat that last lay-by party."

"It'll be about laying by," Sam Payne had said.

That wasn't all he'd said that day. While he and Leighton rode home through the woods, he predicted that one day Leighton would find himself in these woods or others like them, fighting with cold steel. "That's one thing you can count on: sooner or later somebody'll try to take from you."

"Take what?"

His father reined up and pointed a finger at the ground. "Take this, by God. Calling it yours don't make it yours, boy. Taking's what makes it yours—and you don't just take it once. You got to take it again and again."

If there was one thing his father understood, it was how

to take. He'd taken this land away from the panthers and the bears, and he'd taken the lives of more than a few men in the war. He'd also taken the life right out of Leighton's mother. Leighton had watched her grow pale and dispirited, watched her lose her love of sunlight and silk, of books and bright colors.

As much as he missed her, he sometimes found himself wondering if the cottonmouth that killed her hadn't done her a favor.

CONTRARY to what his father would come to believe, the girl's mother wasn't the first person on the Deadening to hold counsel with the Negro who called himself Dr. Sellers. Nor was Markham. The first person to see and speak with him was Tandy. Leighton knew because he watched.

He was upstairs in his mother's room, looking through her books. She had Washington Irving's *Tales of a Traveller* and Augustus Baldwin Longstreet's *Georgia Scenes,* as well as a good bit of James Fenimore Cooper and Charles Brockden Brown. She'd read to him and Tandy at night when they were younger. He could still hear her voice, the way it would rise when she reached an important moment.

You could see a long way from her room. His father had burned a stand of trees south of the house, intending to plant there in the spring, so now the road was visible right down to the river. Glancing out the window that day, he saw Tandy standing beside the road, looking up at a Negro on horseback.

He was the best-dressed colored man Leighton had ever seen. His boots gleamed. He wore a nice-looking saddle coat, though it was still too warm for a coat, and a nice hat. He was smoking a pipe and gesturing with it while they spoke.

It looked as if they were discussing the Negro's horse.

Tandy pointed at one of the forelegs, careful not to get too close; he'd been thrown several times and was terrified of horses.

The Negro laughed. He leaned down and, before Tandy could shrink away, grabbed his hand. As if he weighed no more than a kitten, the Negro lifted him off the ground. For a second or two, Tandy's legs flailed in the air; then he quit struggling and the Negro pulled him into the saddle in front of him.

They sat like that for several moments, the Negro talking, removing the pipe from his mouth from time to time and gesturing with it. Then he turned the horse to the side and spurred it into a gallop across the clearing.

That afternoon, as Leighton went through the front gates, with a fishing pole on his shoulder, he saw Tandy coming toward him, his hands in his pockets.

Leighton said, "What were you doing with that colored man?"

"What colored man?"

"On horseback."

"I ain't seen no colored man on horseback."

"It was Dr. Sellers, wasn't it?"

"I don't know nothing about no Dr. Sellers." Without even a glance back, Tandy went on through the gates.

Some time would pass before Leighton realized that was where his brother found his inspiration: a horseman with no history, a traveler who could move about as he pleased and talk folks, especially women, into the most foolhardy things.

THE DAY his father received the information that Dr. Sellers had been talking to the Negroes on his place, he claimed not to believe it. It was Percy Stancill who told him.

"I got wind of it yesterday," Percy said. He didn't sit down, just stood there holding the whiskey glass Sam Payne had handed him. "He had quite a little crowd gathered around, from what I hear tell."

"From what you hear tell. Who told you?"

"One of my niggers. One that can be trusted. Insofar as a nigger ever can be."

"A nigger can't be."

"I reckon you ought to know."

His father walked stiff-legged over to a chair, then sat down and crossed his arms over his stomach and looked over at Percy. "What's that supposed to mean?"

Percy turned the glass up and drained it. "Sam, he held the meeting up there on that woman's porch."

"What woman?"

"You know who I mean. The only one on your place that's got a porch."

"And you saw this with your own eyes?"

"You just heard me say I didn't."

"That's why I'm having trouble believing it. If you was to say to me, 'Sam, I set right there and watched,' why, it wouldn't be nothing for me to do but pay full credence. But when you tell me a nigger says he seen it—well, now that's a different donkey."

"We got a problem here, Sam, and it's gone affect every damn one of us. That Sellers nigger got forty or fifty tenants to walk off the Sheffield place over on the Bogue just last week. And don't nobody know what become of 'em. That many niggers can't just vanish like that—but they did. So when this black bastard's over here on your place, preaching whatever message it is that gets 'em hot to trot, it ain't just your problem. It's my problem, too. So what I'm here to ask is, what you aim to do? Because if you don't aim to do nothing, then by God I'm going to."

Nobody had ever talked to his father like that before, unless you counted old Bessie.

2

"How's that wife of yours liking it out here?" his father said.

"Liking it fine."

"She come from Atlanta, is it?"

"From over to Savannah."

"Tell you what," his father said, rising, towering above Percy. "Why don't you go on home and let her cook you a good supper."

"She don't cook."

"She play the piano?"

"Passable."

"Then go on home and let her play you a nice tune. Something calmative. And I'll ride over to your place in the morning, then you and me'll talk, and if it turns out that we got a problem, we'll solve it."

Percy seemed tempted to say more, but he must have realized this was not in his best interests just then. So he set the glass down on the sideboard and left.

For a long time, Leighton stood at the top of the stairs, not daring to move. His father, who'd sat back down, was smiling. "Lord God," he said, as though to himself. "If that ain't entertaining. Just pure goddamn theatrical."

Leighton hadn't realized that his father knew where he was, but then he called, "Get down here, boy."

His legs shook as he went downstairs.

"Ride up yonder to her place," his father said, "and tell her I want to see her within the next ten minutes."

"If you want to see her in ten minutes, I better take an extra horse."

"No, that's not what I told you."

"But she can't get here in ten minutes on foot. It's—"

"Tell her I said she'd better be here in ten minutes. And after you've told her, ride off and don't look back."

. . .

HE WENT out and saddled his mare, wondering whether he was supposed to go up to the woman's door and knock on it or sit there on the horse and call her out or just wait and hope she'd come out on her own. How he handled it, he guessed, would say a lot about him.

He'd spoken to her before. Whenever he passed her on the road, he would nod and greet her. In the earliest of these encounters, probably back when he was five or six years old, she'd passed by without speaking or acknowledging his presence. But then one day she nodded, and another day she said hello, and finally she began to use his name. She never said *Mr. Leighton,* like the others did. Just *Leighton.*

He needn't have worried about calling her out. When he came around the bend, she was standing on her porch, staring up the road as if she'd known he was coming and meant to be ready.

He rode over to the steps and reined up. "My father said he wants to see you. Said to ask you to get down there in ten minutes if you could."

"Are you sure he said *ask*? Not *tell*?"

She was a tall, slim woman with high cheekbones; she probably had some Choctaw blood. Her fingernails were long—half an inch, he'd bet. She could hurt you with those nails if she wanted to.

She had a way of looking at him that made him feel confused. Sometimes he wanted to slap her face, or else he felt like putting his arms around her to hug her like he'd once hugged his mother. But most of the time, he just wished she did not exist and never had.

He started to ride off, like his father had told him to, but she was too fast for him.

She stepped down off the porch and grabbed the bridle. Her lips barely moved. "I will ask you to tell your father that I said I will get there when I get there."

The curtains were closed. But he knew the girl was in there watching. He made a tentative effort to free the horse from the woman's control, kicking with his heels. The horse stood right where it was.

"Now, what are you going to tell him?"

The words came from someplace farther down than his throat, in a part of himself he could feel but not name: "That you said you'll get there when you get there."

She stepped back a few inches, so as to study him better. "You're going to be a big man," she said. "Other than that, you don't have much in common with your father."

She let go of the bridle, then slapped the horse in the mouth. "G'on!" she yelled.

He was standing where his father had told him to when she walked through the front door—by now, he'd been standing for quite some time. His father had stayed seated downstairs in his favorite chair, drinking whiskey, holding the glass up to the light once or twice to study its color.

She didn't bother to knock. She entered the foyer, but didn't see Leighton on the landing at the top of the stairs. She'd changed clothes. Earlier she'd been wearing a plain brown dress. Now she wore a long-sleeved white blouse over a lavender-colored skirt that looked like silk. A gold shawl was thrown over her shoulders.

She walked into the living room and stopped before the chair.

His father set the glass down. "I hear tell of dusky doin's."

"Somebody probably made it up. If Negroes did half of what white people think they do, they'd be too busy to sleep.

Of course, they will go to great lengths to keep white people entertained."

"I hear tell a prophet's come among us."

He took to his feet now. Instead of moving away, she stepped closer, until they were just inches apart.

"Prophet done come to lead the chosen to the promised land," his father said. "I'm told it's somewhere way east of Tupelo and north of the South Pole. Which is to say that it exists mostly in the mind of one misguided nigger."

"Maybe not. Maybe he's planted that idea in some other minds, too."

"All God's chirren got feets made of fire?" To Leighton's amazement, his father was grinning. He looked genuinely amused.

She put her hand on his father's chest as if she meant to stroke it. The grin stayed on his father's face, but he batted her hand away.

She turned her hand over, looking at it as if it had somehow failed her. Then she made a fist and punched his father in the rib cage, but she was standing too close for the blow to have much force. His father didn't seem to have felt it. "One nigger," he said.

She hit him again.

"Two niggers."

She hit him a third time.

"Three niggers."

She drew her arm back but then held it there. Though Leighton couldn't see her face, her body had begun to quiver.

His father waited to see if she meant to hit him again. When he saw that she wouldn't, he said, "If he comes back onto the Deadening again, he'll be here to stay. Even if he don't come back, somebody's gone pay for every last poke you just took at me. I'm liable to practice my multiplication tables—whatever number strikes my fancy, times three. Could be this evening, could be next month, could be Christmas Eve. You can't never tell. Old Saint Sam may wiggle down somebody's chimbly and take hisself a special present."

His father stared at the woman a few seconds more. Then he cocked his head and hollered, "Son?"

"Yes sir?"

"Come on down here."

He took the steps one by one and walked across the foyer, then stood at the entrance to the living room.

"How would you characterize her deportment," his father said, "when you told her to get her ass down here?"

"Sir?"

"Did she show you proper respect?"

The woman stood in profile to him, looking out the window at the corral across the road.

"She said she'd come as fast as she could. Said she needed to change into cleaner clothes."

"She did?"

"Yes sir."

"And that's all?"

"Yes sir."

"You sure?"

He nodded. "Yes sir."

"Good," his father said. "Then I reckon we'll let her drag her ass on home without no punishment."

His father stepped past her into the foyer and walked down the hall. Soon, from a distant corner, his voice rang out: "Tell her when you're ready for her to go."

In that instant, Leighton knew for the first time what it meant to be a Payne. His mother had never been one, though she'd taken the name. This woman could never become one, because she could not take the name.

"Please," he said. "Go on. When you're ready."

"Sometimes . . . ," she said. She picked up his father's glass, drained it of the whiskey and left without completing her sentence or closing the door behind her.

IF YOU knew her—and he realized, looking back, that he'd known her better than he'd known himself—you might have predicted what would happen next. She didn't slip off in the middle of the night. The time when she could have left the Deadening had long since come and gone. She stayed on. Waiting.

For several weeks, there were no sightings of Dr. Sellers anywhere close by. Word reached his father that the Negro had ridden all the way down to Natchez and was canvassing plantations in Adams County. That he was down there was too bad for those folks, but as his father told Percy Stancill, better there than here. Eventually, if he found followers, those planters would have to deal with him. Leaving pride aside, his father said, it was a matter of economic necessity.

Percy Stancill said he wondered if it wouldn't be wise to place advertisements in countries like Italy or Ireland. People were poor over there, he said. You might bring a few of those folks over and work them instead. Maybe they wouldn't have the tribal mentality.

No, his father said, they might not have the tribal mentality, but it wouldn't be any time before they started wanting to be treated like white men, and what would be the advantage then? There were not enough riches in this world to go around, and if you meant to have anything, you had to work folks right into the ground. That had always been the truth, it always would be, and anybody who claimed otherwise was a goddamn dreamer.

"Me," his father said, "I do my best dreaming when I'm sleeping. When I'm wakeful, I'm watchful. May I never be nothing less."

His FATHER was nothing less than vigilant the day Dr. Sellers reappeared.

Given his reported intention of leading an exodus to Africa, Dr. Sellers was traveling in an altogether puzzling northwesterly direction. Puzzling, that was, unless you figured he'd promised someone that he'd return—so that even after he'd collected his followers near Midnight and Silver City, Hard Cash and Tilton, he still had to cross the Sunflower one last time.

Leighton was upstairs, doing sums, when he heard a group of men ride into the yard. His father, whom he hadn't seen since morning, was at the head of the party, followed by Percy Stancill, Ferriday Stark, Newcomb Teague, George Baskett and several of their overseers.

His father jumped down off the horse. A moment later, Leighton heard heavy footsteps on the porch before the front door crashed open.

"Leighton. Come on down here, goddamn it, right now. That nigger's on the place."

He wore a revolver Leighton had seen only once or twice before; it had a longer handle than most, and the trigger was oddly shaped. Though he couldn't say where his father kept it, he knew he'd used it during the war.

"Get your rifle."

When he failed to move, his father shoved him. Leighton almost lost his balance.

"Make haste, by God."

He ran down the hall to the gun room. His father had told him to go nowhere without the key, so day and night he wore it on a piece of twine tied around his wrist. He pulled the twine loose, dropped the key, then bent to pick it up. His hands shook. He wouldn't have been able to hit a thing with any gun right now, and that gave him comfort. He went in and pulled the rifle off the rack.

In the stable, he saddled his mare, then jumped on and rode her into the yard. The men's horses were nickering and shifting around in excitement.

"Percy," his father said, "you and George and Ferriday take your men and swing around by the river and then come up from the east. Me and Newcomb and our folks'll cross the creek and cut through the old Zollicoffer place. We ought to catch 'em over there."

Several coils of rope dangled from his pommel. He pulled one loose and handed it to Leighton.

THE PLANTERS and their overseers trotted through the fields as if they were all headed for a party, one of those three- or four-day affairs where everybody ate and drank and fell asleep and woke up sick and then ate and drank some more. Leighton followed at a distance.

He couldn't see a Negro anywhere. Children who normally would've been running through the middles or playing in their dusty yards were inside now, or else they were gone. Not a soul was in the fields. He saw several sacks and baskets lying half-full where folks had dropped them before taking off.

The party arrived at the woman's house, and she stood there on the porch, watching. Wearing old clothes now, she looked like any ordinary Negro.

His father raised his hand, and the men halted.

"Where are they?"

"Gone."

"Where to?"

"I don't know."

"How come you didn't go on with 'em?"

She just looked back at him.

"Treated you like Moses, did they? Let you take 'em so far. And not no farther."

"It was God who decided Moses had to stay. There's no god around this place."

The others—Newcomb Teague and the rest—all dropped their heads, studying the ground as if looking for spoor.

"Sinned and fell short," his father said.

"Fell short," she said. "That's for sure."

"Where's the girl?"

Her eyes scanned the wall of woods that had once marked the property line between Zollicoffer's place and Payne's Deadening. "I don't know."

"Before the sun sets today," his father said, "you'll be glad you fell short. You better hope the girl did, too."

He kicked his horse and led the riders away.

LOOKED at from a certain vantage, they had the law behind them. State and county statutes established that it was illegal for anybody who worked land on your place to move away until certified debt-free. And like most planters, Leighton's father made sure everybody owed him.

"Kept 'em alive during the cholera," he said as they entered the dense undergrowth at the edge of the old Zollicoffer place. "Come to me saying, 'Mr. Sam, my baby be just about to pass.' And me, I hitch the buggy up and haul 'em in to see Doc Lewis. Like the world's gone end tomorrow if another little nigger rows over Jordan."

Newcomb Teague said, "It's the Lord's curse on us."

"What is?"

"The nigger."

"You think the Lord cursed us? That's foolishness, man. We cursed ourselves. We brought 'em here, made 'em multiply and knew it all the while we was doing it. With everybody always tryin' to shove the blame off on acts of angels or folks from Vermont—well, it turns my stomach sour. We come in here and killed the trees and all them snakes, and we made the niggers sweat blood. So now they gone have to sweat a little more. Goddamn it, Newcomb, don't start actin' like some kind of Russian mystic. You want cotton, put seed in the ground. See a weed, you cut it down."

At that moment, with his father's words still hanging in the air, the bushes ahead of them began to rustle and an old Negro man stumbled onto the path.

He had thick side-whiskers. On his neck was a goiter the size of a grapefruit. "I tried to tell 'em," he said. "Yes sir I did, but them niggers, they flat wouldn't listen. I talked at 'em all the way from Mr. Ferriday Stark's. But Dr. Sellers got 'em bumfuzzled. Ain't nobody can outconvince that one, sir."

"They up yonder, I reckon?" his father said.

"Yes sir. I think a lot of 'em realize they done made a mistake."

"Them suffering that realization wouldn't coincide with the arrival of a group of gentlemen led by Mr. Percy Stancill, would it?"

"No sir. Mr. Stancill ain't arrive yet. But there's them sayin' he's comin'."

"Sound to me like they got Percy confused with Jesus," his father said. "And if that ain't a case of mistaken identity, I ain't never heard one." He turned the horse sideways, whipped his rifle from its scabbard and struck the Negro across the bridge of his nose. The old man fell backwards into a patch of wild berries.

His father sat on the horse, looking down at him. "That Dr.

Sellers done captured my imagination," he said. "He a medical doctor or the educational kind?"

Nobody answered. He shook the reins, and they went on.

MANY OF the Negroes had already slipped away. Some had stolen off across the fields, crawling through the middles so the cotton stalks would hide them from the eyes they knew were watching. Others had hidden in the house and outbuildings on the Zollicoffer place. But the ones who kept the faith that day clung to it even after they heard the horses moving toward them. They walked along behind the man on the sorrel gelding.

The man was telling a story in a loud, clear voice.

"The letter C," he said, "and the letter X. They're two steps closer to one another than B and Y. Four steps closer than A and Z. Now whereas A and Z only glimpsed one another once in their whole lives and thus were completely unfamiliar, C and X see one another from time to time down at the stream. This stream itself is an unusual waterway. The current on one side is ice-cold, in the middle it's lukewarm, over on the far side it's boiling. Now they shout at one another sometimes across that creek, but the creekbed's full of rocks, and the water's always rushing over and around those rocks and making a mighty noise, so they can't hear. Each is begging the other to come on over. They both are lonely and have no neighbors. And each of them even wonders if that's not what the other one's saying. But since X knows the water on his side's freezing, and C knows the water on his side's scalding, neither one's willing to get in that creek.

"One night, C is feeling forlorn, and he takes a pistol, puts it to his head and squeezes off a shot. Meanwhile, X climbs onto a chair, ties a rope to a ceiling beam, loops the rope around his neck and kicks that chair over.

"Brothers and sisters: what brought *C* and *X* to their sad, untimely ends?

"Was it the water that divided them? Was it the noise of the rushing water? Was it the presence of those rocks in the stream—which, after all, had rendered their voices unintelligible when they cried out? Was it simply the temperature?

"No, brothers and sisters, they met those unhappy ends because neither one of them was resourceful enough to survive. Cypress trees overhung the banks of that stream. Had they climbed onto tree limbs and swung down into the middle of that stream, where the temperature was pleasant, they might have comfortably conversed. Motion was the cure for their misery, but they stood around and stood around until there was nothing for either of them to do but take his own life."

His father rode into the crowd, which parted just enough to let him pass. Old Bessie had remained with the group, as had Markham, as had the girl and the young Negro named Blueford.

"What the good doctor ain't telling y'all," his father said, "is that it was goddamn deep out in the middle of that stream, and neither of them poor bastards could swim. *C* wasn't meant to be *X,* and *X* wasn't meant to be *C.* Y'all wasn't meant to be me. And right now, I'm sure thankful I ain't you."

Dr. Sellers never looked back. "Brothers and sisters, keep moving. That's not Satan on that horse. It's just a white man. Or to put it another way: he's *M,* we're *N.*"

Through the undergrowth, you could see Percy Stancill and the men who rode with him. They spread out in a line, their horses picking their way through the bushes and vines. Tandy rode behind Stancill, his arms encircling the man's waist. Later on, Percy would tell Sam Payne that he'd discovered his son hiding behind a tree at the edge of the woods. Tandy claimed he was spying on the Negroes.

Dr. Sellers rode right on, toward the row of approaching white men. "Keep moving," he said. "They have this dream in which a large number of Negroes move in unison right toward them. They'll step aside, brothers and sisters. They've never had the dream without doing it."

His father pulled the revolver out and aimed it at Dr. Sellers' back. "I'm about to put a buttonhole on the wrong side of your jacket."

Jesus, no, Leighton prayed. *Jesus, please.*

"Would they shoot their horses while they were gathered in a herd?" Dr. Sellers said. "No, they would not."

"A horse costs more than a nigger," his father said. "A nigger's horse is worth ten dollars a month. Nigger hisself ain't worth but five."

Percy Stancill and his men were getting closer. Tandy let go of Percy's back, clamped his hands over his ears and shut his eyes. Leighton wanted to shut his own, but some force he couldn't master kept them open.

Dr. Sellers said, "We already know Mr. Payne's opinion concerning the relative merits of Negroes and horses. He's just a white man, brothers and sisters. And right now, he's frightened."

Negroes and horses.

After holstering the revolver, his father lifted one of the coiled ropes, did something to it and drew back his arm.

For a moment, during which the gelding continued to move beneath him, Dr. Sellers seemed not to realize that he soon would no longer control the mount. He even prepared himself to say something else, probably beginning with the phrase *Brothers and sisters.* Then the rope snapped taut, and he toppled backwards off his horse.

The fall stunned him. He lay on his back, his eyes open wide, all the air gone from his lungs.

"Y'all go to him," old Bessie said, but nobody did.

As if self-help were a doctrine his bones had somehow

absorbed, Dr. Sellers rolled onto his side and struggled to rise. Sam Payne jerked the rope.

This time, Dr. Sellers fell forward. Lifting his face from the mud, he began to speak. "Everybody keep walking. Liberia can be a state of mind. I'm there now. Been there for some time. But you have to keep moving or you won't ever find it."

"Just like I said," Sam Payne said. "It's all in your mind."

Two Negro men in their late teens moved off through the trees, heading back the way they'd come. They slipped right by Leighton, so close he could have touched them. One of them had a pink sore on his lip.

Dr. Sellers tried to rise again, but the rope pulled him down.

"I don't know what brand of doctor you are," Sam Payne said. "But seems to me like when you was talking about white folks' dreams, you got kind of dreamy your own self. Wasn't too much science in what you was saying, nor much common sense, neither. Because the fact of the matter is, every damn one of these gentlemen here's ready to shoot his own momma if need be to keep y'all picking that cotton. And if they'll shoot their mommas, just imagine what they're willing to do to you and yours."

He handed his end of the rope to Newcomb Teague and dismounted.

One by one, the Negroes were stealing away, slipping off through the woods while old Bessie and Markham and Blueford and the girl and three or four others just stood there.

Sam Payne pulled loose another coil.

"Take off now," old Bessie said to the ones who'd remained, but none of them moved. "Take off now," she said again.

"Keep moving," Dr. Sellers said.

Glancing at Markham, Leighton's father began to fashion the rope into a lariat.

"Go on now," old Bessie said. "Run, y'alls."

Blueford grabbed Markham's arm and tugged at it, but the man stood firm. Blueford looked at the girl, but she didn't move, either, so finally he turned and ran off through the woods.

Taking a step toward Markham, Sam Payne raised his arm. Old Bessie shrieked, "Run!"

At the last moment, Markham decided to. The rope whipped out, missing him by a good three feet. He jumped over a downed cypress, ducked a low-slung branch. Then there was a loud crack, and Markham sprawled facedown in the mud.

Sam Payne lowered the pistol and looked over at old Bessie. "He had the makings of a good nigger," he said, "and might have been one if you wasn't his momma."

Leighton would never figure out why his father had bothered to speak to her. Anybody with eyes could see she was dead, too, that she was nothing more than a corpse which somehow had remained upright.

ZOLLICOFFER had built his house six feet off the ground to protect against high water. The overseers now piled brush up under the floorboards, then lit it with a torch. Within moments, the old house was ablaze.

Black faces appeared at the upper-story windows. A woman held a baby up and started to scream. Leighton's father shot the baby in the chest. An old man crawled through a dormer window, his hands in the air. He squatted on the sloping roof, waiting for the men to tell him what to do, but they just sat there on their horses, watching. The old man duckwalked to the edge, but before he could stand and step off into the air, Percy Stancill shot him.

Several others jumped, then tried to run or crawl into the bushes, but the overseers rode them down. The woman whose baby was shot finally leapt out, her skirt on fire. When she got up off the ground, a white bone shard stuck out of her leg. She hobbled across the yard toward Sam Payne, her upper lip curling, exposing her teeth. She was growling.

Leighton's father turned to Newcomb Teague. "Ain't she one of yours?"

"Yeah," Teague said, sounding apologetic. He pulled his gun out and shot her.

They'd never know how many had died in the blaze, but in the yard they counted thirteen bodies. It was what they called a paradox, his father said: you had to subtract a few to keep all the rest; and the rest, he added, would be back in the fields come morning.

He stood over the body of the old man who'd squatted on the roof. "Add them two back there in the clearing to these," he said, "and you got fifteen. And fifteen ain't a thing in the world but three niggers times five."

THEM TWO back there in the clearing.

When Newcomb Teague had tried to drag Dr. Sellers, he'd struggled to his feet and charged into Teague's horse and knocked him off. He might've kept on going had Percy Stancill not raised his rifle and shot him in the leg.

As it was, he spat in their faces: his father's first and then Percy Stancill's. Percy spat back, but his father just stood there as the spit dripped from his chin.

By then, they had Dr. Sellers roped to the trunk of a hickory. Tied up like that, he'd ceased to look very imposing. His leg must have pained him greatly, and he'd lost a lot of blood. Sweat had broken out on his forehead.

"What's your real name?" Sam Payne said.

"Immanuel Kant."

"Funny name for a nigger."

Dr. Sellers glanced over at old Bessie, who lay in a lump on the ground. She and the girl were the only ones left. She'd tried a run at Sam Payne, as Dr. Sellers had at Teague, but he'd backhanded her three straight times, knocking her off her feet, and she'd finally stayed down.

The girl stood still. Watching.

"The day will come," Dr. Sellers said.

"By the time it does," Sam Payne said, "you'll be long gone. And I will, too. Them that's left'll have to try to figure out what happened. But for now, it's either y'all or us. Between the hills and the river, there ain't space enough for both to prosper."

For the first time since he'd spotted Dr. Sellers and his followers, Sam Payne took note of his sons. Tandy had jumped off Percy's horse and was cowering behind the log Markham had leapt. Leighton was still sitting his horse. Right where he'd been the whole time.

"Son," his father told him, "get down."

His feet felt glued to the stirrups, they were so hard to move. Their contact with the ground came as a shock.

His father reached into his pocket and pulled out an object, from which a shaft of sunlight glinted. He tossed it to Leighton, who looked down and found a bone-handled straight razor in his hand.

"You know what I aim to do with that?" his father said.

The razor felt light, almost weightless. He couldn't peel his gaze away from it.

"I asked you if you know what I aim to do with it."

He never heard himself speak, never heard the word *Yes* come out of his mouth. But it must have.

Because his father said, "Then bring it over here and let me do it." And then again: "I said bring it."

Four steps. The difference in the distance between *A* and *Z* and *C* and *X,* one foot moving, the other following.

A single hand rising. The flesh of his father. His flesh.

"So long," Sam Payne said, "Dr. Immanuel Sellers Kant."

SITTING there across the desk from the mayor, Henry Mead-ows marveled at the man's stiffness as he told this horrific story without betraying whatever feelings he'd had, if indeed he'd had any. If such blankness in the face of insanity was a requirement of manhood, Henry Wheeler Meadows would never qualify. Nor did he want to.

"You handed him back the razor, knowing what he meant to do with it?"

The mayor looked down at his own hands, which lay locked together atop his desk. They looked like the hands of a man deep in prayer. Meadows noticed the ink stains on them.

"I expect I did," the mayor said.

"You expect so, do you?"

"There are days I don't believe it ever happened. Other days, I know it did."

"But why?"

The mayor continued to study his hands. "So why are those men squatting out there in the alley, ready to maim and dismember? That's what brought you to my office, isn't it? You were worried those men might take vengeance on the colored community. Believe me, they'll do it with grim plea-sure, should the opportunity arise."

"But those men aren't like you. They're the scum of cre-ation. You're a man who reads books. You said you read them even as a child. Your shelves over there—they're full of them!" Meadows got up and walked over to the burnished bookcase. With his finger, he thumped spines. "Dickens. Tolstoy. Tur-genev. *Leaves of Grass*." He regarded the mayor through a film of tears. "*Leaves of Grass*! My God, sir. My holy God."

The mayor's head was bowed. "Like the woman said, God wasn't out there on the Deadening."

"So because He wasn't, you just go on and live as if none of it ever occurred?"

The mayor rose. The room suddenly was very crowded.

Meadows watched while the other man walked over to the woodstove, picked up the coffeepot and sloshed it to see if it was empty. He poured himself a cup, then recollected his good manners. He held the cup out, offering it to Meadows, who could only shake his head.

"I wouldn't call what we do around here living," the mayor said.

WHITEHILL

I N LATER years, whenever anybody asked why he'd decided to enter politics, Tandy would offer various explanations for his transformation from gambler to public servant, none of them true. People started asking during the war years, when he was locked in a tight race for his congressional seat—a seat he would eventually lose, to an opponent who'd branded him an opportunist and an isolationist—and the truth would not have squared with the tenor of those times. Nor with any other, either.

The decision, at least in his own mind, was made the same morning he hired a teamster to carry the mail from Garrison to Loring, a distance of fourteen miles. Because that was when he'd first understood two general truths which previously had lain just beyond his ken.

First, that folks could easily be manipulated with the right set of symbols. The sight of an ace—nothing, really, but a red or black pip against a white background—had for many years produced in him a feeling of sheer possibility. Yet nothing in the shape itself, nor in those colors, had the slightest bit of meaning. He'd been trained to respond to the image in a particular way; he moved in circles where other men, too, were trained to respond in this very manner. And if ever he'd turned up his hand to behold an ace, queen, jack and ten of the same suit, he could only have felt one way: euphoric.

Second, that good luck was readily available, far more so

than most folks believed. The problem was that when good luck lurched into your life, you still had to recognize it for what it was and bet accordingly, or good luck would have to wait till a better day. And for most folks, a better day would never come.

His day came on a rainy morning in early December of the year 1902. It came in the form of an old man who wore a patch over one eye, had a wild shock of white hair and a long white beard and smelled of bodily processes too seldom arrested. When he got up off a chair, your first impulse was to throw down a match and be done with it.

Rosa hadn't wanted to let him in the house, but he said he'd heard Tandy needed a means of conveyance and a driver to do the conveying, and he didn't aim to leave until he'd seen him. He sat on an overturned milk crate at the foot of the stairs, too close to the woodstove for Tandy's olfactory comfort.

"Me," the old man said, "I ain't scared of Yankees. They's just regular people with irregular ways. I got a oozing in my old stomach from where one of their minié balls hit me. Come from the same direction as the one killed Albert Sidney Johnston, and not no more than five or ten seconds later."

"You were up there?" Tandy said. "At Shiloh?"

"I was the first one reached the general. He looks at me and he's gritting his teeth, but he says to me, says, 'Soldier, you're in far worse shape than I am,' but you could tell that was flawed thinking on his part. We'd a won that battle for sure if we hadn't of lost him. We's madder than they was right then, though later on they got madder."

"Why do you want this job?"

The old man wheezed, then broke into a fit of laughter. "To get some of that money you been collecting. See, son, I'm gone be dead soon, I can feel it way down in my bowels, and before old death takes me I want a few more good rolls in the hay. I have my principles. I wouldn't ask nobody to do it with somebody as broke-down and dragged-out as I am unless I could pay 'em good wages. Right's right, fair's fair."

He told Tandy he owned a good strong pair of steel grays and a grocery wagon he'd be happy to show if he cared to see them. Tandy had intended only to get rid of him; but instead of an old man, he was starting to see an ace, so he followed him outside.

The horses were more dirty white than gray, almost the color of the old man's beard. The wagon, which had canvas top and sides, was also white, with the legend WHITEHILL'S DELIVERY on the side plank.

A Confederate veteran who'd offered succor to the dying General Albert Sidney Johnston, a man who himself had suffered and bled. White hair, white beard, white horses, white wagon. Hezekiah Whitehill, at your service. This was the closest thing to a royal flush he'd ever been dealt.

"Mr. Whitehill?" Tandy said. "How do you feel about niggers?"

"Niggers?" the old man said. "Left to myself, son, I don't have no problem with 'em, but whoever aspired to be left to hisself? Man's a sociable animal, but so's them two horses. Difference is, a horse can't hate. But I shorely can—if you pay me to."

"Can you take a bath?"

"If they's a good reason. Hell, I could soak ten time a day."

"At the outset," Tandy said, "that might be what it takes."

AT THE outset, there wasn't much mail, because it was still being sent to people at their regular addresses and being held by the railroad in Greenville. But by the middle of the month, just in time for the Christmas excitement, folks had gotten word to their friends and relatives. Parcels and envelopes and cards were pouring into the post office box Tandy had rented in Garrison.

Whitehill made his pickups there on Monday, Wednesday and Friday, and he carried mail back on Tuesday, Thursday and Saturday. Tandy handled the distribution in Loring. He held court, as it were, in the lobby of the Loring Hotel, passing out mail and receiving it from ten in the morning until four in the afternoon. Garton Shanks, the proprietor, supplied him with coffee and fried cakes and, along toward late afternoon, bonded whiskey and spiced rum.

Whitehill—freshly washed and groomed, in a new wool suit and ulster of Confederate gray, with a .44-caliber Colt strapped to his leg to forestall any dark intentions—often sat beside him, regaling the townspeople with stories of battles lost and won, of retreats under cannonade and forced marches at dawn. The truth was that after being wounded at Shiloh, he'd spent the rest of the war doing what he was doing now—driving a delivery wagon—but he had long since tired of mere facts. Tandy heard him place himself at both Vicksburg and Gettysburg on the same day in 1863. At Peachtree Creek, he told Catchings Stark, he'd drawn a bead on William T. Sherman, but for once, his aim was high—he'd shot the devil's hat right off his head. He was the only man, as far as he knew, who'd ridden with both Forrest and Stuart.

As Christmas grew closer, Whitehill rose in rank, until he finally topped out on the twenty-third of December at captain, serving on the staff of General John C. Pemberton during the withdrawal from the trenches at Petersburg. Pemberton had not been at Petersburg, nor by that time was he any longer a general, but when Tandy pointed this out, Whitehill acted aggrieved.

"That don't mean nothin'," he said. "Old John C. would of been there if he could. Besides, you asked for a memorable impression."

"Yeah, but don't overdo it," Tandy told him. "Being a captain's fine, as long as you remember you're still just my lieutenant."

He needn't have worried. He and Whitehill sold well. And what pictures they posed for. In Chicago, on the front sheet of the *Tribune,* they appeared together. In a drizzling rain, Whitehill sits with the reins in his hands, water dripping off the brim of his hat, while Tandy stands beside the grocery wagon, a cigar clamped between his teeth and a mail sack clutched in his arms. The caption says *Loring Whites Defy T.R.*

Tandy posted the photos all over town. His brother followed after, pulling them down.

A COCKROACH, *according to the dictionary that somebody left open here on the desk, is a member of an order of nocturnal insects called blattaria, many of which happen to be considered domestic pests. that kind of sets me apart from all of y'all who happen to be reading these words.*

i eat scraps, all manner of low leavings, stuff that has names you can't print in a paper like this one. i dine on refuse, would be a fancy way to put it. i make my repast out of that which was fresh in times past, would be another.

terry says there's a major difference between him and you. i crawl around at night with a low-slung belly, looking for stuff that stinks. i'm not capable of appreciating the finer things in life.

with christmas coming on, i hope all of y'all will stop and ask yourselves what the finer things are.

is it finer to have everything your own way, even if it means taking from others them things they hold most dear.

is it finer to move forward or is it better to slide backwards, into times that nobody wants to talk about, when things were done that nobody wants to acknowledge.

is it better to live with them that are different, or is it better to tread upon their backs and smash them, as if they were nocturnal pests of the order blattaria.

folks, terry says terry's a cockroach, and as such is no doubt deserving of your boot upon his back. grind him to paste in the mud of your fair streets.

but when people commit no sin save that of walking erect, for GOD'S SAKE let them walk in peace.

S TRANGE that it came down to Miss Bessie, who'd done her best to get herself killed so many times in the past. But it did. It came down to Miss Bessie and Blueford.

Or, as Seaborn put it, to old times on the Deadening.

He said that on Christmas Eve, while he stood before a fireplace in which no fire burned. The man they bought their wood from claimed he'd run out. The coal company said they were way behind schedule.

They were bundled up, both of them, Seaborn bedecked in a fur overcoat, with heavy pants and vest underneath. He'd slept in the overcoat last night. She'd slept in hers, too.

"North Carolina," Seaborn said. "Somewhere up around Raleigh. In the Piedmont. That would be a fine place to settle. Dean Williams, if you recall, went there when he quit Cold River. There's a fine Negro college in that town. A burgeoning Negro business community. We would fit right in."

"Like we fit in here?"

"What's happened here," Seaborn said, his breath smoking in the cold air, "is an unfortunate convergence of several negative traits peculiar to this place." He raised his hand, meaning to enumerate said traits on his fingers, then realized he was wearing mittens. He put his hand back in his pocket. "First of all, there's no real white aristocracy. They like to *think* they're aristocrats, but they're nothing of the kind. They're blunt people, poorly bred. Many of their ancestors came from Georgia. You have a different kind of white person up there in the Piedmont. Second, the land itself around here—it's harsh. All these swampy lowlands crawling with cottonmouths. The *landscape* brings out the harshness of the people who inhabit it. Third, the Negro population. There are too many freedmen and sons and daughters of freedmen. You need more of a mix. There were many more free Negroes in North Carolina. Therefore, self-sufficiency among the members of our race is much higher there. There's less work to be done, but oddly enough, more can be accomplished. I've been in contact with Dean Williams, and he assures me that this is the case."

"How did you get in contact with Dean Williams?"

"Rode over to Greenville and mailed him a letter. He mailed me one back. You and I could leave the day after tomorrow. We can stay with him for a while and settle our affairs here later."

He pulled off his mittens and laid them on the mantel, then reached into his pocket and withdrew an envelope. He removed the letter and was unfolding it when Loda said, "Don't bother."

"Don't bother? Whatever do you mean?"

"We're not leaving. At least I'm not."

She told him she'd been paying the girl to take care of Miss Bessie, that she visited her almost daily, did her washing sometimes and her cleaning, too. When her mother died, she said, Miss Bessie had gone to Sam Payne and reminded him that he'd made her a promise. "Go back on it," Miss Bessie had said, "and she gone haunt you from Hell if she have to." He lived up to that promise, but for her trouble, Miss Bessie received a broken jaw.

Seaborn listened, the letter grasped in one hand. When she finished, he said, "Old times on the Deadening. Good Lord, can we never escape them?"

"Maybe you can. I can't."

He sighed. "What was the promise?"

"That he'd make sure I received an education."

"So that's where the money came from."

"I thought you knew."

"How would I know," he said, "when I was never told?"

The question confirmed what she'd believed for a long time: that he and others like him had turned anti-intuitiveness into the Negro state religion. Because either the evidence their eyes and hearts provided was dead wrong or there was no reason to believe in better times to come. So they kept their eyes closed. And if they could, they made their hearts cold.

"What else don't you know?" she said.

He remained there before the empty fireplace, looking with a bemused expression at the Christmas tree in the corner. He had purchased the tree from Rosenthal, bringing it home rolled up in a tarpaulin. They had not decorated it, for this entailed lighting candles or placing bright-colored baubles on it, and that, seen from the street, might be judged show-offy.

"What else don't you know?" she said again. "Let's say it all right now, Seaborn."

"There is nothing left to say," he said. He slipped the letter into the envelope and put it back in his pocket.

G IFTS.
He'd always liked to give them, even though he rarely managed to buy either Sarah or Will what they expected or desired. To ask what they wanted would never have occurred to him, a fact Sarah pointed out to him many years later, the day he left the house for good. That day, when it came, would be the last of many days on which each assessed the wreckage the other had wrought on their marriage.

The gifts they gave and accepted on Christmas morning in 1902 came to acquire special significance for her, as they did for him. Neither of them ever forgot what was underneath the tree that morning, and while they'd never know whether or not Will remembered—given their rare mutual agreement not to recall that particular holiday in his presence—Leighton always supposed those gifts remained every bit as vivid in his son's mind, and that the texture of that time had thus become thicker for all three of them.

The saddle he bought Will had cost thirty-five dollars. It had a bound cantle, wool-lined skirts, cinches made of Angora hair, with leather chafes and straps and B. C. Baxter's malleable iron stirrups. Will got excited about the saddle long enough to take it down to Uncle Billy's and put it on Leighton's mare and go for a trot, so his friends could see it and admire him. But before long, Leighton would spot his son riding through town in a doorless, roofless aluminum Buick, the first car to defile the streets of Loring, Mississippi, and from that moment forward, Will would rarely be seen on horseback again.

For Sarah, he ordered the Empire Grand Peerless Graphaphone. With its forty-two-inch horn, it was said to be the loudest talking machine yet produced; it came with twelve cylinder recordings of arias and would have probably sounded just fine in an opera house. She listened to these recordings thousands of times. As the years passed, and she began to care less and less about sleep, and still less about propriety, she would listen to them in the middle of the night.

For him, she bought a stereoptican—apparently on the theory that as both mayor and newspaper editor, it was his responsibility to educate the public. The instrument was accompanied by a large white screen and several complete sets of slides with bound notes. He could have conducted lectures on "The Boer-English War," "The Life of Christ on Earth," "A Typical Day at the Chicago Stockyards," "The Pan-American Exposition" or "The Assassination of President McKinley." And for a moment that morning—as he sat beside the tree, running his finger over his name where it was engraved on the polished wood case—he considered the possibility of doing just that: scheduling a town meeting, erecting the screen at the front of the room and beginning his lecture. "This is Jesus," he would say, "or a graven image thereof."

But this was a lecture he would never give. The stereoptican and the assembled views and notes would remain in their carrying cases, stashed away for some years in an upstairs closet, then moved to the storage shed out back. They would finally disappear during the '27 flood, washed away by water or removed by a looter—he would never know which. Nor would he care.

Indeed, he would never call another town meeting, though he did not know it that morning. The next meeting, when it occurred, was not called at all. It simply happened, as if decreed by an authority superior to the municipality, and it would become the subject of a few lectures itself, before it faded from public memory, consigned to the dark corners where personal grievances are nursed.

THEY REMAIN there in his musings for more than half a century. Sarah sitting by the window in her dressing gown, her long, slim fingers resting on her knees. Will straddling the saddle, his legs splayed out on the floor. The tall cedar tree smelling of hot candle wax. Through the window, he sees the gray morning. Rain, he knows, is on the way. What he cannot tell is that the rain—after it finally begins to fall, around one in the afternoon—will quickly turn to sleet and that by evening a film of ice will cover every tree limb, sidewalk and street. Pipes will freeze and burst, power lines and telegraph lines will fall; a mongrel will be found downtown, in front of Tucker's Dry Goods, frozen into a fury ball.

But all that happened later and remained interesting and exotic for no more than a day, because on the evening of the twenty-sixth, a hominy snow started to fall, and the next morning they woke to a world turned white and downy. Children who never before had seen snow were in it up to their elbows, making snowballs and pummeling one another, and Rosenthal did a brisk business selling galvanized frame doormats for use as sleds.

Right now, though, it's Christmas. Will rises, grabs the heavy saddle by the horn, drags it toward the door. "Can we take it down to Uncle Billy's," he says, "and put it on Gracie?"

Leighton sees himself stand. "Yes indeed," the man he used to be replies. "Just let me get my coat."

IN THE lobby of the Loring Hotel, Tandy reclined, his boots up close to the fire. They were dry now, all the snow having melted off them and run onto the hearth.

Garton Shanks handed him another cup of coffee. "No mail yet?"

Tandy took out his pocket watch and looked at it: half past one, and still no sign of Whitehill. "Not yet." He stretched. He was feeling good. A group of planters had taken up a collection for a hefty Christmas bonus. "A gift of gratitude," Catchings said, "small thanks for all you've done."

"The snow must've slowed old Whitehill down," he told Garton. "Everything's in chaos right now, folks slipping and sliding like a bunch of drunken baboons. I was out walking through town yesterday, right after the snow quit falling, and I saw Miss Lavinia riding by in her carriage with that crazy Scheider driving. Something in the window at Rosenthal's caught her attention. She tells the old nigger to stop, and when he tries to, both horses fall down and roll over in the shafts, and Miss Lavinia and that nigger just went flying. Miss Lavinia come up out of a snowdrift looking like somebody had pitched her into a binful of flour. Nigger tries to dust her off, but she pulls off that mourning hat she's always wearing and starts whacking him on the head. Whipped him a good five or ten minutes, not saying nothing, the powder flying everywhere."

"Old Scheider may be crazy," Garton Shanks said, "but he ain't a bad nigger. I can't see that he deserves our Miss Lavinia."

"Ain't no man, nigger or white, done nothing bad enough to deserve her."

Garton looked out the window. "I don't envy Whitehill," he said. "It's a hard day for an old man like him to be travelin'. He's about my daddy's age. I'd hate for *him* to be out in this."

"Shoot. Old Whitehill's tougher than you and me and your daddy put together. You know that old man rode with Forrest?"

"Yeah, I know he did. Other day, he told me how they swooped down on the Yankees from behind at Pea Ridge. Wiped out about a hundred of 'em. Said he remembers it like it happened yesterday. There was this boy wasn't no more than thirteen or fourteen years old, down on his knees in the trench, begging Whitehill not to shoot him, calling on the angels above for good measure. Whitehill said he still remembers the name of the town that boy claimed he come from. Ardena, Indiana. Course, Forrest wasn't one to take prisoners, so there wasn't nothing Whitehill could do but put a hot one right between the poor boy's eyes."

"We got turmoil in our own times. But at least the Good Lord in His wisdom saw fit to spare us that."

"Yeah, and I'm mighty thankful of it." Garton shook his head. "Funny thing, though," he said. "For Christmas, my wife got me a book called *A Southerner's History of the War Between the States,* and when I'm lookin' at it yesterday, it don't mention Forrest being nowhere near Pea Ridge."

"Garton," Tandy said, "there's history—and then there's the *essence* of the times. If it was me, I'd place my faith in Whitehill."

IN FACT, he had placed his bet on Whitehill, and Whitehill had never let him down. But by three o'clock, he was worried.

A few folks had been in several times, checking to see if the mail had come yet, and a couple had started acting impatient. Worst of all, Henry Meadows had passed through the lobby twice; the second time, he'd had the nerve to frown at Tandy, who at that moment was trying to explain Whitehill's absence to Miss Lena Grider.

Tandy waited until the old lady left, shaking her head and muttering about incompetence; then he got up and walked over to the desk. Garton was back there, sticking a room key into one of the slots. Tandy said, "I'm actually feelin' a mite worried."

"About Whitehill?"

"Yeah. He's normally solid. You reckon maybe he's had a problem with one of them nags?"

"Could be. Either that or maybe they quit delivering mail out to Garrison. Old Teddy ain't one to take defeat laying down."

The last was a possibility Tandy had given some thought to. The system he'd worked out with the postmaster at Garrison was that all mail intended for citizens of Loring would be addressed to Mr. T. A. Payne at Box 34, with the true intended's name printed in pencil on the flap. This was perfectly legal, but the federal government still could do, or at least try to do, whatever it damn well wanted. And he figured, further, that it would not necessarily be a bad thing if the mail were intercepted. He could already imagine himself standing before an angry crowd at the town hall, denouncing everyone who'd drawn his first breath north of the Potomac. While he did not yet know where all of this was leading, he foresaw a silver future in the offing.

"I believe I'll ride over toward Garrison and see if maybe Whitehill ain't had some kind of problem," he said. "Sometimes in icy conditions, a horse'll come up lame."

Garton leaned forward, elbows on the hotel registry. "You better not get caught out at night, else you liable to turn up lame yourself. Or worse."

"If I turn up lame, I turn up lame," Tandy said. "Folks are countin' on me and Whitehill. If need be, I'll walk up Pennsylvania Avenue on hot coals and nails, then drag old Teddy out of bed and make him lick our goddamn stamps."

Evidently, Garton liked the way that sounded. He picked up a pencil and began to jot it down.

WEST OUT of town, the fields looked like white bedsheets, with an occasional pillow under them where the snow had drifted. Crossing the wooden bridge over Choctaw Creek, Tandy looked down and saw a calf that must've wandered into the creek and broken its leg; frozen into the ice, with only its head and shoulders protruding, it had a sleepy look in its wide-open eyes.

Icicles hung from the eaves of the few houses he passed; the chimneys bellowed smoke. People had hung tarps over their windows, trying to block the wind; the tarps, too, were covered with ice. Even folks who normally wouldn't have let their dogs set foot in the house had taken them in, in an effort to keep them from freezing.

It was colder than he'd thought—colder than he'd been anywhere, including Denver and Helena, Butte and Cheyenne. The wind howled across the fields, cutting through his macintosh. He felt sorry for the horse. Something he rarely did.

He rode on for six or seven miles as darkness began to fall. He wondered if maybe Whitehill might still be in Garrison, lying in a warm bed, in a warm room, wrapped up with some whore who wanted money bad enough to suffer close exposure to his "oozing." Whitehill had confessed doubts as to whether or not such whores existed, but Tandy knew they existed in great numbers. There were folks who would do anything for the right amount of money. And there were folks who would do anything for no money at all, for the pure and simple pleasure of perversity.

Just as he was about to give up and turn back, something up ahead caught his eye. At first, he thought it was a big snowdrift right out in the middle of the road; then he realized it was moving, and not one object, but two or perhaps three. Drawing closer, he saw the clouds of smoke rising from the horses' nostrils, saw the grocery wagon behind them advancing through the dusk.

The steel grays came on. He heard the springs creaking, the crunching noise the wheels made as they rolled over the ruts. The horses blew and snorted, laboring hard, though they were barely moving.

Except for the fact that his good eye was open, Whitehill looked as if he'd fallen asleep. His mouth was wide open, his head lolling off to one side, resting against the canvas. The reins were clenched in his left hand. His right hand dangled in the air, registering seismic vibrations. The shock of the cold had been too much for his heart.

Garton Shanks's words rang out in Tandy's head. *A hard day for an old man like him to be travelin'.* They all were bound to say he should've done it himself, that he should've been the one to brave the elements. They'd remember how the panther had killed those folks years ago, how he'd slept through their screams while Leighton responded.

They would shake their heads, each and every one. Uncle Billy Heath beat him out of a horse, they would say, and him claiming to be a professional gambler. Anything he touches turns to dung.

He jumped down, pulled the reins loose from Whitehill's grip and stopped the horses. Though he hated to touch a dead person, especially this one, he put his hand on the old man's cheek to see if he'd frozen. Whitehill was still fairly warm.

Tandy shoved against the body, intending to make it sit up straight, but instead it lurched sideways and fell out of the wagon onto the frozen road.

"I'll be goddamned," Tandy said out loud. "If he wasn't dead, I'd kill him."

He walked around the wagon to where Whitehill lay on his back, staring up at the sky. Lifting him would be no easy matter.

Right then, as he stood there considering how best to get the body back into the wagon, Tandy's eyes lit on the pistol. It was strapped to Whitehill's thigh, the butt protruding from the holster.

He looked toward the west, then toward the east. Nobody on the road as far as he could see. Darkness was coming on. Night had always been the time when he felt bravest.

He squatted down beside Hezekiah Whitehill—veteran of Shiloh, Pea Ridge and Peachtree Creek, Vicksburg, Gettysburg and Petersburg, Forrest's cohort and Johnston's confidant—and pulled the pistol free. It was loaded, though he'd feared it might not be.

This would bother him. He never thought otherwise. This would come back from time to time—as well as the smell of burning horseflesh. By then, though, he would know exactly why he'd done it. He'd work his way backwards from the action to the reason, discarding all the garbage in between.

SOME folks would remember it as a scene from a motion picture, though nobody in Loring had yet seen one. The background was white, the borders black, and within this frame the steel grays appeared, their hames ice-encrusted. Tandy followed, occupying the seat where folks were used to seeing Whitehill. The wagon passed. Behind it, tethered to the tailgate, came Tandy's horse, bearing its morbid burden. Whitehill's arms hung down almost to the ground. There was blood in his hair, in his beard and on his coat. There was blood on the seat of his pants.

Nobody thought to wonder why the corpse had been strapped to Tandy's horse, exposed to the wind, when it might have been laid inside the wagon, where it could rest with whatever dignity remained available to a corpse that looked as if somebody lately had taken target practice on it.

Nobody was doing much reasoning right then. Everybody was looking out the window, waiting for somebody else to make the first move.

SEABORN sat counting pennies, now warm inside his house. Last night, Loyal Taylor had transported a wagonload of locust to their doorstep, refusing to accept payment.

"Us niggers got to stick together," he'd said, and for once, Seaborn did not dispute use of this word. Indeed, in recent days, he'd begun to feel like a nigger. He felt it deeply, and the worst thing about feeling this was realizing that in some basic way he had always felt it, that his children, should he ever father any, would feel it, too, and their children after them.

Niggerhood, as he'd come to think of it, had many aspects, the most powerful of which was its infectiousness. It could be transmitted by blood from father to son, from mother to daughter, and it could be passed on to mere acquaintances with a word or a glance. A man who was a Negro today could become a nigger tomorrow, just because he'd lost his resistance or encountered one who had.

He had lost his resistance, or was losing it, and he harbored few illusions about how to get it back. The best thing he could think of to do right now was to count the pennies. Because if you held enough pennies in your hand, you ended up with a dollar, and if you held enough dollars, you ended up with a fortune. He still believed that folks who held a fortune could rise above niggerhood. The difficulty lay in the accumulation.

Loda had been standing in the living room, looking out the window. She let the curtains fall closed. "Seaborn," she said.

"Wait a minute. Forty-seven, forty-eight, forty-nine. Fifty." He made a neat stack of the last ten pennies.

"Seaborn?"

He pulled another handful of coins from the cash box and dropped them on the table. "Yes?"

She'd turned away from the window and was obviously trying to compose herself.

"What is it?" he said. "What's the matter?"

"That old man. The one who's been going to pick up their mail. Tandy Payne just rode by. He was driving the wagon. The old man's dead. I could see his head hanging down off the horse. He looked pretty badly shot up."

Seaborn rose, stepping toward her.

"Seaborn," she said again. And then he knew that while his

name was the one she kept saying, her mind was not on him. "I have to get the horse from the stable."

"You're not leaving the house now."

"Then you have to. Tell him to go. And not to come back."

"Tell him to go? Go where?"

"Anywhere."

"He's to leave, but we're not to?"

He would have said more, but when he looked at her closely, he could see that for the first time since that day on the steamboat, when those little white men stepped out of the woods and fired their weapons at the excursion, she was completely dependent on him: he could do, or he could refuse. But if he chose the latter, he would go right on feeling like a nigger. No matter how many pennies.

"Where," he said, "am I likely to find him?"

"He's probably already left Rosenthal's—he goes home every evening about this time. He still lives out there with Scheider, in that little shack where the road bends back toward the Deadening."

He was already reaching for his coat. "Sooner or later," he said, "it seems that every road leads you to the Deadening."

ROSENTHAL stood near the plate-glass window, gazing out through the inverted letters. The wagon stopped across the street, in front of the post office. The townspeople who'd followed behind the wagon now halted, keeping their distance from the trailing horse and the body bound to it.

Tandy Payne got down and walked over to the hitching post and tied up the draft horses, then stood for a moment with his back to the crowd. His head was bowed. Rosenthal could appreciate the effect. "When you know you cannot convey an emotion," his old drama instructor used to say, "just stand with your back to the audience and keep your mouth shut."

"Blueford?" Rosenthal whispered, moving away from the window. "Blueford, where are you?"

Blueford stepped through the curtain. He'd been in the back room, tidying up, preparing to leave for the night.

"What you gonna do, Blueford," Rosenthal said, stepping over to the corner where he kept the urinals and washbasins and other bathroom fixtures, "is help me with that tub."

The bathtub had arrived the week before Christmas, the largest tub currently being made: six feet long, almost two feet deep, a white enameled roll rim. It weighed nearly four hundred pounds.

"We gonna tip this thing up on its side," Rosenthal said, squatting and getting ready to lift, "and then when we got it up there real good, balanced just perfect, what you gonna do is crawl under and lie down, and I'm gonna push it over. You better lie flat, too, because that thing come down on your head, you gonna forget stuff you don't even know yet."

"How come you want I should lay down under there?" Blueford said, looking toward the front. From back here, you couldn't see the street.

"I want you to lie down," Rosenthal whispered, "because I value your presence. See, lying down under this thing gonna make it possible for you to continue being present. Not here— not no more. But somewhere."

"No sir," Blueford said. "I'm not gone lay down under no bathtub."

Rosenthal said, "Then don't call this item no bathtub, Blueford. It's a heavy white protective object."

TANDY was no longer cold.

He felt the same hot flush he felt when he'd had several shots of whiskey and a good-looking woman whose name he didn't know yet was close by. He'd told more than one woman not to tell him her name right away. "You can tell me later on," he'd say. They believed he didn't want to know their names so he might forget them more easily, but it was himself he needed to forget, and to do that, he had to reduce them to hot flesh and low urges.

He couldn't even name the men who stood in a circle near his horse, which was still loaded down with the remains of Hezekiah Whitehill. He knew only that they represented the riffraff, as everybody with any quality or sense was inside keeping warm. But riffraff would do just fine for now. The moment didn't call for bonded whiskey; it demanded plain old rotgut.

He pulled the curtain back at the rear of the wagon. "Empty," he said, stepping aside so all could see. "The stuff was scattered all over the road, across the fields. White pages scattered around them windswept middles, dead cotton stalks whistling, them and the pages singing a damn dirge. Whoever done it pulled the bags out and tore 'em open and threw our mail to kingdom come. And that was after they'd murdered this brave old soldier."

A big red-faced man in a dirty duck coat said, "Had to be a nigger."

"Either a nigger or the goddamn federal government."

"Couldn't kill the old man in the war, so they waited fifty years to blow his guts up."

"And him not doing a thing in the world but trying to help folks."

For a moment, nobody spoke. Then the man in the duck coat said, "Well, y'all, let's go."

After they left, Tandy untied his horse and led it down the street. He intended to unload the body and spend the evening huddled up with the town marshal beside the fireplace in his office, sipping whiskey and telling stories about Whitehill, building further on the old man's lies, while outside the wind blew ever colder.

BENEATH his clothes, Seaborn wore a pair of thick honeycomb underwear, but the first blast of wind cut right through them. "My goodness," he said to himself, reaching up to pull his scarf higher. His teeth were already chattering disturbingly; he associated this phenomenon with illness, specifically with processes beyond all save medicinal control.

He stepped down off the back porch, but his feet found no purchase and he fell flat on his back, then slid into the pitcher pump.

Ice crystals were embedded in his pants and underwear. He rolled over, put both hands down on the snowy ground and pushed himself up. He glanced at the kitchen window to see if Loda had seen him fall, but the window was dark. She was probably still in the front room, looking out the other window, her mind somewhere else.

He brushed himself off as best he could and set off across the yard, testing the ground ahead with one foot so as to avoid any slick spots. At the rear of the yard, the thick hedgerow was covered with ice and snow. There was nothing to do but push into the prickly mess and shoulder and weave his way through it.

A frozen branch tore at his face, poking him in his right eye, and as soon as it began to water, his lashes froze. "My goodness," he said again, then heaved forward once more, and his head, shoulders and legs came out the other side.

Gasping, he stepped into the alley, which was frozen solid as a brickbat and deserted. Nobody in his right mind would have been out tonight—not that folks were in their right minds lately. As he proceeded toward the bayou, he allowed himself to wonder who had killed the old man. He didn't believe Blueford had done it, or any other Negroes. Nor did he believe for one moment that suspicion would fall on anyone with white skin.

It would be a strange and constricting brand of suspicion that the white folks would entertain. He almost pitied them. They would have to pin the crime on a Negro, but they could not allow themselves to blame *the Negroes*—of whom, in Loring County, there were four for every white—because those Negroes were necessary. You could get mad at one horse and shoot it, but if you shot the whole remuda, then who would pull the plow?

The obvious answer—that other horses would be found—was not one he chose to consider. Right now, he needed to maintain a positive outlook. He wanted to get across the bayou and out to where Blueford lived with that crazy old Scheider and tell him to get on that silly bicycle and pedal till he reached the Pacific. He would not mind if Blueford were to keep pedaling right into the ocean, but that was up to him and whatever spirits moved him.

He crossed Main Street, turned right on Loring, then stepped onto the bridge over the bayou. The boards were slick. The wind, unimpeded, raked the folds of his overcoat. His scarf blew into his face, blinding him for an instant.

While his eyes were covered, he heard a whinny and the sound of hooves beating a tattoo on a hard surface.

LOGS CRACKLED in the fireplace, and her son sat in the armchair, his legs drawn up under him, his ragged copy of *The Wilderness Hunter* open in his lap. Earlier, when Leighton walked in and saw what Will was reading, he hadn't expressed disapproval, even though the author of the book certainly disapproved of him. "That's a hard book to beat, isn't it, son?" he'd said.

Now he was sitting beside her on the couch, leafing through a catalogue of printer's supplies. He'd been excessively kind since the night she'd remarked on his failure to stand up for the people of Loring, but he hadn't touched her. She was wondering if he would, ever again.

"How cold do you think it is right now?" she said.

He closed the catalogue and laid it down, as if to devote his full attention to the question. "When I came in, it was five degrees. And that was two hours ago. I bet it's close to zero by now."

"Inside," she said, "or out?"

He sighed and studied the floorboards for a while. Then he said, "Son, why don't you go on upstairs and get ready for bed. You can read for another hour, okay?"

"Yes sir."

He waited until Will had gone upstairs. "Inside," he said, "and out. And I don't guess there's much we can do about the temperature in either place."

She didn't think so, either, but she said, "We could try."

"We have tried—*are* trying. We're sitting here behaving like married folks. If somebody happened to look through the window, he'd know that's what we were."

"I doubt our mothers and fathers ever had to have this conversation."

"My mother and my father never had any conversations. My mother would've made a marvelous Confederate officer. She spent her whole life in graceful retreat. My father drove her, and plenty of other folks, right into the ground."

Because she wanted to hurt him and believed she knew how to, she said, "You've always got ink on your hands. Don't you ever wash them?"

"Some things don't wash off," he told her.

At that moment, they heard footsteps on the porch.

SEABORN P. Jackson would have looked like a snowman were it not for his black face. Snow and ice clung to his eyebrows and hair and clothes. Blood trickled from a cut in the corner of his mouth. The sleeve of his overcoat was torn.

"Seaborn," Leighton said. "Come in. What happened to you?"

The man made no move to enter. "Nothing," he said. "Nothing's happened to me, sir." Seaborn's gaze darted past him and lit on Sarah, who was standing in front of the fireplace now, staring at him as if at a bandit. "You see, sir, that old gentleman who was driving the mail wagon for your brother? Well, sir, it seems that he's met an unfortunate end."

"What kind of unfortunate end?"

"Well, sir, a *most* unfortunate end. It seems that somebody shot him. That's what my wife said anyway, and she saw your brother bringing the corpse into town. She said . . . she said, sir, that it looked as if the old . . . as if the old gentleman was shot up pretty badly, and that's why I'm here, because to tell you the truth . . ." Breathless, Seaborn foundered. He was shaking.

Leighton grabbed his coat sleeve and pulled him inside and slammed the door. "What is it?" he said. "Did somebody threaten you?"

"No sir, but we are somewhat worried—worse than somewhat, even very. She's worried about . . . Threaten us? Oh, my goodness, I've left her at home alone." Turning, he reached for the door.

Once more, Leighton grabbed his arm. "What did you come to tell me, Seaborn?"

"My wife is worried about Blueford Lucas. And I do believe she has just cause. I heard horses—quite a few of them. You see, sir, they're going to think . . . that's just how white folks—and I'm not trying to say anything you might find . . . But what they'll think, can't help from thinking—"

Leighton waved the explanation off and grabbed his overcoat. "Can you show me where he stays?"

"Yes sir."

"Leighton?" Sarah said.

She stood there in front of the fire, her arms crossed just below her breasts, her color high, the light from the lamp glinting off the silver clasp she wore on her cravat. She'd never looked more desirable. Or more unreachable.

"You're going to escort a colored man out into the night, without knowing whether or not he's telling you the truth?"

"That's one way of looking at it," he said. "But there's another way, too. You could simply say that I'm going out for a stroll with my brother-in-law. Or has that yet to enter local lore?"

STUMBLING along beside the mayor, Seaborn felt calm.

He did not reflect, as he might have, on his earlier fears about Loda being alone. Loda could and would take care of herself. A few days earlier, he had examined the contents of her purse—something, God help him, he'd always done from time to time—and in the process discovered the pistol.

Neither did he worry about what might happen when they got to Blueford's place. Unless the men on horseback had already gotten there, which was unlikely, since white people rarely knew where a Negro of Blueford's station lived, the mayor would take things in hand and send Blueford Lucas scurrying into the fields from whence he came.

He didn't even reconfirm the desire he'd expressed some days ago to leave Loring. That he and Loda would leave town no later than tomorrow morning went without saying.

What he pondered instead was the manner in which white people appropriated the Negro's every endeavor to suit their own ends. He had appeared at the mayor's door half-frozen, shaking and stammering as if someone had put an electric wire up his rear, and duly issued his plea; and in responding to that plea, the mayor had resolved whatever argument he was having with his wife by announcing that Loda Jackson, Seaborn's wife, was the bastardly offspring of his own evil daddy.

The mayor had not considered the effect this information might have on the man who stood in his living room, because that man, brother-in-law or not, was the trembling apostle of Negro subservience.

Reborn there on the icy road, Seaborn resolved to put the needle in and see how deep it went. "I'll tell you what," he said. "These women, they drive a man half-mad, don't they?"

The mayor did not reply. Nor did Seaborn desist.

"That Loda of mine, when she makes up her mind about something—*watch out!* She comes in there and says, 'Seaborn, it must be this way' or 'Seaborn, it must be that way.' Not a thing in the world for Seaborn to do but drop his head and say okay. But you know how that is. I was watching through the window. I saw you drop your own head."

So succulent was the fare of which he'd just partaken that he might have licked his lips, but for the knowledge they would freeze.

He stole a glance at the mayor: he was marching along with his collar turned up, obscuring the bottom part of his chin; he leaned ever so slightly into the wind, as if daring it to blow him over. Though Seaborn had always suspected Leighton Payne was a blood relation of Loda's, he had searched in vain for physical resemblance. Now he understood that the true resemblance was not to be found in their respective features, but in the attitude with which they greeted trouble.

"I'm sorry about telling my wife what I did in front of you just now," the mayor said. "I should've told her, and then told you. Or you and then her. Or maybe I shouldn't have told anybody, since everybody already knows everything anyway. Except that if we don't start saying what we've never said before, we're going to continue having nights like this one."

Seaborn had never heard of a white person apologizing to a Negro for anything, and it left him feeling vaguely uneasy, as if the rules of engagement had been altered without his knowledge.

"Well, sir," he began, and then realized he'd slipped right back into the same old behavior. "Well, Mr. Mayor—or Mr. Brother-in-Law—or whatever it is you are—may the Lord spare us another night like this one."

"I don't think He will. We'll have to spare ourselves."

"And how would you suggest we go about that?"

"For a start, we're going to have to quit lying."

"That won't be easy," Seaborn said. "There's not much around here that's not built on one kind of lie or another."

"Well, that itself is surely the truth."

To Seaborn's amazement, the mayor laid a gloved hand on his shoulder.

"You and I may be about to freeze to death or get ourselves hanged," the mayor said, "but at least we're moving in the same direction."

AND SO they move: a tall white man who can fill a room by himself, and a shorter, stoutly built black man growing short of breath.

VISIBLE SPIRITS

They stride along the icy way, each one faltering occasionally and grabbing the other one's elbow, neither of them absolutely sure what the moment would require of him—how much it would cost, in what currency—if the other slipped and fell into the road ditch.

WHAT Scheider sees and Scheider says verge toward agreement.

But what Scheider saw that night he'd never say. Come morning, he was miles away. He'd stolen out the back door into the cotton fields, where he would have frozen except for the alcohol in his blood. Any man who spent most of his waking hours around Miss Lavinia needed to be numb.

That night, he felt just about right. Almost numb. He was on that little cot in the corner, opposite to where Blueford slept. Whereas Scheider's stayed cluttered with old jars and bottles, Blueford's corner looked like the shelves at Rosenthal's, with everything just so.

Lying on the cot, his head resting against the wall, Scheider had both blankets pulled up to his chin. Just studying the fire, knowing that if Blueford came home soon, he'd go over to stoke it and then bring some more wood from the pile out back, busting the ice off with a mallet if he had to. Blueford always knew what to do.

Scheider heard the voices the wind was blowing toward him as if from far off. Then they sounded right up close, and then off again.

"Blueford?"

A knock on the door. That door hadn't ever been knocked

on before. Hadn't anybody been inside this place in years, as far as he knew, except him and Blueford Lucas.

"Who that is?"

"Mayor Payne."

Didn't sound like Mayor Payne. Sounded like somebody trying to sound like Mayor Payne. Not that Mayor Payne had ever spoken to him. But he had in his head an idea of the way Mayor Payne would sound if you heard him.

"White folks, what y'all want?"

This time, the door rattled. "Scheider?"

Now he recognized the voice. "The policy man?"

"Scheider, for goodness' sakes, open this door."

He rose from his cot, steadied himself against the wall, then stumbled over to the door. They kept it locked at night with a piece of wire snaked through one hook on the door and another on the wall.

He undid the wire and opened the door. Hugging himself, Mr. Seaborn P. Jackson leapt inside. Behind him stood the mayor, who took a long look at the opening, then ducked down and stepped through.

Mayor Payne pushed the door closed. "Where's Blueford?" he said.

Scheider couldn't speak. He had no idea what the right answer might be, and he didn't want to get caught giving the wrong one.

Mr. Jackson grabbed him under the arms and shook him. "Goddamn it, Scheider, come together."

"Ain't seed him since last night," Scheider said. "Yes sir. That's right. He gone when I got up this morning."

"Gone where?"

"To work, I 'magine."

"And he's usually home by now?"

"Show is."

It dawned on all of them at about the same time. Scheider

read it in the mayor's face first, because he'd spent his whole life reading white faces. Then he saw it in Mr. Seaborn Jackson's face, too. And Mr. Jackson saw it in his.

"Horses," he said.

And the mayor said, "Yes."

WHAT *Scheider sees.*

Acting like it's something more than his sworn duty to go out and deal with mischief—more like it's his birthright—the mayor says, "Y'all just stay put. And be quiet."

He opens the door and steps out.

The shack has no windows, but there's a good-sized chink in the front wall, covered by a flattened-out can that once contained Blue Ribbon Liquor Cure. If you want to see out, you turn the can on its nail. Scheider and Seaborn squat there, peering through the crack.

There are several men on horses—five or six or seven. The horses are not the kind you stable down at Heath's. These horses look like they last ate around Thanksgiving.

The men's faces are hard to see, but Scheider recognizes two or three. He doesn't know their names, just as they would not know his. These are men who work for other men.

For a moment, the mayor just stands there looking at them. Then he steps closer. "Can I help you gentlemen?" he says.

The man on the first horse—a big red-faced man who will always try to walk right through you if you're too slow jumping down off the sidewalk—this man says, "We ain't here to talk to you. The old man that drives the mail wagon's been killed. That Lucas nigger did it."

"What makes you think so?"

"We don't think. We know."

"The first statement's true," the mayor says. "You don't think.

You don't stop to wonder what's going to happen in the morning when I walk down to the marshal's office and swear out a complaint against every last one of you. I don't know your names, but I know your faces. You work for Catchings Stark. And that man back there, he lives on Newcomb Teague's place. The fact that you're here, instead of the folks you work for—well, I guess that represents some progress. They used to have to do this kind of thing themselves.

"You probably figure they'll protect you, but they won't. To them, you're worth less than a breaking plow. Which means you're worth a good bit less than a colored person, and that's what makes y'all so mad. But killing Blueford Lucas won't change it.

"Now, you men can turn politely around and head on home. Or if you've just got to do it, you can go on back to that alley behind the Feed and Grain and build a fire in that old washtub and drink every drop of moonshine in Loring, Mississippi. But if you choose to do the latter, try not to disturb Mr. Meadows, who's sleeping up above you in the hotel. He's formed a mighty bad impression of us all, and I believe he's communicated it to Mr. Roosevelt."

The red-faced man hangs his head. You can tell, if you know much about white folks, that he's one of those who's hung his head a good bit. But you'd have to know more about white folks than the mayor does to understand that the man on the horse has gotten tired of it.

Scheider thinks, but does not say, *Mr. Mayor's done fell behind times.*

The big red-faced man jerks the reins, the horse rears, the mayor takes too long to move. The hooves come crashing down.

The mayor falls. Though he does his best to cover his head, the horse tromps him into the frozen ground.

"Y'all get in there," the man yells, pulling a rope out, slashing at the mayor. "Get that goddamn nigger."

Scheider's moving toward the back door, moving fast and breathing hard. "Mr. Jackson," he says. "This way!"

LIKE HE was tired of running, Scheider will often think but never say. *And him not having run before, far as I know, up till that very night. But he run then, did Mr. Jackson. Grabbed that old post maul been laying by the front door.*

Says you sorry white rubble good for nothing troublemaking trash.

Mr. Jackson he go forward, out that door into the night.

VAPORS

ON THE screen, the figure faded, then coalesced once more into the image of a man wearing a black cowboy suit, a guitar hanging from a strap on his shoulder. He was moving his mouth, bobbing his head up and down. Behind him, several similarly clad young men and women sat on haystacks, boots kicking to a beat she couldn't hear. The set made a noise like the sound of bacon frying.

"Miss Loda?" The girl's voice came in through the window. "Do I got it now?"

"I can see them," she said. "I just can't hear them."

"Miss Loda! I say do I got it now?"

She gathered her reserves. "Not really, dear. Only the picture." She heard a creaking sound as the girl tried once more to rotate the antenna.

"Now?"

This time, she didn't answer.

In a moment, the screen door slammed shut. The girl came through to the bedroom and stood there in front of the set, hands propped on her hips. "Ain't nothing on good no way. Just them peoples from over in El Dorado. Wonder how do they make a living and not singing no better than they do? Them peoples need to get out and pump some gas or pick they cotton."

She walked over to the set, turned it off, then sat down on the chair in the corner and picked up one of the pamphlets her mother had brought home the day before. They were from a minister named Reverend Truitt, who'd told the girl's mother he was collecting for a tabernacle, one that would serve the black people of the entire Delta. A rolling tabernacle, it would travel from town to town, county to county, spreading the Gospel to all those who labored in the fields. The End Times were coming, Reverend Truitt had told the girl's mother. But not the End Times some folks expected. The way he'd described it, and how she'd described it for Loda, was that one day all the white folks would just disappear. As if they'd been vaporized. Nobody would miss them; they wouldn't even miss themselves, he'd said with a laugh. And what would be left was a core of black believers. It would take the rolling tabernacle to spread the word to the brothers and the sisters, Reverend Truitt said. Those who didn't hear it would not be vaporized themselves, though their period of labor in the fields would be prolonged.

"Now, far as I'm concerned," said the reverend, "anybody that's spent one hour out there picking those folks' cotton has labored long enough. So what I'm asking of all the brothers and the sisters is for them to dig down—not into their pocketbooks, but all the way down into their hearts. Because when the heart gets in line, the pocketbook's sure to follow."

Celia's pocketbook was almost empty, and that was why she'd come with the pamphlets, seeking support for Reverend Truitt from one she knew could give it. That and one other reason. "Being as you a little closer to the gates of Eden, Miss Loda, than most anybody I know, I figure you got less of a need for what the reverend call 'the trappings of mundanity.' Help him out, Miss Loda. I sure want to see that tabernacle when it roll through Loring."

There was no point in suggesting to Celia that the reverend might not be righteous. Everybody had to fall in line behind someone sometime. Loda told her to go get the cash box. "Take whatever's in there," she said. "Give it to the reverend and tell him I wish him luck."

"Oh, the reverend don't need luck," Celia said. "The reverend got them vapors on *his* side."

LIKE THE picture on the set, she faded in and out. There were days when she could tell you what day it was, even the exact time, when she could recite the names of all the principal shareholders of Piedmont Life and Casualty, the insurance company she'd founded with Robert Williams. She could have directed you to the house she'd lived in on Pettiway Street in Raleigh, not far from the college where Robert Williams had worked until he felt he could quit and devote himself to the company full-time. She could tell you the names of all the dogs and cats they'd owned.

Other days, she didn't know where she was. She would look around the room, and it would seem to her that she was seeing it for the first time. The pictures on the wall of two men— one plumpish, balding; the other thin and light-skinned, with a delicate nose that looked as if it belonged on a woman— were the images of strangers.

"Who are those men?" she once asked the girl.

The girl said, "Now, Miss Loda, don't go scaring me like that. I'm gone have to be callin' Momma."

"Who are those men?" she said again, and when the girl didn't answer, she said, "Where's Blueford?"

So the girl called her momma, and her momma called the doctor, and he came with a leather bag, a young man who smelled as if he'd sprayed himself with women's fragrance. He placed a cold instrument against her chest, and when the cold metal touched the skin, her lucidity came rushing back in.

"Dr. Ormesby," she said.

"Yes ma'am."

"How's your grandmother?"

"Just fine, Mrs. Williams. You and she ought to get together when you're both feeling better."

"She used to be my bridge partner. She and your grandfather. And my husband, Seaborn."

"Yes ma'am, she speaks fondly of those times."

She grew quiet then, resentful. She remembered how they'd canceled their policies. She would say no more. Before leaving, he wrote a prescription and told the girl to send her mother to the pharmacy, and to call him if they encountered any problems getting it filled.

Now she lay in bed, looking across the room at the girl, who was paging through another of the pamphlets. The television was quiet, the radio, too. But outside, from somewhere close by, she heard music, loud voices. Hoping to see where the noise was coming from, she looked out the window, which the girl had left open to catch the evening breeze. But the window was completely black, and she couldn't see a thing.

She realized she couldn't move her feet. She tried to remember how long it had been since she'd moved a foot or a hand. Days, it seemed like. There was no feeling in her legs or feet, nor in her arms, no hurting in her chest where she'd hurt for so long.

"Johnnie Mae?" she said.

The girl laid the pamphlet down and looked at her. "Miss Loda, now you worrying me. You know my name ain't Johnnie Mae. Who in the world she was? I believe you done made her up. That's what Momma say."

She had called her by the wrong name one time too many. The girl got up and went outside and stood on the porch and screamed "Momma" until she came running.

THE WOMEN'S ward in the Negro wing consisted of four beds in a room not much larger than a broom closet. It stank of antiseptic. They sent a young Negro woman in to mop it once a day.

They put her in a bed beside the window. From here, she could see across a vacant lot to the highway. The first day, she determined to count all the cars and trucks that stopped at the red light. She drifted off a couple of times and couldn't remember what number she'd been on when she quit, so she had to start over. Then she wandered away again.

She believed she'd seen Blueford on a street in Memphis, '23 or '24. After the war, at any rate. She and Robert Williams had gone there to look at some property for a hotel they thought they might open. He walked away when she spoke his name. She called it again, louder, and he walked even faster. He disappeared around a corner, and a second or two later, a dog trailed after him.

She danced at an auditorium in Raleigh. The whites had it mostly, but they used it sometimes. That night, Duke Ellington played. Though she was too old to be dancing, she did it anyway. Danced with Robert Williams, too old to dance himself and not much inclined to, and his heart gave out the next night.

"When I was checking her in," she heard one nurse tell another, "that colored doctor said she owns her own insurance company. Somewhere over in North Carolina."

"My granddaddy told me about some colored man that used to sell insurance around here," the second nurse said. "Way back before World War One. Said he made a mint doing it, too, owned businesses in the white part of town, and everybody loved and respected him. Problem was, he sold whiskey on the side. One night, two other colored men killed him."

She sees herself standing in tall weeds raked by a breeze—cold or warm, she doesn't know which. Stepping into a clearing, she confronts a tall gray-faced man who holds a razor in his hand. He asks her to use it on him. She says she can't. Why not? he says. She's lost her license, she tells him.

"They took my license away," someone was saying, "back in '51. They should've taken it sooner. I ran smack into the scout hut. Fortunately, none of the boys was inside. I don't know how it happened, I must've gone to sleep. I went to sleep one day at a stoplight—the policeman got a real kick out of that. You probably saw me driving around town. It was a big purple car. I forget the make. I never was interested in cars. I used to see you. I knew when you came back from North Carolina. I know why you did it, too. I thought about leaving, but where can you go?

"My son, Will, got killed in the Argonne Forest. He'd been to West Point and was commanding artillery. I went over there to France to see where it happened. I couldn't tell much about how it'd been. You can't ever tell what it was like unless you were there, and about half the time, you can't even tell then. Teddy Roosevelt lost a son over there. When Teddy himself died, a Negro was with him. It was his manservant—I forget the fellow's name. But it's in a history book somewhere, and that's important. I know where Seaborn's buried. I've been out there a few times. I saw the flowers you left. Carried some myself.

"My brother died a pauper in Birmingham—1931. He'd been dead a month before I found out. A woman and her daughter paid to have him buried. While I'm ashamed to say it, I forget their names, too. A reporter wrote him up in the Birmingham paper, but it was just a paragraph, and he got a few things wrong.

"They always get things wrong in the paper. I always got things wrong in my paper, too. If I wrote my own obituary, I still wouldn't get it right. Mine least of all. I wouldn't even know how to start it."

She opened her eyes then and saw Leighton Payne. She'd thought he would be sitting on a stool, but he was standing. A tall man with sandpaper skin and an old man's odor you could smell even over the antiseptic. He had one glass eye, and his nose was bent askew. He held his hat in his hands and leaned forward just a little, as if uncertain of his position and the space he'd taken up for so long.

ACKNOWLEDGMENTS

During the writing of this novel, the following sources were invaluable: Herbert Asbury, *The French Quarter: An Informal History of the New Orleans Underworld* and *Sucker's Progress: An Informal History of Gambling in America from the Colonies to Canfield;* John M. Barry, *Rising Tide: The Great Mississippi Flood of 1927 and How It Changed America;* H. W. Brands, *T.R.: The Last Romantic;* James C. Cobb, *The Most Southern Place on Earth: The Mississippi Delta and the Roots of Regional Identity;* Eric Foner, *A Short History of Reconstruction, 1863–1877;* John Hope Franklin and Alfred A. Moss, Jr., *From Slavery to Freedom: A History of African Americans;* Willard B. Gatewood, Jr., *Theodore Roosevelt and the Art of Controversy: Episodes from the White House Years;* Louis R. Harlan, *Booker T. Washington in Perspective: The Essays of Louis R. Harlan;* Harlan and Raymond W. Smuck (editors), *The Booker T. Washington Papers,* volumes 6 and 7; Marie M. Hemphill, *Fevers, Floods and Faith: A History of Sunflower County, Mississippi, 1844–1976;* William F. Holmes, *The White Chief: James Kimble Vardaman;* Nathan Miller, *Theodore Roosevelt: A Life;* Frank Luther Mott, *American Journalism: A History, 1690–1960;* Ted Ownby, *American Dreams in Mississippi: Consumers, Poverty, & Culture, 1830–1998;* Hortense Powdermaker, *After Freedom: A Cultural Study in the Deep South;* Theodore Roosevelt, *The Rough Riders;* Richard Schweid, *Catfish and the Delta: Confederate Fish Farming in the Mississippi Delta;* John Ryan Seawright, "Slavery

ACKNOWLEDGMENTS

Onstage," in *The Oxford American,* number 21–22; Vernon Lane Wharton, *The Negro in Mississippi, 1865–1890,* and C. Vann Woodward, *Origins of the New South, 1877–1913.* The conceit of the cockroach jumping on the typewriter keys is derived from Don Marquis's Archy and Mehitabel poems, which first appeared in the *New York Sun* in 1916.

I owe debts of gratitude to the many people who offered research help, as well as support and friendship, during the time when I was writing the book. I'm especially grateful to Luis Costa, S. Gale Denley, Scott Ellsworth, John Evans, Gail Freeman, John and Renee Grisham, Caitlin Hamilton, Sloan Harris, Jere Hoar, Lisa and Richard Howorth, Kathi Lamonski, Hugh and Mary Dayle McCormick, Teri Steinberg, Sarah Williams and J. K. Yarbrough. Thanks also to California State University, Fresno, and the University of Mississippi.

Lastly, special thanks to my editor and friend, Gary Fisketjon, for making a difference in more ways than one.